LAWLESS

King Series Book Three

T.M. FRAZIER

Copyright © 2015 T.M. FRAZIER
All rights reserved.
This is a work of fiction. Names, characters, businesses, places, events and incidents are either the products of the author's imagination or used in a fictitious manner. Any resemblance to actual persons, living or dead, or actual events is purely coincidental.

LAWLESS
Cover photo by: Lane Dorsey
Cover model: Josh Mario John
Cover design by T.M. Frazier
Formatting by T.M. Frazier

Created with Vellum

Author's Note

This is Bear's story and book three in the King series. It is recommended that you read both King and Tyrant in order to fully understand and enjoy all that goes on in Lawless. I hope you enjoy reading LAWLESS as much as I loved writing it.
—T.M.

Acknowledgments

Thank you so much to my husband for making this dream of mine a possibility. I honestly can't tell you enough how much I love you and without you I'd never have typed the first word of my first book. Forever and ever my love. In you I've found a friend, a husband, and my soul mate. Not to mention you are a kickass dad to the most kickass baby in the world. #TEAMTLC

To all the members of my Frazierland Facebook group, you guys are amazing and give me reason each and every day to keep typing away. You are the reasons I write, you are the people I write for. I love all of you.

To my agent Kimberly Brower, thank you for all you do for me. I appreciate you more than you could ever know. Thank you for believing in me and taking a chance on me.

To my parents, Anne & Paul, thanks for understanding that I needed to pursue this craziness and thanks for accepting my resignation. I miss seeing you guys every day and no, Dad, Matt Lauer hasn't called yet.

Thanks to my sister Cindy for reading Lawless and for cheering me on and for always telling me I can do it.

Thank you to my editor Ellie for understanding my last minute tendencies and for loving me anyway.

Thank you to Julie Vaden, my assistant, beta reader, and first and foremost, my friend. This book wouldn't exist without you and I'm not sure I would either. Love you hard.

To Rochelle, Jenny, Joanne, Bri, and all my other beta readers who read parts of Lawless completely out of order and suffered through my craziness as I loved and labored my way through Bear and Thia's story.

To the blogs, both big and small, for supporting me and cheering me on, thank you for sharing your love of my books. Thank you for bringing your love of reading to others. You are my superheroes.

To Milasy, love your face.

To Crystal, I love you. I am so honored to call you my friend.

Thank you to photographer Lane Dorsey and model Josh Mario John for an amazing cover and giving me a fabulous physical concept for Bear.

For Logan & Charley

"We're lawless my friend. Civilians can't wrap their little fucking brains around that without getting their frilly panties in a fucking twist."

—Bear, TYRANT

Prologue
BEAR

I was born a Bastard.
A soldier, in the lawless army of the Beach Bastards Motorcycle Club. Groomed to one day take the gavel from my old man.

Duty came before my conscience, before family, before everything.

I didn't choose the life, it chose me, and living it came with knowing, and accepting, that every morning I got up to take a piss, could be my very last day above ground.

Or, depending on my orders...someone else's last.

Being a biker, a Bastard, wasn't just in my blood. I didn't just live it.

I breathed it.

I drank it.

I fucking loved it.

It was everything.

Until it wasn't.

I don't remember the exact moment it happened, maybe after my first kill, maybe on the day I was patched in, but it happened. Motor oil, leather, violence, and a penchant for laying down enemies of the club, replaced the blood in my veins.

I became more biker than man.

And I was proud.

I never thought of it as a problem, but I also never thought there would come a day when I wouldn't be a Beach Bastard anymore.

But it came.

And I wasn't.

On the day I laid down my cut and walked out the door of the MC, I'd turned my own hourglass and set the expiration on my life.

Once a Bastard, you were always a Bastard.

Or you were dead.

They'd come for me. But the fucked-up thing was that it wasn't the thought of my brothers trying to put me to ground that bothered me most, it was the uncertainty.

I knew everything about being a biker.

I didn't know shit about being a man.

I've been tortured and on the verge of death, violated for the amusement of my captors. Through it all I'd never lost that edge that kept me alive. That fight. The thing inside that makes your heart beat so fast it feels like it's going to beat its way right through your chest, and tells you that no matter the situation, you'll not only get the fuck out of it, but that you're going to burn every motherfucker alive who tried to take you down.

I've been beaten, but I'd never been broken.

Until Thia...

Chapter 1
THIA, TEN YEARS OLD

I *don't know where it all went wrong.*
I never understood that saying. Because looking back on my life I can pinpoint the exact day, the exact hour, when it all changed and took a turn that no one could have predicted. Especially me.

Three weeks away from my eleventh birthday, I had just ridden my little red bicycle the three miles to the Stop-n-Go. Dad wanted me to drop off a crate of oranges so I'd tied them to a skateboard and tied a rope from the front wheels to the seat of my bike with a rope I'd found in my dad's old boat. "Will you watch the counter, Cindy?" Emma May asked, swaying her hips from side to side, she shimmied her way over to the door, clutching her little square purse in her hand. "I'm just going to pop next door to the salon for a bit. No one will probably even come in," she added, leaning over the counter she opened the antique cash register using a series of button pushes and a slam of her fist on a spot at the bottom. She removed some cash and smiled back at me, pushing through the glass door that chimed when she opened it and again when it swung shut.

Emma May was right. She'd asked me to watch the store before and no one had ever come in.

Until that day.

It's not like I was eager to get home. Mom had started acting weird. Cleaning the floors for hours until the wood lost its shine. Talking to herself in the kitchen. Anytime I asked her about it, she acted like she didn't know what I was talking about. Dad told me that it would be okay and to just stay out of her way and give her some space.

I did what he said and stayed away as much as possible, most of the time not getting home until just after the sun set.

Watching the store was a good reason as any to prolong going home.

After an hour I got fidgety. I straightened the wall of cigarettes behind the register, turned the hot dogs on the rollers that didn't work, and tried to read a magazine, but I didn't understand what 'Seventeen Positions to Make Him Ache' even meant.

If someone was aching why didn't they just go see a doctor? Or a dentist? That's where I went when I had a toothache.

I'd given up on magazines and was leaning back on an old bar stool that creaked every time I swiveled on it. With my feet up on the counter, I turned the channel dial on the little black and white TV that was propped up on a phone book sitting on the corner of the counter. The only two channels that came in was some western one and the weather channel. Both pictures were fuzzy and the only sound coming out of the speakers was the sound of static and white noise. I tried to turn the entire thing off but nothing was working, if anything I'd only managed to make it louder. It became so loud that I didn't hear the motorcycles pull in the parking lot or the chime of the doorbells against the glass.

I pulled the plug from the outlet. I was still holding the cord when I looked up into the eyes of a dark-haired stranger.

And his gun.

"Everything you've got," he ordered, pointing with his gun to the register. He was swaying from side to side and his eyes were rimmed in red.

"I don't know how..." I started, but the man interrupted.

"Just fucking do it!" he ordered, making the gun click, he hopped up so that his chest was resting on the counter and the gun was only inches from the side of my head. I slid off the stool and pushed it over to the register, climbing on it I sat back on my knees and attempted the complicated combination of buttons that Emma had used when she'd opened it.

Nothing.

"Come on! Now kid!" The man yelled, growing impatient.

"I'm trying, maybe I'm hitting it in the wrong spot." I tried again, this time hitting it more at the bottom than the top. The man came over to my side of the register. He smelled like the time my baby brother got sick in the backseat of the truck on our way to Savannah.

"You listen here you little bitch," he said, raising his gun in the air like he was going to hit me with it. I jumped off the stool and wedged myself under the counter.

The front door chimes announced the door had opened and a voice boomed through the room, rattling the display case filled with glass jars of homemade beef jerky. "What the fuck are you doing?" The voice asked. The man with the gun froze with his hand still in the air.

"I'm getting paid, motherfucker," the man slurred.

A colorful arm came across the counter and grabbed the man by the neck pulling him over the counter like he weighed no more than a bug. There was a commotion and again the bells announced the door opening and closing.

It was another few minutes before I came out of my hiding spot from under the counter, crawling back onto the barstool I leaned across just as the doors opened. In walked a blond man wearing the same type of leather vest as the man with the gun, except he wasn't wearing a shirt underneath. He had muscles you could see under his skin like the wrestlers on TV, except not as enormous, his skin was decorated with tattoos, one large one across his shoulder and down one arm. The same colorful tattoos on the arm that had just pulled away the guy with the gun.

His bright eyes were the same shade as the Maxwell's new above ground swimming pool. A deep shining blue. His sandy blond hair was slicked backwards, longer on the top and shaved on the sides. A Mohawk I think they called it in the movies. "Are you the only one here?" he asked, scanning the room, peering into all three of the little aisles.

I nodded.

"You are the one that Skid just..." he didn't finish his sentence. Leaning forward he braced his hands on the counter and took a deep breath. His colorful tattoos extended to the tops of his hands and his fingers. He wore three big silver rings on each of his hands. He had hair on his face and up until that moment, when someone talked about beards, I'd always imagined the long white wire hair growing from the chins of old and ugly wizards wearing long robes and huge blue pointed hats. This man's beard was a little darker than his hair and only an inch or so long.

He was no wizard. Or old.

Or ugly.

"You have cool hair," I said. He had cool everything. More than cool, he was...

Pretty? Could a guy be pretty?

No, he wasn't pretty.

He was beautiful.

"Thank you, Darlin'," he said, leaning on the counter. He smelled like my father's truck when he was changing the oil and the lilac soap Mrs. Kitchener made from scratch every summer. "Your hair is pretty cool too." It was the first time in my life I think I blushed. My cheeks got hot and when the man noticed, he just smiled brighter and leaned in closer.

"Why are you in here all alone? They don't believe in child labor laws in Jessep?"

"I don't know what that is, but no one really comes in here much since they opened up the new highway. I was just minding the store while Emma May went to the beauty parlor. She said she'd be right back, but if they are going to make Emma May beautiful I think she's gonna be a while."

The man laughed and leaned on his elbows. "Listen, sweet girl. I'm sorry about my friend." He shot me a small smile. "He's very sick from a long ride and was being really stupid."

"Looked more like drunk to me. Maybe hungover, but you should tell him not to drink and drive."

"Where did you come from?" He looked amused. I wanted to do whatever it took to keep that look on his face. "Yeah, long rides can do that to people. But you're okay? He didn't hurt you at all did he?"

I shook my head. "No, I'm fine and you don't hafta be sorry. I was reaching for Emma May's shotgun just when you came in." I lifted the shotgun off its hooks under the counter so he could see it and pumped the shaft. The man took one look at the gun and bent over in a fit of laughter. I put it back under the counter. "What's so funny?" I asked.

"Oh man, I can't wait to tell Skid he almost got put to ground by a little girl." His eyes teared up as he continued to laugh, deep and loud.

"I'm not a little girl." I argued. "I'll be eleven next month. How old are you?"

"I'm twenty-one." He smiled even brighter and suddenly I was no longer angry over him calling me a little girl. If he kept smiling at me like that he could call me whatever he wanted.

"What's your name, Darlin?" he asked.

"I'm Thia Andrews," I said proudly, extending my hand out to him like my dad had taught me to do when introducing yourself.

"Thia?" he asked, giving me the same weird look most people did when they heard my name for the first time.

"Short for Cynthia, but not like Cindy. There are twelve girls in my class and three of them are Cindy's so I'm glad I'm a Thia and not a Cindy." I stuck out my tongue and mimicked sticking my finger down my throat. I hated the name Cindy, although when my dad proposed Thia as an alternative my mom refused to use the new nickname and had stuck to calling me Cindy. "What's your name?"

He took my hand in his. "They call me Bear, Darlin'." His skin was warm, except for the cool metal of his rings. I looked so small and pale compared to Bear, my hand looked like doll hands. "I got a buddy who shook hands as a kid too."

"Daddy says it's polite."

"Your daddy is right."

"Your friend who shakes hands, is he nice like you?" I asked.

"I wouldn't exactly say I'm nice. But my friend? He's...let's just say, he's different," Bear said with a laugh.

"Different is good. My teachers say I'm different cause I got pink hair, although they also say I have a speaking-out-of-turn problem," I said, with all the prolific knowledge of a ten-year-old.

"Sometimes different is real good, kid," Bear agreed.

"Is your real name Bear?" I asked. "Is your last name Grizzly or something?"

"Nope," he said. "Bear is just a nickname my club gave me. All the members go by nicknames, except we call them road names."

"You're in a club?" I asked with excitement. "That's so cool! If your real name isn't Bear though, what is it?"

"Can you keep a secret?" he whispered, looking around to make sure no one was listening. "I haven't told anyone my name in years. Even my old man calls me Bear. But my real name? It's Abel. And now you're one of the only few people who know that."

Abel.

"That's a really great name." Although Bear fit him too. He was taller than my dad and he had a lot of muscles and his hands were huge like Bear paws.

He reached into his back pocket and pulled out a clip with folded bills in it. More money than I'd ever seen.

More than what was in my Buzz Lightyear piggy bank in my room at home.

More than what was in Emma May's register.

Bear pulled off three of the bills and set them on the counter. "What's that for?" I asked, looking down at his hand which was partially covering the money as he slid it over to me and released it.

"That, is three hundred dollars."

"What do you want to buy? I can run over to the hair place and get Emma 'cause this dang register—"

"I'm not buying anything. It's for you. For your help today. For not—"

"Three hundred bucks for not calling the sheriff?" I asked, catching on to what he was offering.

Three hundred dollars to a ten-year-old might as well have been a million.

"Consider it a thank you for not shooting him," Bear corrected.

"That's okay. Emma May would have been mad about the blood anyway." Emma May hated a mess.

Bear laughed again and I smiled. "You're funny, kid. You know that?"

"I am?" I'd been called crazy, weird, strange, talkative, but never funny. I decided that I liked being called funny.

"Yeah," he said pushing the money closer to me. He looked up and around the counter. "No cameras in here?"

"I never seen one, but Emma is cheap, that's what Mama says 'cause she used fake flowers at her wedding, so maybe she didn't buy cameras." I blurted, eager to say anything to elicit another smile from Bear.

"Make sure you keep this money safe. Hide it somewhere. Don't tell anyone. It's a secret between you and me," he said with a wink. I tried to wink back but only managed to blink both my eyes at him like the genie on the old reruns of *I Dream of Jeannie*. Bear reached over and pushed some of my crazy stray hairs out of my face, tucking it back behind my ear. His fingers were rough but gentle, and when he withdrew his hand I wanted nothing more than for my hair to spring back out so he could do it again.

"I don't want your money," I blurted. I'd gone to the dollar store last week with my three-dollar allowance and couldn't find a single thing I really wanted. Three hundred some things were way more than I could ever want.

"Well in my world when someone does a favor, we repay that favor," Bear said, resting his chin on his hand. My eyes darted to the ring on his middle finger, a skull with a shiny stone in the center of the eye. Bear looked down, following my gaze. "You like that?" he asked, taking the ring off his finger.

"Yeah, I never seen nothing like it."

Bear held it between two fingers and looked down at it like he was seeing it for the first time. He was quiet and his forehead scrunched like he was thinking about something the same way mine did when I did my math homework. "I have an idea," he said, setting the ring on the counter. "This ring? It's a promise. In my club, when we give this to someone it represents a promise."

"A promise for what?" I asked, staring down at the ring, amazed, as if it were hovering in mid-air.

"A favor, whatever you need. It means I owe you."

"Me?"

"Yes," he said, tucking the bills back into his pocket. He slid the ring onto my thumb, it was so big I had to close my fingers around it to keep it in place.

"Wow. Cool!" I looked up into his eyes and smiled. "Thank you. I'll keep it safe I promise and I won't use it unless it's super important."

"I know you won't," Bear said.

A throat cleared and we both looked toward the sound. Standing by the open door was yet another man wearing the same type of vest. "We gotta go, man. We gotta be back at the MC in twenty minutes."

"Gotta go, Darlin', You make sure you keep that safe okay?" Bear tapped his finger over my closed fist.

"I'm not gonna tell no one. I swear it," I said, making a cross over my chest, something you only do when you are very serious about the promise you were making and I wanted Bear to know how serious I was about keeping quiet.

With a wink and a clamoring of the bell against the door, he was gone.

I watched as he slapped the back of the head of the dark-haired man who tried to rob the store. They exchanged some angry words before putting helmets on and heading back down the road. The third man following close behind.

Not thirty seconds after the last biker had left, Emma May sauntered through the door. "Anything exciting happen while I was gone?" she called out, heading for the back room.

I set the ring in the back pocket of my shorts. Then I crossed my fingers behind my back.

"No ma'am. Not a thing."

Bear

The sunlight of midday was blinding. Skid wasn't the only one hungover. We had partied in Coral Pines with some spring break chicks until the sun came up this morning. Skid just hadn't yet learned the value of eye drops and strong coffee.

The fucker is lucky I didn't lay him out right there in the parking lot of that fucking gas station.

"Are you out of your fucking mind holding up a gas station? Especially one in the same fucking county as the club. I don't know what they told you when you patched in brother but we're not a bunch of fucking juvenile delinquents. We don't ride around holding up gas stations or doing anything else that runs the risk of bringing huge heat down on us. We got big shit going on right now and dumb shit like this could land us all serving real fucking time. And who the fuck holds a gun on little fucking girls? I should shoot you to teach you a lesson. Where is your brain man?" I smacked Skid upside his head and knocked his sunglasses to the ground. "Prospect," I shouted over to Gus. "Why don't we do stupid shit right now? Why don't we point guns at little girls?"

"Got big shit going on. Gotta keep a low profile," Gus answered flatly. "And cause that's just kind of fucked up in general."

"Dude," Skid said, rubbing his eyes. "I'm still drunk from last night or this morning or whenever. I'm sorry, it was fucking stupid. Just don't fucking tell Chop okay?" He bent over to pick up his shades and I seriously thought about kicking him in the head. But then I calmed down a bit when I thought about all the stupid shit I'd done when I was first patched in, shit that would have brought hell down from my old man if he ever knew. "This one time and one time only. That's all you get. Your only pass. You pull shit like this again and you're dealing with Chop on your fucking own and I won't be there to come to your rescue." I straddled my bike.

"What was all that talk about the ring?" Gus asked. "That's the first time I heard about it. Did I miss something I'm supposed to know about? Am I supposed to give away a ring too? Cause I don't have one as nice as the skull one you gave her." Gus was always eager to learn and the possibility that he might have missed something made him look twitchy.

"No man, that was all fucking bullshit. A ring in exchange for her not calling the fucking law or her mommy and daddy to tell them what the big mean bikers did," I said.

"Creative," Gus said, pulling on his riding gloves.

"You gave the girl your skull ring? Didn't that thing have a diamond in it?"

"It sure did, and you'll pay me back every fucking penny." I turned on the engine, the roar of the bike coming to life between my thighs.

I laughed all the way home at the look on Skid's face when I said he owed me.

Bear

I never thought about that day or that girl again.

Until seven years later, when it all came back and bit me in the ass.

Chapter Two
THIA, SEVEN YEARS LATER

Silence. Scarier than any gun blast or cannon fire. Louder than thunder and ten times more terrifying.

Carrying one of Mrs. Kitchener's famous apple pies with one hand and holding onto the handle of my bike with the other, I navigated the rocks and holes on the narrow dirt road that led up to the small farmhouse I lived in with my parents.

Every day when I got home from my part-time job at the Stop-N-Go I was greeted by the bickering voices of my parents. With no other houses around for miles their voices carried over the tops of the trees and I heard them well before I saw the light in the window.

Before my little brother died I'd never heard them fight at all. When Sunlandio Cooperation decided to import their oranges, canceling their long held contracts with my family's grove, the bickering turned to full-blown hatred filled screams.

I set my bike down in the dirt, carefully shifting the pie from one hand to the other. Unable to bend down to retie my shoelace that had come undone on the ride, I shook out my foot as I walked, making sure not to trip over the hanging strings.

Chills broke out over my damp skin causing it to prickle with little bumps, making the little hairs on the back of my neck and my arms stand on end like I was moments away from being struck by lightning.

That's when I noticed it.

The silence.

"Mom?" I called out, but there was no answer.

"Dad?" I asked as I swung open the screen door. The lamp on the side table was on, the lampshade tilted on its side like it too was questioning what the hell was going on.

I heard a scuffle from the back room. "You guys back there?" I asked, setting the pie down on the counter. I made my way down the hall, pushing open the door to my parent's room, but it was empty. Same for the only bathroom and my room.

At the end of the hall, the door to my brother's old room was cracked open. My mother, having kept Jesse's room as a shrine to him since he'd passed, had always kept the door closed and whispered when she was in the hall like he was in there taking a nap and she didn't want to wake him up.

"Mom?" I asked again, slowly pushing open the door.

"Come on in, Cindy. We're in here," she said cheerily. It was the first time I'd heard my mom's voice take on a happy tone in years, although I hated that she'd called me Cindy.

It made my stomach roll.

Something was so wrong I almost didn't want to see what was waiting for me on the other side of that door.

And I was right.

I didn't.

Because there was my mother, sitting in the old rocking

chair she used to read to Jesse in, clutching his favorite dinosaur, rocking back and forth and back and forth, clutching the stuffed animal to her chest and nuzzling up against it.

Her eyes were rimmed in red with dark circles underneath, yet she had a smile on her face. "I'm so happy you're home Cindy-loo-hoo," she said, using the Dr. Seuss nickname she hadn't called me in years. "Are you ready to go?" she asked.

"Where? Go where, Mom? Where is Dad?"

"Your father didn't want to wait so he left already, but I wanted you to come with us so I waited for you." Her smile was big, but her eyes were glistening and were completely void of any emotion.

"But where did he go?" I asked again, stepping further into the room.

"Don't worry, we'll be joining him soon. I just wanted to talk to Jesse first," she said, stroking the dinosaur.

"Mom, Jesse is dead," I reminded her. "He died years ago."

Mom nodded and her eyes darted to the Star Wars themed wallpaper and then to his stack of Legos in the corner. "I know that, silly."

"Okay, because I thought for a second you were saying that..."

"I just wanted to let him know that we'd be joining him soon," Mom said. It was then, when she shifted the stuffed animal from one arm to the other, that I noticed the gun on her lap.

"Mom?" I asked, my entire body starting to shake with awareness of what she was really saying. "Tell me where Dad is," I whispered.

"I told you. He's gone. He left without us because he couldn't wait. He was always the impatient one." She shook her head and rolled her eyes. "You're a lot like him in so many ways," she sang.

"Why do you have a gun, Mom?"

"Silly girl, how else are we going to meet up with Jesse and your father? I mean I know there are other ways but I think this is the quickest and most efficient. After all, we don't want to keep them waiting too long," she said, patting the dinosaur's back like she was burping it. Back and forth she continued to rock, never breaking the slow and steady rhythm. The chair creaking with each roll over the hardwood floors.

I took another step toward her hoping to snatch the gun from her hand, but she saw where I was looking and picked up the pistol, waving it in the air. "Nah ah. Your father wanted to be the one to hold it too but I insisted. This is a job for Mommy and no one else. It's about time I took some control and took care of this family. Having us all in the same place is the first step."

My foot on the floorboards sounding as quiet as a beating drum. "Now, now, Cindy. You were never good at waiting your turn, but the good news is that you'll be first."

"Where did you send Dad to meet Jesse?" I asked, tears prickling behind my eyes but the adrenaline coursing through my veins prevented them from spilling.

"I don't see why that matters," Mom said, blowing off a strand of dark curls that had fallen into her eyes. "But if you must know he left in our room. It was a lot messier than I expected. When I send you I think it should be in the tub, then I'll just climb in after you. Maybe I'll leave some bleach for the sheriff, red stains are the worst, especially in the white grout," she said with the same eerily cheery voice she'd greeted me with.

I took a step back and Mom continued to stare up at me,

smiling a full-toothed smile from ear to ear. She didn't follow me when I turned and opened the door to their bedroom. It was empty.

Mom's gone crazy. That doesn't mean Dad is dead. She could be lying. She could be making it up.

I rounded the bed.

Please be alive, please be alive.

On the floor on the side of the bed against the wall was my father's lifeless body, his eyes and mouth both opened, frozen in surprise.

I gasped and covered my mouth. "No, no, no, no, no!" I shouted.

I backed away from my dad into the hallway and when I looked down the hall my mother was no longer in the rocking chair. I turned to run out the door but ran directly into the soft satin of my mother's pink nightgown.

"You ready honey?" she asked, cocking her head to the side. The gun was in her hands but it wasn't raised.

"I, I, I need to say a few things to Jesse too," I said, scooting past her toward his room.

She smacked herself in the forehead with the barrel of the gun. "Silly me, of course you do. I'll be waiting right here and then after we meet them we'll have ice cream."

"Yuh yuh yeeaaaahhh, ice cream is good, Mom," I said, sniffling. I sidestepped her and pretended like I was turning down the hall to Jesse's room, she shifted her shoulders to make room for me, and I took the only chance I knew I had and burst into a sprint, dodging her as I made a run in the opposite direction toward the door.

The wall beside the door exploded as a bullet tore into the hundred-year-old plaster. My mother was laughing as I leapt down the porch steps. One of the laces of my shoes caught on the railing and I sailed forward through the air, landing on my chest. The air whooshed out of my lungs and I turned on my back, desperately gasping for air.

"You talked your way out of that trip to Nana's last year, you're not getting out of this," my mother said as she looked down at me from the porch. In my peripherals I spotted my father's old rifle against the front of the house. He used it to scare the critters away from eating the oranges. I don't think it had been used since the previous harvest. It had been out in the elements for months.

Chances were that the thing didn't even work.

"I'm not talking my way out of it, Mom," I said, as I could finally draw in a breath. Slowly, I crab-walked on my hands and feet, sideways toward the house.

Toward the only shot I had of surviving.

"I just thought that maybe we could do it together, you know, go at the same time," I said, mirroring her cheery voice as best I could.

"Oh, Cindy that's a lovely idea. You were always my sweet one, you know. Headstrong. And a holy terror at times, but you could also be very sweet. I loved the way you used to play with my necklaces and earrings when you were a baby." Mom set the gun against her chest and sighed.

"Can you do me a favor though, Mom? Can you use Dad's old rifle? That way I have something to talk to him about when we get there. And I can use the gun you sent him to Jesse with. It will be fun and you know it's hard for me to find things to talk about with Dad."

"You know," she said, picking up the rifle off the house. I climbed to my feet and wavered, holding onto the chipped siding so I wouldn't fall. "I wish your father would have thought of something nice like this. It would have been so much easier. You should have heard him screaming and yelling." She let out a quick burst of laughter. "Begging." She inspected the gun to make sure it was loaded then tossed it to me. I caught it and made sure it was loaded just as she had. "Can you believe it? Your father...begging. It was quite ridiculous."

Under the moonlight my mother's ivory skin glowed. I'd always envied her long dark curls and naturally pink lips. To me she'd always looked like Snow White. I used to watch her pick oranges in the grove for her famous orange marmalade and wonder why I got stuck with pinkish hair, green eyes, and freckles, instead of her good looks.

Snow White stood tall in her satin blood splattered nightgown and aimed the rifle at me. With my heart hammering in my chest I raised the pistol at her. "I love you baby, see you on the other side," she said. Tears welled in my eyes. I would only have a split second. Even if the gun jammed like it often did on the first pull of the trigger, it wouldn't on the second.

My mother smiled manically at me with wide eyes.

Then Snow White pulled the trigger.

I held my breath, but nothing happened. She tapped on the side of the gun as she'd seen my father do a million times before and just before she was able to get her finger around the trigger again, I fired.

Blood splattered against the siding, turning peeling white paint to shiny red.

Mom had been right about one thing.

It was quick.

I dropped to my knees and clutched my chest. My mind blanked. I couldn't form a coherent thought. Both my parents were dead and I didn't know what I should do. Who I should call.

Both my parents were dead.

You killed your mother.

I wailed into the night; lost, afraid, and utterly alone.

I reached under my shirt and sought comfort the way I often did when my parents had been fighting, by clutching the ring I wore on a chain beneath my shirt.

I rubbed the cool metal between my fingers. A bolt of lightning hit the water tower and it was at that moment when the answer came to me. I knew where I had to go.

Who I had to go to.

Chapter Three
THIA

It was raining.
It was summer in Florida.
It was always raining.

Somewhere during the forty minute bike ride from the farmhouse in Jessep to Logan's Beach I'd lost all feeling in my feet as I pedaled wildly against the force of the sideways rain.

I'd tried to take my dad's old Ford. The key rack by the front door was empty, which left only one other place they could've been. I willed my legs forward and back into the room that held my father's lifeless body. Seeing him earlier didn't lessen the impact of walking around the bed and finding my father splayed out at an awkward angle against the wall, his hair still wet with his blood.

"Daddy," I cried, stepping over the red river that started as a pool behind his head and grew thinner and thinner until it left the room my parents shared and seeped into the space between the wall and floor, spreading both left and right, lining the white baseboards in fresh red.

My entire family was dead, but I didn't have time to think

about it and I was grateful because the weight of what happened was threatening to crush me where I stood.

Something inside me, a final ray of hope, told me that if I could just get to Bear, then it would be okay. He could make all this go away.

But he could make it okay.

He made you a promise. He will help you. He can do the thinking for you. You just have to get there.

I couldn't bring myself to look in my dad's pockets. Touching him would just make it more real.

Without another option, I picked my bike out of the dirt and headed out.

Each rotation of my legs made the muscles in my thighs feel heavier and heavier. The only thing propelling me forward was the salvation I'd hoped to find when I reached the Beach Bastard's clubhouse.

When I reached Bear.

Chapter Four
THIA

The rain hadn't let up by the time I got to the gate. A skinny kid stood guard outside on a stool. Through his clear plastic poncho I could see the patch on his cut that read PROSPECT. He watched me as I laid down my bike and limped over to him, the muscles in my legs hadn't yet gotten the message that I was done pedaling. "I need to see Bear," I said. "Please. Can you tell him that Thia is here to see him? Thia from the gas station. I need to talk to him. It's very important."

"How important?" The prospect asked, moving the toothpick that hung from his lips from one side to the other with his tongue.

Pulling off my chain I held it up so he could see Bear's skull ring dangling from it. "This important."

The prospect eyed the ring skeptically before slithering off his seat. He took the chain from my hand and disappeared behind the screeching metal gate. When he came back ten minutes later it was like he was another person. "I'm Pecker," he announced, stepping aside so I could enter. "What did you say your name was again?" A smile replaced his earlier scowl.

"Thia," I said, stepping into The Beach Bastard clubhouse, although I would have called it more like a compound. It was an old motel or apartment complex. Three stories high with rooms open to the elements circled an open courtyard below where an empty pool sat in the center. Off to the side was a clear glass door that looked like it used to be an old bar or restaurant and it looked as if the Bastards still used it for its original purpose. The bar was fully stocked and several men, all wearing cuts, played pool at one of three pool tables.

"Where is Bear?" I asked again. Out of the rain and under the protection of a series of overhangs, my jaw began to shake and my teeth chattered. My wet tank top and shorts clung to my body. My hair lay flat and lifeless against my forehead and cheeks, dripping water into my eyes.

"Bear's busy right now, but he told me you can wait for him in his room," Pecker said as I followed him up a flight of stairs to the second floor, holding onto the jagged aluminum railing for support. I nicked my middle finger on an especially sharp point, sucking off the drop of blood that pooled on the surface. "Sorry, should have warned you about that."

Rain streamed down into the courtyard with such ferocity that the Bastards wouldn't need a hose to fill their empty pool. The small overhang was no protection from the sideways rain.

Pecker stopped in front of a dark green door and opened it, motioning for me to go inside. "He'll meet you in here," he said with a laugh. I stepped inside the dark room but spun around again when I heard the door slam behind me.

"Where did you get this?" a menacing voice asked. My throat squeezed tight and slowly I turned to face the owner of the voice. On the edge of the bed sat a man who looked very much like what I remembered Bear did, except this man had graying hair and a face filled with hard lines.

He held up Bear's ring.

"Where is Bear? Are you his dad?" I asked, hugging my arms around my waist. The man stood up and laughed, closing the distance between us. I backed up to avoid contact, my head banged against the door.

"I'm not sure you heard me, Darlin'," he said with mock sincerity, "But I asked you a fucking question and I don't know who you think you are or where you think you are, but I'll fill you in..." He leaned down to stare at me with familiar blazing blue eyes. "I'm Chop. Stands for Chop Chop because..." He chuckled and ran a calloused finger down my cheek, I pulled away and he grabbed my face so hard my mouth opened and he squeezed my cheeks until they touched in the middle. "Well, you don't need to know that story, now do you? I run this shit. The patch on my cut says so. You're in my house so you'll tell me where the fuck you got this before I shove it down your fucking throat and choke you with it." Chop held up the chain again, the light from the lamp glinted off the diamond in the eye of the skull.

Chop might have had the same color eyes as Bear's but they held none of the beauty. Chop's burned with instability, rage, and violence.

This was a mistake.

I'd gone to the compound seeking... what exactly had I been seeking? Help? Protection? Safety? All I knew was that in that room, with Bear's old man only a few inches from my face, I felt anything but safe.

When I didn't answer right away, Chop shrugged. "Okay have it your way." It was when he pressed the ring to my lips when I suddenly found my voice.

"Bear gave it to me," I blurted out.

"Bullshit! Where did you get it?" he roared, again trying to force the ring between my lips.

"I was ten!" I screamed and when I opened my mouth the ring slipped in and smacked against the back of my throat. I gagged and Chop took a step back, examining the ring in the light of the lamp. I didn't know if he meant for me to continue but I did anyway. "He gave it to me in Jessep when I was ten years old because I did a favor for him." I didn't know if I would get Bear in trouble by telling Chop exactly what happened so I kept it vague. "He told me that if I ever needed his help to come here and show the ring and he would help me."

Chop waved me off. "Shut up," he commanded, still twisting the ring around in his hand like he couldn't believe it was there. A twisted smile took over his face and he let out a burst of laughter. "He's a dead fucking man walking but the kid has always been funny."

"What does that mean?" I asked, not sure if the new round of teeth chattering was from being freezing or from fear.

"It means that my boy gave this to you because he never expected you to show up and take him up on it," Chop said, putting the ring in a pocket sewn to the inside of his cut. "He wouldn't have done shit for you, except maybe show you his cock."

"No! He said that it's a biker promise. It's your way…"

"Darlin' we ain't got no such code and I know that because all of our codes have to do with killing. Like what, where, who, and when."

Bear lied to me?

Yes, Bear lied and I was a stupid little girl who fell for it. He never wanted to help me. He just didn't want me to tell on him.

"Can I at least talk to him?" I asked with one last shred of hope. It didn't matter that the ring that I'd been clinging to for seven years was a joke. I still needed help. "I just need to..."

"Bear isn't a Beach Bastard anymore. He took off his cut like the cunt pussy he is and walked out that gate because he's a coward. He's not a biker anymore. He's not a friend. He's not even a fucking man. Do you know what he is?" Chop asked, stepping back in front of me. I shook my head, frozen in place by his stare. "He. Is. Death. A dead motherfucker who just happens to still be breathing." He pressed his nose into the space between my neck and shoulder and inhaled. I cringed, and tried to pull away, but his big muscular body kept me trapped. "But I'm gonna fix that real fucking soon," he whispered, his hot breath against my ear made me feel like I was going to puke.

"If he's not here, then I should just go," I said, every internal alarm I had reaching deafening volumes inside my head.

Run. Run. Run.

I felt behind me for the doorknob and when I found it I gave it a twist, but it didn't budge. "Locks from the outside," Chop said wickedly, his eyebrows jumping suggestively.

Grabbing me by the shoulders he threw me onto the floor. I landed on my side and pain tore through my ribs. Chop knelt down and straddled me, his thighs holding me prisoner on the dirty carpet. "He chose that motherfucker King over his brothers. And he's going to fucking pay."

"Let me go!" I wailed, writhing underneath him, trying to break free, but he was as stuck in place as the doorknob. I tried to beat my fists against his chest but he grabbed my wrists and twisted them painfully. "Please just let me go!" I cried out.

"Don't worry, little one. I'm not going to kill you. In fact I'm going to make sure one of the boys gives you a ride out."

"You are?" I asked, knowing that he wouldn't be on top of me cutting off circulation to my hands if his only plan was to drop me somewhere else.

"I am. Boys are going to drop you off first thing in the morning."

"Morning?" I asked, only half the word audible, the rest came out as a breathless whisper.

"Yes, morning. Because first we want to make sure that if Bear sees you that he knows that he's a dead man but anything he wants to keep breathing better not be stupid enough to step over onto this side of the causeway."

"Okay, let me go. If I see him I'll give him the message," I promised.

"No, you stupid girl. You are the message." Chop pushed my hands above my head with one hand and leaned down, biting my nipple through my shirt.

Hard.

I cried out and Chop sat up and laughed, admiring the fresh stain of blood on my shirt where his teeth had just been. "The brothers and I are gonna have some fun with you, bitch."

"Brothers?" I asked, or at least I thought I asked because Chop balled his fist and slammed it into my jaw, making me see stars. His smiling image above me flickered like someone was turning the lights in the room on and off. One second I saw him and the next second it was all black, although I knew he was there because the crushing weight on top of me never left. "He doesn't know me. He won't care. Don't do this. Please don't do this!"

Chop ignored me. "Wait until Murphy gets ahold of you. He likes to break little girls like you," Chop sighed. "When we saw you come in, I'd already promised him that I'd save your pussy for him, though I think a taste won't hurt." He sat back on his knees and just as I thought he was about to get off me, he flipped me over with one arm, my head crashing against the dresser. He pulled my wet shorts and underwear down my legs with one rough yank.

"No!" I screamed, kicking my legs out.

Chop used his knee to spread my legs and using one of his fingers he roughly forced it inside of me. I felt his too long fingernails scrape against my inside walls. I felt every ridge of his finger until his ring prevented him from going any further. "So fucking tight. Really is a shame that I'm a Bastard who keeps my promises to my brothers. You'll have to remind Bear of that when you see him." He pulled his finger out of me and my insides pulsed from the injury. I picked my cheek off the carpet and turned around to look at Chop who winked at me before popping his finger into his mouth. "You taste so fucking good, Darlin'. It's too bad we are going to ruin this little body of yours, because we could use some new pussy around here."

Chop unbuckled his belt and pushed down his jeans with one hand, still leaning over me, his one hand still keeping me prisoner. His enormous erection sprang free from his jeans and I turned my head back toward the floor not wanting to see what I was about to feel. I clenched my thighs and tried to push my legs together, but another blow to the side of my face stripped me of the will to fight. Replacing it with the dizzying image of the spinning room as my head landed against the carpet. I tried to lift my head again but my neck couldn't support it. My head was too heavy. It was too much.

It was all too much.

Chop released my arms when he felt the fight in me die, nudging my legs open wider with his knee. I felt his hot and heavy erection on my back. He whispered into my ear, his words beyond cold. Beyond callous. "I'm going to wreck this pretty little asshole of yours. I'm going in dry so this is going to fucking hurt." He ran his teeth down my ear, biting down on my earlobe. "But first a little test to see how tight this ass really is."

He pressed his thumb into me and pain shot up my spine over and over again like I was being stabbed. The further he pressed the more pain I felt.

The more jagged the knife became.

I used all the strength I had left to speak, "And you say Bear isn't a man, anymore."

"What was that little girl?" Chop asked, pressing further inside of me until I collapsed against the arm holding me up.

"You told me that Bear's not a man. It's you who isn't a man. You're nothing. You're fucking garbage!" I wailed as the pain intensified.

"Here I was nice enough to give you a warm up," Chop removed his thumb, but any relief I felt was temporary because he grabbed his shaft and pressed it firmly against the tight bundle of nerves he'd just finished injuring. "No more of that." I tried to mentally ready myself for the pain, but there was no amount of preparation I could do to be ready for what was to come.

He was going to split me apart.

I felt him start to push in, sharp stabbing sensation.

Then it was gone.

Chop was gone.

Glass flew through the air as the window exploded, shattering into a million pieces, coating every surface in the room, including my skin, with tiny prickly shards that stuck to me like little Chinese stars.

Spinning. The room. Everything was spinning.

Shouting, shuffling and banging sounded from outside the room. The door opened and slammed shut several times.

The solid floor underneath me disappeared and was replaced with swaying, bumping, and a slight vibration of a vehicle.

I pried open one of my swollen eyes. "Who are you?" I asked. Shadows concealed the driver. Rain pelted the windshield faster than the wiper could clear it.

"I'm Gus," he said flatly, with zero emotion in his voice.

"Hi, Gus," I sang deliriously, as the spinning returned. My head fell back against the passenger window.

Gus, the rain, the clubhouse, Chop, parents, everything started to fade. Further and further away until I was surrounded by nothingness. Delicious nothingness. I wanted to exist in it for as long as it would have me.

Living in a permanent state of nothing sounded like a good idea.

Maybe, this is what death feels like?

Was I dying?

I didn't know, and in all honesty, at that moment...

I didn't fucking care.

Blackness came for me. I didn't fight it. Closing my eyes I allowed it to swallow me whole, welcoming it to take me in. A part of me hoping it would keep me there forever. I never wanted to wake up to face the reality of what my life had become in such a short period of time.

It wasn't a life at all.

It was a nightmare.

Chapter Five
BEAR

I wasn't wasted.
I was beyond fucking wasted.
A new word needed to be invented for the level of fucked up I was.

Twisting dark hair in my hand, I pulled back hard, eliciting a moan from whatever her name was who was licking my balls. Her friend, who had the same color hair, just shorter, rolled a condom onto my cock and sank down onto it.

The motel room was dark, the curtains so thick it could have been noon and I wouldn't have known.

Day, night. It had all blended together.

The place reeked of cum, sweat, and weed. There was no questioning what had been going on for the last however many days I'd been there.

Sleep was pointless because whenever I did fall asleep there was nothing restful about it. Which was partially due to the recurring dreams I'd been trying to avoid, and a lot-a-bit to do with the mass quantity of blow I was shoveling up my nostrils.

Did I come? How fucking sad is that?

Even sadder?

I didn't fucking care.

It didn't matter that there was two of them, there could have been two-thousand, all wet and ready to go, bent over and waiting, and it wouldn't have changed a fucking thing.

Whatever had happened, at least it was over.

I didn't even remember where I met the girls or even when, and I didn't know their names because I never bothered to ask. From the looks of them this wasn't their first rodeo. They may not have been club whores, but I could spot their type from a mountain top, and these girls had BBB written all over them.

I had the sudden and immediate urge to be left alone.

Now.

I lit a cigarette and tossed the lighter back onto the nightstand, watching it spin around and around until it fell off the edge. "Get the fuck out!" I snapped, waving my hand in the direction of the door, squinting to make sure I was waving at the exit, and not the bathroom.

Yup. Exit.

Nailed it.

Scurrying around the room like a cockroach after flipping the lights on, the short haired one searched for her clothes and shoes. Once she found what she was looking for she shook the shoulder of the other girl who was still on the bed, naked and on her stomach. "Clarissa, we gotta fucking go." She looked back at me and my expression remained hard. "Now, Clarissa, we gotta fucking go, NOW!"

Clarissa groaned and turned onto her side, clutching the sheets to her ample chest, "I'm fucking sleeping, Julie. Leave me alone. Grandma's not picking us up for church until twelve. I can sleep in today."

Julie kept trying to wake her friend, with no luck.

With each tick of the old clock on the wall I felt my blood beginning to boil. As the second hand approached click number ten it was like thunder in my ears.

I picked up a heavy glass ashtray from the side table and launched it against the wall, creating a basketball size hole in the sheetrock and a sound that exploded through the silent space like a tornado had crashed through the window. Ashes billowed from the hole in the wall, clouding the small space with the stench of stale cigarettes.

Clarissa leapt from the bed, alert and awake like she'd been up for hours. She grabbed her purse, and her sad excuse for a dress from the floor on her way out—leaving her shoes behind, and the door open. Julie was close on her heels as they both ran naked out into the daylight, which was so fucking blindingly bright that all I could see was white.

I guess that answers my question about it being night or day.

Swaying on my feet I got up from the bed, shielding my eyes from the light I stumbled over to the door and slammed it shut before turning back around and falling onto the hard mattress.

I ashed my cigarette onto the floor, and from state of the holes in the carpet I could tell I wasn't the first one. The half empty bottle of JD beckoned me from the side of the bed. Grabbing it by the neck I tilted my head back and poured the amber liquid directly into my mouth. I didn't bother to wrap my lips around the bottle in fear of slowing the flow of whiskey. I swallowed it down in huge gulps until my throat burned like it was on fire, and the bottle was empty. I let my head drop again, this time onto a pillow that smelled like pussy. I threw it to the floor and pressed my face into the bare mattress.

Well, you're handling this shit real fucking well, Care Bear. My dead best friend said in my head. Preppy was as clear in my mind as he would've been if he were sitting on the edge of the bed. *I'm one for a party but this isn't a fucking party. This is where parties go to die. This motherfucker is about to need one of those Pulp Fiction shots to the heart.*

"Shut the fuck up, Prep. Aren't dead people supposed to be quiet? Because if so, you, my nonliving friend, are failing at this whole dead thing," I said out loud.

Awe, it's so cute you think that being dead could get me to shut the fuck up. And I'm not fucking done yet, Care Bear. You were really mean to those whores and whores are like my favoritest people ever. Not cool, man. Not cool at all."

"I'll make a note of that," I said, as the room began to spin. I closed my eyes in an effort to make the spinning stop, but it didn't work. I kicked one of my legs off the bed and anchored my foot to the floor but my level of sobriety was way past that old trick working.

When I opened my eyes again not only was the room spinning even faster, but I could almost swear that I saw Preppy standing over me, looking down with a frown on his usually happy face, his bow tie swirling around and around growing darker and darker as black halos filled my vision.

I was seeing my dead best friend.

I was right.

A whole new level of wasted.

This wallowing in your own shit is starting to fucking depress me and I'm fucking dead!

It was the last thing I heard, or thought, or however this

odd communication between my fucked up brain worked, before my vision became completely black and the darkness swept me under.

But even copious amounts of whiskey couldn't save me from the dreams.

I feel heat against my side so close it burns. I hear the fire crackle and when I open my eyes I can see the embers from the fire pop into the air. I feel the singe of my skin when one lands on the back of my neck.

I try to get up, but I can't. I can't move my arms either.

I'm on my stomach, laying across a set of cheap plastic lawn chairs.

I'm tied down.

Men, several of them surround me. They're laughing. Poking at me. Punching me in the face. Kicking me in the sides. At one point the chairs fall to the side and I go with them, positive I cracked a rib against the brick of the bonfire in the process. There is an order to set me upright, and it's done immediately.

When they set the chairs back up I lift my head and I see Eli, the man responsible for my current state, sitting with his legs crossed and a cigar in his mouth. When the smoke clears from around his face it reveals his amused smile.

The one I was going to cut from his face.

My pants are tugged down. I try to scream, to protest, but there is a gag in my mouth. One of the men puts his fucking hands on the cheeks of my ass and spreads them apart. They are poking at my asshole with the end of something and I scream through the pain as they penetrate me over and over again. I concentrate on the things I am going to do to them when I'm free to avoid passing out from the pain.

Because I will be free.

This was not the way I was meant to go out.

I think of revenge. Removing all of their teeth one by one with pliers. A guy in the club knows how to do it in a way that maximizes blood loss. The victim dies a slow painful death by tooth loss. That's of course only after I remove their intestines through their assholes with a wrench.

They think what they are doing to me is torture.

These fuckers have no fucking idea what torture is.

I'm so still that one of them asks another if I've passed out. My eyes are closed when I feel the presence of someone in front of me. He pokes his finger into my eye and I don't react. I'm in the worst pain I've ever felt in my life, but I've found my place of calm and I'm not leaving it until I can kill every single one of these motherfuckers. I'm saving my energy for when I can actually use it.

I'm a fucking Beach Bastard.

Bitches have been gunning for me since the ink was still wet on my birth certificate.

This isn't my first time being bound and tortured.

Chances are it wouldn't be my last.

Never is there a doubt in my mind that I'm going to die there.

Never.

My gag is removed and I hear the unmistakable sound of a zipper being lowered. I almost laugh to myself because I know what's about to come.

But he doesn't.

He laughs to his friends when he shoves his fat little cock in my mouth. I fight the bile rising in my throat. My reflex to fight. I stay perfectly still for one, two, three seconds.

The longest three seconds of my life.

I close my teeth around his cock until they meet in the middle. When he screams and tries to pull away I hold on tighter and jerk my head to the side.

Warm copper fills my mouth and I can't help but laugh as the man hops around in pain.

My laughter is out of control as his blood pours down the sides of my mouth and I spit out what's left of his little cock onto the ground.

The sound of gunfire erupts and bodies around me start to fall. There is an explosion and the bonfire sends me sailing into the air. I land with a dull thud on the grass and wait to be untied.

Because I know it's King.

I know he's come for me.

And I know it's just killing time now.

In a flash King is dragging a tied up and half conscious Eli into his truck and I'm putting a bullet in the last of Eli's men on the dock when I hear a voice. And then suddenly I'm not covered in blood and ending a life. I'm sitting next to the most beautiful girl I'd ever seen in my life.

My best friend's girl.

King's girl.

"I would have been a good biker whore for you," she says, and my cock practically leaps to attention inside my pants. Her large blue eyes are unfocused. Her pupils the size of the fucking moon, but somehow the way she's staring up at me makes me believe that she is looking past me. Past my bullshit. Past the biker and to the man inside. At that moment she's the only person in the world who can see past the cut and I must be suicidal because I'm willing to suffer the wrath of King to be with her.

I don't even care that she's drunk, it will make what I have to tell her easier. But right now I don't care about anything but putting my lips to hers. Pink, plump, beautiful. I imagine them wrapped around my cock and my jeans get tighter when my cock decides that he likes the idea as much as I do. When I hear the click of a gun behind me I know it's King. The click is a courtesy because I'm a friend. I know first hand that most who find themselves at the end of his gun aren't extended the same courtesy of a warning. I look back at the girl they call Doe and I want her so bad I can almost taste her on my tongue.

I contemplate ignoring my friend and taking the bullet.

I think she could be worth it.

She's angry at King, and has every right to be. She just walked in on him and some bitch. I almost want to deck the motherfucker myself for making her so upset. But oh the fuck well.

I'm going to tell King to fuck off. Tell him to shoot me if that's what he really wants. As I see it, I'm about to right a wrong. I should have never sent her up to King at that party. I should have taken her to my bed and kept her there the second I laid eyes on her.

Instead my dumb ass sent her up to King to put a smile on his face.

Like that fucker ever smiled.

Doe turns and looks up at King and even through all the hurt and anger on her face I can see clearly how she feels about him. I've never seen real love before, but I know that this is it and it makes my stomach turn because I know right then what I am seeing is the real thing. Shit, I can feel it. Like static electricity zapping the air between them.

It physically pains me to unwrap my arms from around her because I know it's the last time I'd ever touch her because she didn't belong to me. Never did.

Never could.

I walk past King and barrel into him with my shoulder, giving him a polite 'fuck you' shove. When I get back up to the house I almost keel over when I feel the sting in the very center of my chest. It hurts so bad I think for a second that the motherfucker changed his mind and shot me after all. Either that or I'm having a heart attack.

But when I open my eyes and look down I'm staring at my best friend Preppy, blood pours from his chest and he's dying in front of me all over again. The life drains from his eyes and the pain in my chest intensifies. I look down and the blood stain on my chest matches Preppy's. The pain becomes unbearable.
But the pain isn't because of any bullet.
It's because I couldn't save him.
And then a swarm of bees attacked.
BZZZZZ BZZZZZZ BZZZZZZZ
Bees?
Bzzzzzzz. Bzzzzzzz. Bzzzzzzzz.

My burner phone vibrated on the end table, jumping around and playing the same cheesy ringtone all the burners I'd ever had played. Some fucking happy tune that never seemed to match my less than happy mood.

I was thankful when it stopped dancing. I smashed my face back into the mattress.

Three seconds later it started again, and again I ignored it.

Three seconds after that it started yet again.

Only one person had my number and when I first left Logan's Beach he called me every day.

I never answered.

The calls slowed to once a week.

I never answered.

When the calls stopped completely I felt a mixture of both hurt and relief.

The phone buzzed for the fourth time and I couldn't take it anymore. I reached over and pressed the green button, holding it to my ear without saying a word. "Bear? Bear is that you?" a female voice asked.

Doe.

"I'm so glad you answered. You don't have to say anything,

but you need to come home. Something's happened," she said, the worry in her voice cutting through my fog.

I sat up on the bed quickly. Too quickly, and saw stars.

"I don't know where to start. It's just that..." she paused and it sounded as if she'd covered the receiver with her hand. "You're so pushy," she said, but not to me. There was a commotion on the line like the phone was being passed and I knew exactly who it was being passed to, even before I heard him murmur, "I'm going to make you regret that smart mouth of yours after the kids go to bed."

I didn't need to hear that shit. It was hard work sustaining the constant headache that pounded between my ears and I needed to get back to it.

"You there?" King asked. I responded with a grunt and the sound of my lighter as I lit a cigarette. The smoke opened up my lungs and sending just enough nicotine to my brain to make the rusted wheels in my head start turning again. "I'm here," I said in case he didn't hear my grunt, my voice dry and scratchy. I reached over for my bottle of Jack Daniels but it was empty.

I tilted it back and opened my mouth, the remnants dripped into my mouth.

One, two, three, done.

"You sound like fucking shit," King said.

"Well hello to you fucking too," I sang.

"We have a situation here more important than the sound of your fucking voice and as much as I'd like to take care of it for you, I wouldn't know where to start."

"What?"

"Gus was here..."

Holy shit.

I leapt off the bed, and again it was too fast because I fell to the floor with a thud. The phone slid across the carpet. Turning over onto my back I grabbed the phone and again held it up to my ear.

At least I didn't lose my smoke I thought, crossing my eyes to look at the cigarette still dangling from my lips.

"What the fuck is going on over there?" King asked.

I looked over at the clock on the nightstand. "Don't worry about it. What you should worry about is why a brother is at your fucking door at three o'clock in the morning." The MC was after me. As much as they'd love to take out King, killing civilians brought too much heat, but I still couldn't think of a single reason why Gus would be there, other than taking out my closest friend to get to me.

"He's not here anymore. He had a girl with him."

"Gus has a girl? He's an awkward motherfucker, but good for him, I guess," I said.

"No, shut the fuck up and listen..."

"I've got a headache the size of the fucking Grand Canyon so cut the vague shit and tell me what the fuck is so important in the middle of the night that a text wouldn't have been sufficient," I said. The popcorn ceiling above me had blackish mold growing in the corners and if I closed one eye I could practically see the patch of fuzzy spores slowly growing into long-term lung issues.

"It's one in the afternoon," King corrected. "And I just sent you a picture. Check it," King said.

Clicking over to the messages a little red number one appeared over the green bubble. I clicked on the icon and when the picture popped up I sucked in a breath. It was a girl. Naked, bruised and bloodied. Her hair was a weird shade between red and blonde.

Pink maybe? Or maybe that was the blood in her hair.

"You get it?" King asked.

"Looking at it now, but why the fuck are you sending me a picture of a dead girl?" I clicked the speaker button so I could talk to King and look at the picture at the same time. She looked familiar. Her eyes were closed and her crazy colored hair was covering most of her face. "I'm not Preppy, this kind of shit doesn't get my dick hard."

"It's not a dead girl, asshole. She's alive, but she's here and she's pretty banged up."

"So take her to the fucking hospital..." I began, ready to end the conversation and bribe one of the maids to make a liquor store run for me.

"Bear!" King snapped. "She's here, in the garage apartment. Gus saved her before the MC could work her over worse than they already did, but he'd heard your old man say he was gonna dump her here, for you."

Why the fuck would the MC do this?

I didn't have to think about it too hard. Knowing my old man and how he operated, I knew there was only one reason why he'd beat up a defenseless girl. Well, actually there was a few. But there was only one reason why he'd beat up on one and dump her somewhere he knew I would be told about it.

To send a message.

The realization set in as King kept talking, although I couldn't hear what he was saying. It was the pink hair. I hadn't seen it in a long time. Not since...

"Look at her fucking hand, asshole," King barked, bringing me back to the present. I could practically see through the phone the vein in his neck that always pulsed when he was angry.

I used my fingers to zoom in on her hand and my breath

caught in my throat when I saw what she was clutching between her fingers.

A ring. A Bastard skull ring.

My Bastard Skull Ring.

"I'm on my way."

Chapter Six
BEAR

The numbness that had been good to me over the last several months had been replaced with the familiar anger that drove me my entire life. The anger that allowed me to take lives. The anger that allowed me to hate enemies I'd never met. However, this new kind of anger bubbling inside me was for one man and one man only.

Chop.

I was still half drunk. It was hard not to be. If I wanted to be completely sober it would take months to clean my system out. Maybe years.

The broken lines of the highway blended into one long streak of white and yellow as I pressed down on the gas pedal, the engine shrieked and groaned in protest. The red line of the speedometer pulsed with hesitation, climbing higher and higher as I pushed the old bread truck to its limit.

I'd given the ring to the little girl as a fucking joke. A way to placate her, make her feel good for not calling the fucking law. I never expected her to show up to the damn MC. What could she have needed my help with anyway? I honestly thought she'd forget all about the ring and the fake story behind it.

I was so fucking wrong.

Just because it was that same girl in the picture King sent me didn't mean it all wasn't an elaborate trap set up by Chop to get me back to Logan's Beach.

My old man was a cocksucker, but he was a smart cocksucker. He wouldn't come after me in public, and with all the surveillance around King's house he'd be sure to stay as far away from The Causeway as possible.

But the girl?

She could be on the Bastard's payroll for all I knew. All she needed to do was guide me to a quiet spot without surveillance so the Bastards could take me back to the clubhouse and hang me in the middle of the courtyard so they could throw beer cans at my body until I started to smell.

But what if she really was just going to the MC because she needed my help? Needed me to fulfill a promise I'd had no intentions of ever following through with.

In the picture she was clutching the damn ring like it was the most precious thing in the world to her. I felt a pull from the bottom of my fucking gut, but like every unwanted emotion tumbling through my brain, I pushed that shit right back out.

My stupid joke ended up on King's doorstep. The plan was to get to Logan's Beach and quietly clean up the mess I made. Then I would send the girl on her way and head right back out.

Each bump in the road caused me to glance up and look into the rearview mirror. The back windows were blacked out and about as useless as a monk with a ten-inch cock. My bike was strapped down to the back of the truck with heavy nylon straps that attached to hooks in the floor.

A tied up mechanical beast wasting away when it was meant to be flying down the road.

Like me.

I'd rented the truck under an alias from a junkyard that operated solely on paper tickets, no computer system of any kind. I wasn't hiding from the club. I wasn't a fucking coward, but I wasn't about to advertise my arrival and put King's family at risk either.

I wasn't hiding, I just needed time.

Time to do what, I wasn't fucking sure.

Over the last few months the only thing I'd accomplished was being a wasteland for booze, coke, and loose pussy and as soon as I handled my business I was going right back to it.

My old man wasn't stupid enough to take our fight to the streets, but he was stupid enough to send me a message by beating on a girl he knew I'd given my promise of protection to.

How long ago was that? Six, seven years?

It seemed like another lifetime.

One where I was so sure of my place within the club. One where I was content being a naive soldier whose main concern was pussy and a party.

Pussy.

I'd been knee deep in it since I was twelve.

De-virginized the same way all the other preteen boys were who grew up in the club. An older member, for me it was my old man, sat me down in the middle of a room full of brothers already drunk or high or both, while a half-naked club whore twice my age gave me a sad excuse for a strip tease to an old Bon Jovi song, every brother I'd known since I was born looked on. She dropped to her knees and sucked me before sitting back up and turning her back to me. She held onto the armrest for support when she sank down onto me, taking my cock inside her pussy.

The crowd cheered and my old man's right-hand man, Tonk, shook a bottle of Bud, popping the top off with his knife, spraying beer all over me and the club whore after I blew my load in under twenty seconds.

Best fucking day of my life.

I'd give anything to have those days back. To be blissfully unaware of all the fucked up shit that made me eventually turn on my brothers and take off my cut.

I was happy being just another ant in his mound, doing his bidding without question.

My life outside the club always grated on Chop. The fact that I was close to civilians, namely Preppy and King, never sat well with him. He took every chance he had to warn me of letting them in and reminding me of where loyalties needed to lie and how outsiders caused nothing but problems in our world.

I never saw it that way. King and Preppy were useful to the club. The Bastards leaned on them when something was too high profile for us, and they leaned on us when they needed a cleanup. They embraced my brothers and opened up their houses to us and our wild partying ways.

Chop even went as far as offering them cuts. Patching them in. I think he did that because the fact that he had no power over them was driving him ballistic.

Of course they said no. King was a bull who ran in his own direction and Preppy was the wild donkey, running amongst bulls with no direction at all.

I went out of my way and took every opportunity to show

Chop that my loyalties were with him. With the club. I pulled triggers on demand. Buried his problems deep in the woods without hesitation. Lived my life according to our code and no one else's.

But it was never enough.

The more he pushed me on his idea that in order to take the gavel I needed to lose my friends, the less I wanted it. I started spending less and less nights at the compound and more nights in the makeshift apartment in King's garage. We'd throw parties in his backyard for my brothers who embraced King and Prep, not just as my friends, but as friends of the club.

Preppy died at our clubhouse several months back because there was a traitor amongst my brothers.

A rat.

Chop was more concerned about the blood on the concrete than Preppy's death or the traitor in his midst. And that's when it hit me. The reason Chop was worried about my loyalties was because he had a reason to be worried.

When it came down to it. Life or death. A gun held on Chop and one held on my friends. I had to play God and choose whose life I would save, I would choose my friends, the only real family I'd ever had, over Chop.

I think he knew this long before I did.

When he refused to let me help King save his girl he made the choice easy for me. King or the cut.

It wasn't even a decision that was hard to make. King had saved my life at a time when not a single Bastard came to my rescue, when Eli and his gang of pussy ass motherfuckers tied me down and tortured me.

Chop talked a big game about loyalty, but he'd never done a goddamn thing to earn it.

I felt naked without the soft leather of my cut against my skin. And not a good kind of naked. The shameful kind of naked.

I missed it.

I missed my club.

I missed my brothers.

I missed knowing my place in the world and knowing who I was because driving that truck back into the gates of my hell, I had no fucking idea.

All I knew was that I didn't miss Chop.

I may have given that little girl my ring as a joke, but this wasn't a joke anymore.

This was fucking war.

Chapter Seven
BEAR

The day I met King was a bloody one. I chipped two teeth and gained the scar that runs across my left elbow.

We'd gotten into a fight over—over I don't even remember what. Whatever fourteen-year-old kids fight about. Well, fourteen-year-old kids who dealt dope, stole cars, stripped them for parts, and ran from the law.

We'd traded blow for blow until we were so bloodied and bruised neither of us could see past the slits of our swollen black eyes.

Preppy, some scrawny kid who came along with King, sat on top of a nearby hollowed out log and kept running his fingers along the front creases of his pants, sharpening them. He seemed totally unfazed by the mutual beating taking place just feet away.

In fact, he looked...bored.

"You cunts done yet?" Preppy called out with a sigh, letting his shoulders fall. "Ya'll fight like bitches. When one of you taps out I bet it's because you gotta go change your fucking tampon." He shook his head and rolled his eyes.

King had weight on me, but I had speed on my side. For every time he trapped me underneath him, I was quick to maneuver out of his hold and land another blow to his rib cage.

This seemed to go on for hours.

We wailed on each other ferociously, mercilessly. Rolling around on the soft wet ground, I tried to spit the mud out as soon as it entered my mouth so I could catch my breath.

King straightened his arm and punched the heel of his hand against my face, sending my head sailing backward. A rippling pain shot down the bridge of my nose and vibrated against my cheekbones. Blood dripped from my nostrils into the seam of my lips, sending copper flavored warmth into my mouth.

It was the third time my nose had been broken.

A loud shriek tore through the air. King and I both whipped our heads around toward the direction of the sound to see Preppy, who was looking down at his crisp white shirt in absolute horror. His already pale face seemed to get even more pale. "What the fuck?" he screamed, jumping down from the log. He pulled one suspender down to his elbow, revealing the small spec of mud splattered directly above his chest pocket.

I barely registered that King and I had stopped fighting. His hands were still firmly around my neck, my knee was tightly pressed into his stomach. Preppy slowly looked up from the spot on his shirt and back to us. His cheeks reddened, his fists clenched at his sides. Before I could register what the fuck was wrong with the kid he'd launched himself into the air with a yell that could rival the fucking Braveheart call to arms, and landed himself right between King and me, knocking the wind out of my lungs, sending King falling backward into the mud. Preppy then proceeded to come at the both of us with all he had, but since the kid was built of elbows and knees...

It wasn't much.

"You motherfuckers!" he screamed, his pubescent voice cracked *over the vowels as he tried his damnedest to inflict pain on us for dirtying up his clothes.*

King and I burst into laughter and after Preppy had given all the fight he had to give he collapsed onto his back and laughed with us. The three of us spent the rest of the day getting high on top of the water tower. That was the night Preppy drew the giant dick on the water tower.

I learned that day that Preppy had been responsible for all the dicks that had been spray painted on stop signs and light poles throughout the town. "I use special paint, too. Shit's never gonna come off. When I'm long gone my beautiful big black cocks will still be everywhere in this shit town."

"Oh you like big black cocks?" I asked, nudging him in his bony ribs with my elbow.

"Only my own," Preppy said, grabbing his dick through his khakis.

King rolled his eyes. "You're not fucking black, asshole."

"I am from the waist down, motherfucker, have you seen the size of my fucking cock?" Preppy reached for his belt.

"Preppy, if you pull your fucking cock out again I'm throwing you off the water tower," King warned.

"It's your loss." He shrugged, taking his hand off his belt. He sat back down between me and King and leaned over the railing looking down at the scattered lights below. "We're gonna own this fucking town."

Big. Thick. Black.

The Logan's Beach water tower came into view. The outline of the spray painted dick around the letter L was still visible, even though the city had attempted to cover it up several times with cheap thin paint. The smell of the salty air mixed with sunscreen and fish permeated the air through the open window and with the smell of home came the memory...I hoped to fuck the city never invested in decent paint, because I'd climb the motherfucker in the middle of the night and recreate Preppy's dick pics all over again.

When I pulled down the long dirt driveway that led up to King's house, an odd feeling swept over me. It used to feel like home.

Now it was the last place I wanted to be.

A sense of dread lingered inside my chest, growing larger with each roll of the tires propelling me forward.

Get rid of the girl and get the fuck out as soon as possible.

The three-story stilt home to my right was the main house, but that's not where I was going. Passing the fire pit in the backyard made me want to throw up, but I shook that image from my head and instead chose to remember the time Preppy was so high he convinced everyone he could walk over the burning coals.

We were all on board. His feet though?

Second-degree burns.

King stood outside his newly rebuilt garage with his arms crossed over his chest. He was a man of few words and never spoke before he thought it out, which was the opposite of his girl, who was always spouting out the first thing that came to mind. King was always a big motherfucker, but when he was released from prison last year he'd come out even bigger, like he'd skipped being someone's bitch in exchange for doing non-stop sit ups. His hair was short and dark and he had an even darker look in his eyes.

He looked the same as he always had, but there was something about him that seemed ...different, although I couldn't figure out what it was.

King lifted the cover off of a key panel on the side of the garage that wasn't there before I'd left, and punched in a code.

The right side of his neck was covered with gauze. The garage door opened automatically, disappearing overhead. King waved me inside and I drove into the darkened space. As my eyes adjusted I was careful not to hit any of the classic bikes and cars in different stages of repair that I knew were hidden under the multitude of dusty tarps.

I killed the engine and hopped out.

"Do you own anything besides black t-shirts and dark jeans?" I asked, trying to lighten the mood and avoid any heavy conversation he might feel like having.

"This coming from the guy who doesn't own a fucking shirt."

"That's what's been bugging me," I said, pulling the black tank top over my head and tossing it back into the truck. "Much fucking better."

King rolled his eyes but I could see the hint of a smile. Not on his lips but in his everything. He was a hard man to read but I'd figured his ass out. Just took me almost fifteen years.

"Garage looks better than last time I saw it," I said, following King to the back. The actual main garage area was twice as big as it was before Eli crumbled it to the ground. "You get in a fight with a vampire?" I asked, pointing to the gauze on his neck.

"New tat," he said, opening a door that was in the same place my former crash pad used to be.

"Who did it?" I asked. King had done all of mine and they ranged from chicken scratch looking bullshit from when he first started, to my right sleeve which was not a picture, but a portrait of the causeway during sunset, a bike on the top of the bridge.

"Ray," he said and that time he did smile.

"Holy shit you let your bitch tat you?" I asked reaching for the gauze.

"Fuck off. You call her a bitch again I'm drowning you in the fucking bay."

We entered an apartment but it didn't look like the makeshift area I'd used before as my apartment. This was a legit living space. The Beach Bastards decor I had pinned to the walls were gone and those walls were now bare. The smell of fresh paint lingered in the air.

A newer looking couch and TV made up the living room area. A small kitchenette sat to my left. And unlike the studio I had before, this area had an additional door which I realized probably lead to an actual bedroom when it opened and Doe came out.

A small smile crept onto her face. "Bear," she said, her eyes sparkling, her white blonde hair a lot longer than I remembered.

"Doe," I said, unsure of how to greet her anymore. It felt awkward. She was the only girl who I ever thought I could make mine. It wasn't that I was in love with her, it was that she was the only girl I'd even considered spending more time with than the time it took to come. For me? That was a lot.

Doe looked like Doe but also different. Where King's change was something I couldn't put my finger on, Doe's was much easier to spot. She wore bright colored shorts and a black tank and flip flops, her signature style, but this top was looser around the middle than what I was used to seeing her wear and flowed as she walked toward me. When she wrapped around my neck to bring me in for a hug I couldn't help but look down at her ample cleavage. Cleavage that certainly wasn't there before.

"She goes by Ray," King said. I was such a fucking idiot. I'd heard King say Ray but it hadn't registered.

"Ray," I corrected. I wasn't as perceptive as King when he caught me staring at her.

"Stop staring at her fucking tits," King growled. Ray let out a small laugh.

I held her for a beat longer after she tried to pull away and she swatted my shoulder playfully and laughed again before I finally let her go. I missed her voice. Her laugh. It was even nice to have King growling next to me again.

It was all so... normal.

"You get your tits done, beautiful?" I asked mostly to piss off King, I knew they weren't fake because of how they felt smashed up against my chest when she'd hugged me. "Cause I'll tell ya they were always pretty fucking fantastic."

"Bear," King warned and I wondered how far I could push it until he drew his gun.

"Oh come on, Bear, you seriously don't know why?" she asked, cocking her head to the side.

King tugged on her arm, pulling her against his chest.

My chest tightened.

I looked Ray over again, and she was right, they were soft and yet looked like they were about to explode out the top of her shirt. The rest of her was curvier too, her thighs a bit thicker. Even her face had filled out. And yes, her ass had gotten bigger, but hot damn was that a good thing.

Fifteen or so pounds didn't look good on her. It looked great on her.

"You seriously don't remember?" she asked, crossing her arms over her chest which made them pop out of her top even more. King reached out and uncrossed them, and that's when I noticed it through the fabric of her shirt. A slightly rounded belly. Like she'd recently... "Fuck, I'm a dumb shit," I admitted, finally realizing what I'd forgotten. "Congrats, guys, I mean it," I said, pulling Ray in for another hug that was rewarded with yet another growl from King.

Now my chest hurt for an entirely new reason. My friends, closer to me than any family, had a baby while I was away and I hadn't even remembered Ray was pregnant.

A shrill scream came from the other room and then stopped just as fast as it had started.

"She's been doing that every few minutes since Gus brought her here," Ray said, pulling away from King. "Sally, who runs one of the Granny Growhouses. She's a retired nurse. She just left a few minutes ago. She cleaned and bandaged her up best she could where the girl would let her, but every time she tried to take off her shorts to inspect the damage the girl kicks and screams. Whatever happened, I think it was brutal to say the least."

King's eyes darted to mine and I knew what he was thinking. He was the only one who knew what Eli and his group of cunts did to me and he was searching my face for any sort of reaction. I wasn't a chump. I wasn't some chick whose virginity was stolen. It was torture. Plain and simple. Did we kill every last one of those motherfuckers?

Yes, we did.

"Great of you guys to take her in, but you ever think she might be on their payroll? That she's not a victim but out to get info?"

"Crossed my mind. Don't say shit around her just in case. But I'll tell you something. If her beat down was all for show, it's a pretty impressive act," King said.

"You should go in and check on her. If she starts to shake

or anything, Sally said to put her in the warm shower," Ray said.

"Fuck!" I said, running my hands through my hair. "Shock? What if this is real? What the fuck did they do to her?"

"Ray's been with her all night and she's been either sleeping or screaming, but hasn't said anything about what happened," King said.

"She's just a fucking kid!" I yelled. "You don't think that he would…" But I answered my own question. "He would. He totally would. And not just him either…" I trailed off. I walked over to the couch and sat down feeling my stomach turn over and over again when I thought of Chop raping a little girl and then letting the sick fucks, and there were several in the club, have at her.

"How did she get your ring?" King asked.

"I was a dumb kid and I gave it to a little girl because she didn't call the cops when Skid held her at gunpoint at a gas station. I never expected to see her again. I told her a story. A lie. Told her if she ever needed anything to come find me and give me the ring and I had to do whatever she asked of me. Thought she'd forget all about it."

"You should go in and see her," Ray said. "If she really did come to you to seek some sort of help from you, seeing you, knowing that you're here, might do her some good."

"Why?" I asked. "She doesn't know me. I haven't seen her since I gave her the ring years ago." I sprang off the couch. "Chop wanted to send me a message by beating on and possibly raping a little girl. What I'm going to do is sneak back into the clubhouse and slit my old man's throat and then hit the road again. This shit shouldn't be at your doorstep. I won't let it happen again. I'll put her in the van and drop her at the hospital. We'll both be gone by morning."

"Don't you think that if you take her to the hospital you run the risk of ruining whatever it was she needed your help for?" Ray asked.

"Never thought I'd hear you suggest a hospital," King said.

"It was a lie! A joke. I was a dumb fucking kid!" I dropped my head in my hands.

And now you're a dumb fuck pushing thirty, Ghost Preppy chimed in.

"Go in there and you tell me if the girl in there looks like a fucking joke."

"I'll take care of it. I'm not a Bastard anymore. I'm not worried about hospitals or getting caught. Besides, if she's a fucking rat what the fuck does it matter? I'll drop her and be on my way."

"Where?" Ray asked.

"Wherever that's not here," I said.

"That hurts you know," Ray said, disentangling herself from King.

"You can't run forever man," King said.

"I'm not running from those fuckers!" I yelled. Ray's eyes darted to the closed door, I lowered my voice again.

No, but you're running from yourself.

"I have to go check on the baby," Ray said, stepping toward the door. She picked up a radio looking thing off the table on her way out. "Baby monitor," she said, holding it up with a tight smile on her face. The last thing I wanted was to hurt her, but I didn't know how to fix it. I just needed to leave. To be on my own. To figure out my fucking life.

Why didn't they get that?

"What's the baby's name?" I called out to her, but it was too late. Ray was already gone.

King lifted the gauze from the side of his neck revealing an intricate new tat in grey and black lettering that read NICOLE GRACE.

"You named your kid after the whore who shot at your girl?" I asked.

"There was more to that and you know it. Besides, Nicole Grace is a lot better than what Sammy and Max wanted to name her."

"And what was that?

"Baby Pancakes," King said, rolling his eyes and smiling.

"Maybe a little better. But holy shit on the tat man. Ray did that? That's good fucking work."

King ripped the rest of the gauze off and chucked it into a nearby trash bin. "And yeah, it is. She gets better every day. You should see some of the shit she sketches."

"What's HER name?" King asked, jerking his chin at the closed door.

"Thia," I said. "Her mom calls her Cindy, but she hates it," I said, remembering her words to me from all those years ago. "If this is a ploy by Chop, and she's in on it, you best believe that I don't give a shit how old she is. I'm sending her back to the MC in a fucking body bag."

"Agreed," King said. "But how long has it been since you've seen her?"

"Six years, maybe seven?" I answered scratching the hair under my nose. "Why?"

"Cause that girl in there? She's young. But she's no fucking kid." As the last word left his mouth, another shrill scream pierced through the air.

"I'll go get Ray," King said.

"No, let her be with the baby, I'll go in. Better I figure out what the fuck is going on sooner rather than later."

King nodded but then he stopped, again searching my face

for something I already knew wasn't there. "You sure you're good man?"

"Yeah man, I'm sure. Go. Get some sleep," I said, waving him off.

King went to leave but turned back around. "Sit on the 'going to slit your old man's throat' plan for the night. We'll talk it out in the morning. Whatever you need. I'm in."

That's when I realized what was different about King. The anger. The anger that he'd been drowning in since before Ray arrived, was gone. That's why he seemed different. Lighter.

Calmer.

It freaked me the fuck out.

Chapter Eight
BEAR

What the fuck is wrong with me? Maybe it was all the fucking blow or mainlining Jack for months, but I was really starting to question my sanity. The picture King had sent me of the girl had been blurry at best and I couldn't make out her face, but I'd known it was the same girl from the gas station from the weird pink color of her hair.

Thia.

Her name was Thia, I remembered.

I thought I knew what to expect when I entered that room.

I was so fucking wrong.

Thia's long hair was splayed out above her on the pillow and it wasn't so much the pink I remembered, but more of a blonde with a hint of red. Her skin was pale, except for the dark bruising on the side of her lip and the butterfly stitch covering a cut on the side of her eye that was getting darker and darker as the seconds ticked by. The circles under her eyes were a deep purple underneath her thin skin.

She was beat the fuck to hell.

She was also so fucking beautiful. I was so taken aback by her that I felt like she wasn't unconscious at all, but instead had just slapped me upside the fucking head.

When her lips parted she drew in a breath, arching her back off the bed, pushing out her tits against the thin blanket, before collapsing again.

My fucking cock sprang to life.

"Bad fucking timing, asshole," I muttered to myself.

Whether she was a fucking trap or not, someone, probably my old man, had worked her over real good.

Seeing her in person was so different than looking at a picture. Being in the same room as her, watching as she wrestled in her sleep, the anger I felt minutes ago toward my old man amplified by a thousand. The cords in my neck strained and I balled my fists.

I wasn't JUST going to kill Chop.

I was going to gut the motherfucker.

Thia thrashed about wildly, her arms and legs limp and useless as she rolled from side to side. Her mouth opened and closed, her nose wrinkled and her eyebrows drew in like she was having a heated conversation with someone in her dream. She thrashed about again, this time kicking the sheets and blankets off the bed.

I sucked in a breath.

She wasn't wearing a shirt or a bra, her tits were full, high, rounded, and perfect. My cock hadn't gotten my earlier message to tame the fuck down, because again it twitched in my pants as all the blood from my brain rushed to my dick until it was straining painfully against my zipper. Thia rolled over onto her side so she was facing me and I was able to get a better view of her light pink nipples. There was a mark on her left tit and when I leaned in to inspect it I saw red.

Bright fucking red rage.

Teeth.

A fucking bite mark on her fucking nipple.

I stood over Thia as a confused mixture of hate, rage, and lust swam around inside of me. I added decapitation to the list of things I was going to do to Chop and possibly burning off his own fucking nipples beforehand.

On the other hand, if the bitch was working for Chop, it was going to be a shame to have to finish what he'd started on such a perfect body.

I paced the room, cracking my knuckles and breathing fire. If this was King's old place I'd probably have already punched a hole in the fucking drywall and suddenly wished that the old dilapidated garage that used to be covered with my Johnny Cash posters and Beach Bastards flags hadn't been replaced by new, fresh, and white paint.

Thia sat up suddenly and opened her eyes revealing large round and doll-like emerald greens beneath the surface. "Bear," she whispered, locking her gaze onto me. Her one hand flew up to her chest to grab my skull ring which was dangling on a chain between her tits.

I opened my mouth, but I didn't have a chance to say anything, because her eyes rolled back in her head and she started to convulse.

Chapter Nine
THIA

Warmth. I was wrapped in a cocoon of warmth and comfort I never wanted to emerge from.

"You dead, Darlin'?" A deep voice penetrated the silence, calling me back from the darkness.

Warm water cascaded onto my skin. I was sitting down on the slippery surface of a shallow bathtub while strong arms cradled me against a broad hard chest. Something huge and hard prodded my back, causing my eyes to fly open.

Panic poured into my veins like I'd been shot in the heart with adrenaline.

I sat up and turned my head, staring directly into the sapphire blue pools that made my skin crawl and bile rise in my throat.

It couldn't be. I thought I'd gotten away.

CHOP.

"Nooo!!!!" I screamed, scrambling away, trying to hoist my leg over the ledge, but only managing to lift my leg high enough to hit my knee directly into the side of the bathtub.

The same strong arms wrapped around me and tugged me back underneath the spray.

I couldn't breathe.

This can't be happening.

But it was.

It was happening all over again, and I couldn't. Fucking. Breathe.

"Look at me!" the voice ordered, and when I didn't comply he kept one hand wrapped around my shoulders and used the other to turn my chin to face him. I fought him using every ounce of strength I had, but it wasn't enough. I was tired. Weak. The muscles in my neck gave out and I was forced to again look into the eyes of my captor.

There was a hardness and an anger, a violence, lurking in the bright eyes before me. A deep down exhaustion I could relate to, however there was no outright hatred, no malice.

It wasn't him.

It wasn't Chop.

I had gotten away after all.

But where had I gotten away to?

"Bear?" I asked. Despite being surrounded by water my throat was dry and scratchy, my words came out like I'd been in the desert for months breathing in sand. "How are you here?"

"No, you'll answer my questions first," Bear said, peering down at me like he'd never seen me before in his life. "Don't worry about where you are or how I'm here. You need to be more concerned about telling me why you're here and who sent you." Trails of water ran down his face, dripping off of the bottom of his beard which was much longer than I remembered it being. He brushed some of the wet hair from my forehead. I jerked away from his touch, my body still in full panic mode.

Remembering the prodding on my back I looked down to where his jeans bulged. Bear's eyes followed mine. "Can't help that. All my cock knows is that I'm in the shower with someone who has a pussy." I lifted my hands to cover my naked breasts, suddenly all too aware of my nakedness, but thankful I was still wearing my shorts.

My muscles felt like rubber that had been melting in the heat of the sun like a tire in the middle of the highway.

Used, spent, hot, useless.

Broken.

Bear wanted to know why I was there.

Why was I there?

Something had happened before I went to the MC. Before Chop. But my brain was foggy and I couldn't see the images of the day that were just beyond my grasp.

"I don't understand," I said. This time when I spoke I felt a tug at the corner of my lip. I touched the spot with my fingertips, discovering a soft scab over a fresh wound.

"You don't remember going to the MC?" Bear asked, raising a brow. I don't know who the man sitting in front of me was because there was none of the charm and carefreeness that practically dripped off of the Bear from seven years ago. This man was like a vacant version of his younger self.

I closed my eyes and dropped my forehead to my knees. "I remember riding my bike. I remember the rain. I remember going up to the gate. A prospect named...Pick? Peck? No, Pecker let me in."

"Never liked that little twat," Bear scoffed.

Why did I go to the MC?

Think, Thia. Think. Why are you with Bear right now?

The images I'd been reaching for began to flash in my mind like Polaroid pictures being thrown into a stack, each one containing a flash of memory, one after the other.

My mother sitting in the rocking chair in Jesse's old room.

The gun in her hand.

My father's lifeless body.

The shotgun in my hand.

My mother's blood against the white of the side of the house.

I gasped as the photos began to stack up higher and higher, filling my brain with images I never wanted to see again. This couldn't be real. I had to be dead. Mama was right. I was going to hell. Because that's exactly where it felt like I was.

My stomach rolled. Acid and bile rose in my throat. I covered my mouth with my hand.

"Hey! You still in there? Come back," Bear asked, sounding like a faraway echo as the pictures kept flashing in my brain.

A river of blood.

So much blood.

Bear grabbed hold of my shoulders and began shaking me. "Whose blood? What the fuck are you talking about?"

"I killed my mother!" I blurted, leaning over the side of the tub just in time to heave the little I had left in my stomach into the porcelain toilet. "That's why...that's why I came to see you." I wiped my mouth with the back of my hand, opening the scab on my lip, fresh blood and vomit streaked my skin. "I...I killed her."

Bear turned the shower off and leaned over me, grabbing his phone off the top of the toilet tank. "Where?" he asked, pressing a button on the phone. The screen lit up and he held it to his ear. "Damn it girl. Where?"

"Where what?" I asked into the toilet.

"Where? As in where is your mom's body? Where is she right fucking now?" he asked angrily, sliding me forward so he could stand up.

My mother's body.

"Uh. Um she's..." I said, trying to catch my breath long enough to not be sick again. "Home. She's home. In Jessep." Without the hot water against my skin I started to shake violently. The skin on my fingers ached they were so pruned.

"Ray, is King up there?" he barked into the phone. "Tell him to get his ass down here." He pressed a button on the phone and tossed it onto the counter. He stood, lifting me up under my shoulders as he stepped over the rim of the tub and onto the tile. He closed the lid on the toilet and set me down on it. Tearing a towel from the wall rack he tossed it to me and I immediately wrapped it around my shoulders.

"Your jeans are all wet," I said flatly, staring at the soaked through dark denim sitting low on Bear's hips, probably lower than they usually did with the weight of the water pulling them down further. There wasn't a spot on his chest or arms that hadn't been touched by the needle of a tattoo gun. Colorful and vibrant against his smooth muscular skin.

"Nurse said to put you under warm water if you freaked the fuck out, so I made a run for the shower," he said. "Didn't think much about what I was wearing." He leaned over to pick me up off the toilet and I waved him off, freeing my arm from the towel I rewrapped it under my arms to cover my breasts.

"I can walk," I assured him.

I stood up, shaky at first, holding onto the counter for stability. "I got it," I said again, this time saying it more to convince myself when my knees buckled. "Just need a sec is all." Bear growled and bent down, slinging my right arm over the back of his shoulder. "I said I got it!" I yelled, although clearly I hadn't got anything.

"Fucking stubborn, bitch," Bear muttered, walking me out of the bathroom and into a small bedroom. He sat me on the edge of the mattress and went back into the bathroom.

The door opened and a man appeared, his eyebrows knitted together, I could only assume this was the King person Bear had called. Short dark hair, a dark tight v-neck t-shirt stretched against his muscular chest. He was a huge wall of man. At least six feet tall, although Bear was about his height or even taller. He reached overhead and grabbed onto the molding of the door, his biceps and shoulders rippled as he leaned into the room. He was also covered in tattoos but whereas Bear was covered, this guy still had a few spots of bare skin visible amongst the ink. Leather studded thick bracelets wrapped around his forearms. He released the molding and folded his arms over his chest, his new position revealing the buckles, it was then I realized they weren't bracelets or cuffs at all, but belts. His skin was dark and tanned, his eyes a unique fluorescent green.

He didn't look at me. Not once.

"What do you need?" the man asked Bear as he came out of the bathroom, still shirtless but buttoning up a dry pair of jeans. He slicked back his wet hair with his hand.

"Gotta go to Jessep. I need you to help me stock up. I'm taking the bread truck. Too risky to ride," Bear said, slinking past King he walked out of the room then reappeared a moment later.

"Cleanup?" King asked. "That why she's here?" The slight chin tip in my direction, the only acknowledgement of my presence.

Cleanup? What's a cleanup?

Every instinct in my body had told to me seek him out, but I didn't think about what it was I was really asking of him. Probably because I didn't exactly know.

"Seems that way," Bear said, rifling through a duffle bag on the floor and putting on a fresh pair of black socks. He shoved his feet into a pair of thick black boots. He turned to me. "What's the address of the farm?"

"It doesn't have a number. Just Andrew's Farm on Andrew's Farm Road." Like a lot of the groves in Jessep that had been there for as long as ours, the roads came second and were usually named after the farms they connected. "It's the only grove on the street. Mailbox at the end. Little white house. Blood," I said, still hoping this was all a nightmare and that I wasn't giving a biker my address to clean up the body of my mother.

"How long ago?" King asked and Bear again turned to me for the answer.

"I'm not sure," I said because I didn't know how long I was at the MC or when it was I came here. "Ummm... it was Friday after my shift at work. Around six pm, maybe seven?" I scrunched my nose, trying to remember exactly. "I think?" I added as I tried to recall when my life had forever changed.

"Is she inside or outside?" Bear asked again, and instantly I recalled the way her body looked slumped over the side of the house, my throat tightened.

"Outside," I choked out remembering the moment when I convinced my mother to switch guns with me.

"I need to get out there before the smell..." Bear started and my stomach rolled again.

King nodded. "I've got what you need in the garage. How many?" he asked and this time Bear didn't turn to me for the answer.

"One."

"No," I said, tears pricking the back of my eyes. They both looked at me with confused expressions. "No." I repeated, shaking my head vigorously. "Two. There are two," I said, holding up two fingers while staring blankly at the ceiling.

"I'll get started," King said, disappearing from the doorway. "Meet you out in the garage."

Bear knelt down in front of me, hot tears dropped down the side of my face as my gaze darted from the ceiling into the angry eyes of the person who I was stupid enough to think could have somehow been my savior in all this. "This is your only warning, Darlin'. If I find out that you're in any way working for the MC. If you're on their payroll..." His eyes turned dark and I tried to look away again, but he grabbed me by the back of the neck and leaned in so close the tip of his nose touched mine. His breath flitted against my lips in angry bursts as he spoke between his snarl. "If this is some sort of fucked up trap, you better fucking believe that whatever my old man did to you at the club is going to feel like you skinned your fucking knee compared to what I'm going to do to you."

Chapter Ten
BEAR

King and I loaded the bread truck with the plastic tarps, different types of saws, both electric and manual, drills, and enough cleaning supplies to start our own maid service.

"You think Gus went back to the MC?" King asked.

"Yeah that's probably exactly where he went. If he disappeared too long now they'd figure out really quickly that he was the one who took the girl. Chop has always been paranoid about rats in our midst." I laughed. "Fucker's probably having himself a heart attack right now trying to figure out what the fuck happened."

"He didn't do it quietly. Fucker said he set off a pipe bomb as a distraction to get to the girl," King said.

"The crazy thing is that motherfucker had a pipe bomb handy. Probably has a stack of them to the ceiling in his room. He's always been a little off his rocker. One time I was in the shower at the club and when I pulled back the curtain he was just standing there, staring. Scared the fucking shit out of me."

"Creepy fucker," King said.

"Yeah, but he has his uses. And he's loyal, obviously, which is more than I can say for most people these days." King and I each grabbed a door on the back of the truck and slammed it shut.

"What did you do for him that earned that kind of loyalty, cause that's big shit, man."

"I saved his life. Fucker was about to catch a bullet in the head," I said.

"From who?"

"Me. Gus almost didn't turn prospect because Gus almost didn't live past his sixteenth birthday. I'd caught him peering in through a warehouse window where he'd been watching me 'question' one of our rivals for information. The kid was as good as dead. Except when I was about to pull the trigger to put him down, the fucker didn't flinch. Then he asked me if it felt good to gut a man and then he criticized my choice of knife I'd used on the guy before him. I decided he was more useful as a Bastard than dead. He turned prospect the very next day." The little fuck became the best 'questioner' the club ever had. I bought him an entire butcher knife set when he was patched in. He looked down at the knives and I didn't know if he was about to cry or come.

Probably both.

"Ready. Let's go," King said.

"Nah, man. No need to put yourself at risk for this shit. I'm gonna get out there, neutralize the bullshit and get the fucking girl out of your house. The sooner I do that the sooner I can hit the road again."

"Fuck off. I'm going with you." He pointed to the door of the apartment. "You know you can stay, right? That apartment is yours. Always has been. Rebuilt it with you being there in mind. Also, I built something else. A sort of fall out building, it's on the island."

"Fallout building? Like a bomb shelter?" I asked. The back island was an acre of land that blended into the shoreline of the preserve on the other side of the bay. If you looked across the water from King's property you couldn't see that it was even an island. When King and Prep had first moved in he didn't even know it was there until we came up on it by boat.

"Something like that. I'll show you one of these days," King said.

I shook my head. "Won't be here long enough. Just me being here puts you and your family in danger. You've got kids now man. Wouldn't be able to live with myself if something happened to them."

Like something happened to Preppy.

That wasn't your fault, dick slick. It was mine. I literally couldn't dodge that bullet. See what I did there? Oh my shit I'm hilarious.

"Do you think I'm stupid? I'm not. I know the MC isn't in the business of killing civilians," King said, "besides, we're wired up here like there is no tomorrow. See that?" King asked, pointing to a high corner of the garage where a small red light was blinking. "Got cameras everywhere. Everything is hooked to my phone. I also give the local sheriff a cut of the Granny Growhouse operation plus all the fucking weed they can smoke and now they look out for us. MC had a few deals go south lately so they stopped paying off the law. So you can stay here. Nobody is coming to our door. Nobody."

I cringed, remembering when Eli had done exactly that. He didn't just come to the door. He bulldozed his own door and half of King's garage in the process. King must have noticed my reaction. "Never AGAIN," he amended. I hated the way he was looking at me, like he was about to ask me about how I was doing so I changed the subject.

"I thought you were planning on going civilian?" I asked, surprised to hear that King still had the Granny Growhouses operating.

"There's only so much civilian a guy like me can go. I scaled back and I don't bring anything to our doorstep. We keep busy though. During the day Grace has been watching the kids and up until we had Nikki, Ray had been apprenticing for me. She's pretty fucking amazing. Can draw better than I ever could."

"That's why I need to leave," I said. "You got all this shit going on that I have no business being part of."

"Brother, we've had no business being part of a damn fucking thing that we've been doing since we were kids and that's why you need to stay. Shit's not the same without you. At least stay until you figure shit out and clear your head. Then if you still think being on the road is what you want you can go back to Bear's Pussy Parade across America without ever thinking about Logan's Beach again."

I laughed at how well he knew me. Better than anyone.

Better than myself.

He knew me so well in fact that he already knew there was no way I was going to stay. Logan's Beach was my home, it's where I was born, where I grew up. But right now there was nothing for me there except problems, and I wanted nothing more than to put the distance back between me and my bike, and the constant reminders of the shit my life had become that were on every street, every sign, every shell and piece of sand of my hometown.

King ignored my refusal of his help and opened the driver's side door. He set a radar detector on the dash, hooking it into the lighter outlet. Red numbers flashed to life and it made a sound like a metal detector hovering over a nickel in the sand. "Figured it could shorten the drive. Coyotes could be dragging her mama's head around by her neck on main street by now. Every minute counts."

I nodded, time was definitely not on our side. "Good call."

"That girl in there..." King asked, tossing me a package of black tattoo gloves and rounding the truck to the passenger side. We've always had a 'your ride, you drive' rule which apparently applied to the bread truck rental. "...She tell you why there are two bodies rotting in the sun right now?"

I shook my head. "No, she won't say much. She mutters a lot. Rocks back and forth. Lucky we got her address out of her. Seriously, you shouldn't even be coming with me. This entire thing could be a setup. Something happens to you or you go back upstate, Ray would kill me with her bare hands." King had done time for letting his mom, who was an evil cunt druggie bitch, die in a fire that he didn't start. Can you believe that shit? He doesn't do time for killing her. He serves time for not saving the dumb cunt who neglected his baby girl.

It was bullshit to me four years ago and it was still bullshit to me sitting there in that bread truck.

"When I came to you at the MC. After all the shit that went down with Eli and asked you to soldier for me to get my girl back, did you hesitate? Fuck no you didn't. You went there GUNS-A-BLAZING like a badass MOFO!"

"Yeah, because it was Ray, but this isn't my girl. This is just a girl. A wacky, parent-killing bitch who may or may not be sucking my old man's cock. This isn't a life-or-death guns-a-blazing situation," I said, repeating the same words my old friend had just used. "This is just a problem that needs fixing."

King laughed. "You've seen thousands of Beach Bastard

Bitches come and go at the club." He jerked his chin toward the room where I'd locked Thia inside. "Answer me honestly, she look like any BBB you've ever seen?"

"No, but that could all be part of it." Chop couldn't exactly send someone who had 'cum dumpster' written all over her so he sends an innocent looking girl with a fat lip...and even fatter tits.

Down boy.

"Do you even hear yourself right now? You got history with this girl, right? Enough to know her name?" King asked.

"Yeah, but..." I started to argue.

"But nothing. Skid's been in the ground for years. What are the chances he told your old man that story before the cartel took him down, AND that your old man remembered it years later, and then decided he needed to go seek out that same girl, turn her into a club whore, AND then send her back to you to carry out his revenge against you for leaving the MC he practically pushed you out of?" King asked, pointing out the huge and obvious holes in my entire Thia conspiracy that up until a few seconds earlier had seemed like the most plausible explanation for Thia suddenly popping up in my life.

"Well, when you put it that way," I said, realizing how farfetched the idea seemed now that King had said it out loud, but that didn't change the fact that something about the girl didn't sit right with me, although I couldn't for the life of me figure it out. Which was fine with me, I wasn't going to stick around long enough to figure it out either.

"What have you been getting into on the road?" King asked, and again my old friend surprised me with the concern in his voice.

"Nothing good," I answered honestly, but it's better than

being here. "Looking forward to getting back to it right after I see what this crazy bitch did to her family."

"Did she say the second body was a family member?" King asked.

"Nope, just a feeling," I admitted. "She killed her mom, and if she really is an innocent then it only makes sense that the other body isn't some random, so I figured it's probably another member of her family."

"Don't take this the wrong way, but why do you care? You said yourself that you don't even know the girl and that the ring and promise thing was a fucking joke. Why do any of this?"

"I don't care. Not about the girl. It's not about her." I hopped up into the truck and slammed the door. "But I told you already. The sooner I fix this, the sooner I can send her on her way and go back out on the road until I can figure out my next move. If I don't do this she might cause problems, get loud, hang around longer than she's welcome, which was already about the time I had to come riding back into town to see what the fuss was all about," I said, not willing to admit that a little bit of my motivation was the evil five letter word that's been haunting me for the past year.

GUILT.

"That makes a fuck of a lot of no sense," King said, lighting a joint and passing it to me, I took a hit and passed it back.

"Didn't think it did, man," I said, starting up the truck and easing it out of the garage. I turned us around once we were clear of the overhang and started down the narrow driveway.

I pulled out onto the main road and waited for the radar detector to chirp, and even though King said he was tight with the local cops I was still relieved when it remained silent.

"You know what?" King asked, picking a stray bit of weed

off the tip of his tongue before taking another deep drag from the joint.

"Huh," I said. He passed it back to me.

"You might not wear a cut anymore...but you're still a fucking bastard," he said on an exhale, a deep burst of laughter exploding from his mouth in a puff of smoke.

"Haha, fuck you," I spat, as he continued to laugh.

There was a question I'd been wanting to ask him since I'd gotten back that popped back into my head. "Remember the night we were talking about hearing Preppy?" I asked.

King nodded. "Yeah, the night we lit up Eli and his crew." The vein in his neck started to pulse as he recalled the night I was tortured.

The night he saved my life.

"Yeah, that would be it. I was just curious. Do you still hear him?" When King raised an eyebrow I clarified. "Prep. Does he still talk to you? Do you still hear him?"

"All the fucking time man. He grew quiet there for a little while, but as we settled down with the kids it's like he's back with a vengeance. Sometimes when Max and Sammy are screaming at the top of their lungs, I think he's even louder than them. Like a fourth kid who broke into a case of Mountain Dew at nine pm and instead of sleeping has decided to run laps around the living room." King turned to me. "You?"

"Yeah. All the fucking time. Especially when I'm fucked up. Or fucking up. Or when HE seems to think I'm fucking up. You think that's weird?" I asked, knowing damn fucking well how weird it really was to live with a second voice in your head who chimed in when he saw fit.

You flatter me, Care Bear.

"You mean do I think it's weird that we both hear the voice of our dead friend talking to us?" He smirked. "Naaaahhhh."

"Well when you put it that way." I hit the joint again, holding the smoke in my lungs until it burned.

I pressed down on the gas and sped down the road toward the rotting bodies of Thia Andrew's parents.

But all the hurrying was pointless.

We were too late.

We were WAY too fucking late.

Chapter Eleven
THIA

I hadn't meant to eavesdrop. I'd meant to LEAVE. But when I found out that yet another door had been locked, trapping me inside, I couldn't help but to listen when I'd heard voices on the other side.

I don't care about the girl.

When Bear said those words they shouldn't have stung like a hornet to the heart. I already knew he didn't care. It wasn't until after they'd already pulled out that I remembered what Chop had said about the ring and about Bear's making up the whole biker promise as a joke.

This was probably all still a joke to him. They probably weren't going to Jessep. They were probably in the truck on their way to some sort of badass tattoo convention where Bear would tell everyone about the stupid trick he played on a kid who actually fell for his stupid lie and came back years later, still holding onto a ring that had meant everything to her growing up and nothing to him from the moment he'd placed it in my hand.

I knew he didn't care about me. Not then.

Not now.

So why do I feel like someone punched me in the gut?

After my brother died, my dad always told me that under the weight of great tragedy, came great responsibility. I took this to heart and as the years went on I took on more and more responsibility at the grove so my dad could tend to my mother who was slipping further and further into her delirium. Before the Sunlandio Corporation cancelled our contract I was seventeen and running the grove full-time, often skipping school to meet with vendors or make sure that orders went out on time. One night during an extremely rare frost I rallied the workers and we spent all night hosing down the oranges so we wouldn't lose them to the cold.

Under the great weight of that tragedy I took responsibility, but under the weight of the new trudges was too much, too heavy, and it was crushing me before I could make any rational or responsible decisions.

Why did I even leave town? Why didn't I just call the sheriff myself?

I know why. I panicked. Panic and fear clouded any sort of logic, but as logic started to once again take over so did the gravity of my loss. I loved my father. He taught me how to tell when the oranges were ripe for the picking from the way they smelled. He taught me how to fish. He'd let me sit in front of him on the tractor when he mowed the field behind the house, the only space not taken up by orange trees. I don't think losing him was something I would ever be able to move on from. My brother had died when I was young and although it hurt like hell, what hurt worse was seeing my parents hurting.

I loved my mother, but I wouldn't miss her. Not in the same way I'd miss my dad. She hadn't been my mother in a long time. My father picking up her slack on days she refused to get out of bed, refused to take her medication, or after Jesse died, refused to acknowledge she still had a remaining living child.

The night she killed my father she'd been more manic than I'd ever seen her. The look of death swirled in her eyes.

I had no choice and my only true regret was not getting there sooner.

Not being able to save my dad.

Responsibility meant not running away. Isn't that what I'd done? I'd run away.

What if I went back to Jessep? What if I told the sheriff what happened. They knew my mother and although she and my father went to great lengths to cover up her mental issues they had to understand that I didn't have a choice. Isn't that the way justice worked?

Guilty people don't run away. But I panicked and instead of dialing the sheriff for help, the only person who popped into my mind was Bear. Getting to him was my only focus and through my tunnel vision he was all I could see at the end.

That was a mistake.

I didn't want to be this weak girl. I was never weak before and I hated that I was being weak now. I'd go back and face whatever I had coming to me. Hopefully, I'd get back there in time to tell my story before someone stumbled upon the nightmare back at the house.

I also imagined the relief that Bear would feel when he came back and found me gone which made my decision an even easier one.

I didn't have a shirt and it's not like I could walk all the way back to Jessep wearing a towel, so I grabbed a plain black t-shirt from a small pile of Bear's clothes on the floor. Before I could register what I was doing I lifted the shirt to my nose and inhaled deeply. Laundry detergent, sweat, and cigarettes shouldn't have smelled so good. I pulled it on over my head. On Bear it was probably tight, on me it was a tarp.

The little apartment I was in was plain, but smelled like new paint. When we built a new shed in the orange grove and the doors were installed the trim company set the door keys on top of the molding. The door was a taller one and me being only five foot three there was a problem. I slid a chair over to the door ignoring the protesting burn of my muscles as I did so. I carefully climbed the chair and felt the top of the molding.

No such luck.

Although I should have known better since luck and I hadn't seemed to be friends not just the last few years, but my entire life.

I looked around the apartment for something I could use as a key, like a small screwdriver or a nail file when I noticed a paint splattered sheet in the corner of the room covering what looked like a little alcove.

Crossing the room as quickly as my broken body would allow, I tugged on the bottom of the sheet, freeing it from where it had been tucked behind something at the top of the pile it had been concealing. As it fell to the floor it revealed the entire life it had been hiding underneath.

Bear's life.

An older style TV, much thicker than the more modern flat screens, with fake wooden paneling on the sides sat in the center. On top of the TV was a stack of Harley Davidson coffee table books and behind that was a display case with three hooks holding long curved samurai swords with gold handles. A framed poster of Johnny Cash flipping the bird with the title "AT SAN QUENTIN" over his right shoulder sat on the floor against the wall where a huge BEACH BASTARDS black flag was held unrolled with the Beach Bastards logo peeking out from the folds like an uninvited guest.

I was about to search the kitchen drawers when something in the center of the pile caught my attention. A framed picture of three young men.

One I recognized instantly as Bear, his ridiculously blue eyes practically shone through the old faded picture and although I'd met him when he was twenty-one, he was even younger in the picture, I would guess around fifteen or sixteen. He was facial hair free and his cheeks still had that slight roundness to them that would eventually fade and give way to the sharp intensity that Bear was today. The leather cut he wore read PROSPECT across one side in a U shape at the bottom. I recognized another boy as King, but with slightly longer hair that was too short to give way to the budding half curls that surrounded his face. King was also smiling, but unlike Bear, King already looked hardened in the picture, maybe even a bit sad.

In the middle of the two teenagers, who would grow up to be larger than life men, was a boy who was a good head smaller than Bear or King, which by anyone's standards still made him taller than most. He was dressed up, different than the t-shirt and jeans of his friends, although the setting didn't look as if they were going somewhere that required that kind of formal dress. They were sitting on a bright blue picnic table, tall skinny trees and twinkling water in the background. The kid I didn't know wore a short sleeved white dress shirt tucked into khaki pants with a lime green bow tie with checked suspenders and just like the Johnny Cash poster, he was flipping off the camera. The letters FU were tattooed down his middle finger.

With all the shit I had going on and with the need to run

coursing through my very being, I was surprised that a picture of all things had me at a pause. I ran my fingers across the faces of the three boys and wondered if they knew what kind of men they would eventually become.

I found myself jealous of the easy friendship that radiated through the photo.

Socially awkward was an understatement, but after Jesse died and I took on more and more at the grove, friends were no longer an issue because I didn't have time for them. Between my part-time job at the Stop-n-Go and trying not to fold under the pressure, school dances and first kisses were never a priority.

They were never even a consideration.

I did have one friend.

Buck. I called him Bucky. He was the only one who no matter how many times I told him I couldn't hang out, he always made time to come to the grove to check up on me. Bring me lunch. He was the only one who amongst a sea of adults realized that I had taken on more than what any normal teenager ever could or should.

Buck was the deputy sheriff. He and Sheriff Buckingham were the only law in Jessep, maybe if I got to Bucky first then he could help me convince the sheriff of the truth? That this was all just a horrible, horrible tragic accident.

I couldn't go to jail. Not that I thought jail or thinking of being there took any precedence over what had happened to my parents. But because I couldn't sit there day in and day out and stew over what I had done. What I could have done differently. That my entire family was dead.

I wouldn't survive.

The thought of survival brought me back to the present and my task at hand. Setting down the picture, I went to the kitchen where the drawers and cabinets were all bare. Growing frustrated with each passing second I made a decision. I walked over to the samurai swords and removed one from the hooks, unsheathing it slowly so I wouldn't accidentally cut myself on the blade.

I may not be able to unlock the door.

But I can chop the fucking knob off.

And so I did.

With a guttural roar I severed the knob from the door with the sword, revealing the silver mechanism underneath. I pushed my fingers into the small space and pinched the two ends of the small metal bar together, unlatching the bolt.

The mid-morning sun blinded me as I walked out from the cover of the garage apartment and into the light of day. After my eyes adjusted, I followed the driveway past a three story stilt home. I wasn't sure where I was until I got to the bottom of the narrow driveway and spotted the causeway to my right and knew right away that I was still in Logan's Beach and that if I took a left I'd eventually find my way back to the highway.

I wish I had my dad's truck or my bike.

There was no way I'd take a chance of going back to the MC to get it. I shook my head, refusing to acknowledge what had happened to me there. Not yet anyway.

One horrible event at a time.

One tragedy to focus my grief and anger on.

Someday I would allow myself to be upset and angry at the MC, at Chop. I would curse the world for what he did to me, or TRIED to do to me, but not today. I started off down the road. Toward Jessep. Toward home. The injuries caused by Chop and his thumb made each step more excruciatingly cringeworthy.

With newly found determination, I limped forward.

Today was for my parents.
Today was for my dad.
And today I would be strong, for them. For him.
Tomorrow, tomorrow I would cry.
Not today.
Just not today.

Bear

We were turning back into King's driveway when his phone rang. "Pup," he said. There was a short pause. "You see what direction she went?"

I spotted a figure limping down the road and instantly recognized the wild pink hair.

"Never mind, we see her," he said, ending the call.

"Where the fuck does she think she's going?" I muttered, leaning over the steering wheel. I brought the truck to a stop with a squeal of the brakes and considerable effort to throw the shifter on the steering wheel into park.

"I'll take it back up to the garage while you deal with that," King offered. I nodded and hopped down onto the road, quickly catching up to Thia, who was moving a lot faster than her limp should allow. She was wearing a plain black t-shirt.

MY t-shirt.

It was so big and bulky on her I couldn't tell if she was wearing anything underneath until the breeze picked up the hem, revealing the same blood stained shorts she'd worn the night before.

"You're wearing my shirt," I pointed and grunted, matching her furious pace. It wasn't the shirt that was bothering me, but leave it to me to point out something trivial when my blood was boiling because she didn't stay put like I told her to.

"I'll send it back to you," she said bitterly, focusing her eyes on the road in front of her.

"Where the fuck do you think you're going?" I asked, grabbing her shoulder and spinning her toward me. "I told you to stay. Shit, I locked you in. How the fuck did you get out?"

"I'm not some animal you can cage in! I'm going home! Don't worry I won't burden you anymore. I'm going to tell the sheriff what happened, which I should have done in the first place. You won't ever have to think about me again. You're off the hook." She tried to wriggle from my grasp but there was no way in fuck that was going to happen. The more she spoke, the angrier I got and the more my fingers bit into her arms.

"You think it's that easy," I said between gritted teeth. "You think you can go home like none of this ever fucking happened? 'Cause, trust me on this one, it doesn't fucking work that way." I expected her to show a little fear, to cower, even if it was only slightly, but the girl was bold, breathing through her scrunched up nose like she was about to breathe fire, challenging my every word with her stare. "I got news for you, little girl. You can't go anywhere. You seem to forget that the MC knows who you are and now that you have a connection to me, you're as good as dead out there by yourself. So like it or not, you're stuck here, at least for the time being, so get back up to the fucking house before I grab a hold of that crazy hair of yours and drag you there."

"I know it was all a fucking lie!" she snapped, locking her eyes with mine. Fear and anger radiated from her as she stared me down.

"What?" I asked, threading my hand in her hair I gave her a warning tug and her head snapped backward but she stayed strong.

"I told Chop about your promise to me, about the ring, and he laughed in my face. Then I heard you tell King it was all a joke." She lifted up her shirt so high she revealed the rounded underside of her breasts. She pointed to the purple black and blue bruises on her ribs. "Does this look like a joke to you?" Then she pointed at her swollen lip and then the butterfly stitch around her eye. "Do these look like jokes?"

For the first time in my life I was caught off guard. I wanted to pummel the girl for not listening to me, but for the first time realized that her injuries would never have happened if I wouldn't have given her that ring or told her that lie. "I've got it from here." She pushed against my chest but it was useless, I had at least a hundred pounds on her.

She wasn't going anywhere.

"Just let me go! I want to go home!" she screamed, continuing to struggle, wincing when I'd grabbed her by the waist and lifted her off her feet. I loosened my grip but didn't put her down.

"Listen to the words I'm saying," I seethed, leaning down, invading every inch of her personal space. "Did I say that I didn't want you to leave? Am I begging you to stay? What did I just say?" I asked, trying to make the girl see reason.

Thia gasped and her eyes went wide. "You said...I CAN'T leave." She stopped struggling, but I continued to hold onto her like she was. "Why? Why can't I?"

"Reason number one is because I fucking said so. I still don't know if you're working for my cocksucker old man..." I started, even though what King had told me made that possibility highly unlikely.

Highly unlikely wasn't beyond Chop.

"I'm not!" she snapped.

"Shut up and listen. I'm going to show you something, but I need to be able to use my hands. I'm going to let go of your arms. You fucking make a move to run and I won't be gentle next time," I warned, finally letting go when I felt the tension in her arms start to fade, setting her back down onto her feet. I pulled out my phone and clicked on the internet where I'd already had the website for the Logan's Beach News Press queued up. I clicked on the morning's latest news and turned it around so she could see the screen.

Thia paled. Her already white skin fading to damn near see through as she read the headline.

Missing Teen Daughter Only Suspect
HUSBAND AND WIFE FOUND SLAIN IN JESSEP HOME
Police Have Deemed The Killings
THE 'ORANGE GROVE SLAUGHTER'

I snapped the phone shut and answered her honestly. "Reason number two, is because we were too fucking late."

Chapter Twelve
THIA

I was officially wanted.

And unwanted.

All at the same time.

Bear wasn't going to let me go. Going home to Jessep and confessing to what I'd done to the sheriff was no longer an option. The headline was so damning. Would they even believe me if I told them the truth? Would I face charges even if they believed me?

I couldn't do anything at all, yet I wanted so badly to do something that would take away the lump forming in my throat and chest, slowly suffocating me with each intake of breath.

Breathe in, squeeze.

Breathe out, tighter.

Breathe in, squeeze.

Breathe out, even tighter still.

I wish I could say I felt numb. I wanted numb, craved it. I longed for indifference and detachment, because I was a runaway train, racing forward at full speed toward the end of the tracks and a crash I could see clearly in front of me as if it had already happened.

The fight in me faded as quickly as it had built.

I was trapped.

In this place.

In this horrible life.

Tomorrow had come, a day too soon.

Chapter Thirteen
BEAR

Thia sat perched on the edge of the bed, staring at the wall with an unreadable expression on her face. The same place she'd been since hanging her head in defeat and silently following me back up to the garage.

Ray came over and brought some fresh clothes and a toothbrush for Thia who thanked her and disappeared into the bathroom, but when she came back out both Ray and myself noticed right away that although we'd heard the shower and the sink, she was still wearing the same shorts. We shot each other the same confused look. "Ummm, the nurse who checked you out when you got here, her name is Sally," Ray said. "You wouldn't let her check you everywhere. She called earlier and she's worried and wants to know if you want her to come over and take a look to make sure you're okay," Ray offered.

"I'm fine, but thank you." Thia shook her head, offering Ray a small smile that could barely qualify as a smile. She'd been in the same position, staring at nothing ever since.

I followed Ray out, leaving Thia in the bedroom. "Sorry

about the door. I'll take care of that before I go," I said, picking up the sword and the door knob from the carpet. I'd forgotten how heavy the sword was, Thia must have been really determined to leave if she was able to not only lift it, but swing it hard enough to sever the fucking knob.

Ray crossed her arms under her chest. "What's your plan with her?"

"Fuck if I know. She wants to go. I told her the MC was out to get her. I showed her the fucking newspaper article. She's dead one way or the other, but she still wants to go, so who the fuck am I to keep her here?"

"You're a guy who knows a little bit of what she's feeling."

"How do you figure that?

"Oh I don't know, maybe because she's been displaced and has nowhere to go. Maybe because she's had some terrible shit happen to her that she doesn't want to talk about," Ray said, cocking an eyebrow at me. "Any of this sound familiar?"

"I didn't think about it like that," I said, leaning against the wall, running my hand down my beard.

"You boys never do," Ray said with a smile that didn't reach her eyes. "Grace is coming by tomorrow, you might want to pop your head in and say hello so you don't catch hell for it."

"Fuck. Grace. I haven't even thought to see how she's doing." The small radio looking thing in Ray's hand started to cry, she held it up and waved it in the air. Grace had been battling cancer, but around the time I'd left she declared she wasn't ready to die and just like that she suddenly seemed well again.

Stubborn women seemed to be a trend in my life, but I was glad for Grace's stubbornness, if anyone could go to war with death and come out a winner, it was her.

"Gotta go, but you might want to make a plan when it

comes to that girl in that room over there. Either let her go or keep her here, either way, you need to decide what's going to happen, because none of this is fair to her." She pushed open the broken door and made her way into the garage. I hit the automatic opener and followed her out. "Take that from someone who knows what that's all about." I watched Ray leave, following her with my eyes through the window until she made her way into the house by way of the back steps.

Ray was right. I needed to make a decision, but I couldn't think of one that would result in her being both safe and gone. I could sneak her out of town and get her somewhere the MC didn't have reach but if the law caught up to her it didn't matter where she was, if she ended up in a prison or jail somewhere, she was as good as dead.

Unless...

I dug my phone out of my pocket and as my fingers pushed each number I cringed at what I was about to do. "Bethany Fletcher's office."

After my call I found Thia exactly where I left her.

"We couldn't get down your street," I started, rounding the bed to stand in front of her. Her gaze shifted to the floor. "Law already had the place roped off and were lifting up the tape to let the coroner's van through. We put our heads down and kept fucking driving." I kneeled down in front of her and again tried to get her to look at me, but she turned away, this time crawling up the bed and climbing under the blanket. With her back to me she pulled the blanket up to her chin.

"Leave me alone. I just want to sleep," she said, her voice flat and empty.

"Fuck this," I said, pushing off the wall. I wanted to tell her what the fuck happened because I thought she'd want to know. What was I doing? Ray was wrong. I couldn't relate to the girl in any way, and just because she was stupid enough to believe one of my lies a hundred fucking years ago didn't mean I owed her shit. I didn't need to stay to watch some kid turn inward and self-destruct.

Speaking of self-destruction.

I rummaged through my saddle bag on the floor, searching around the internal side pocket until I found exactly what I was looking for. I walked over to the only surface in the room, the little night table Thia was facing.

I didn't care that she could see what I was about to do.

I didn't give a shit what she thought about me.

I tapped some powder out onto the wooden table into three jagged lines. I felt Thia's eyes on me as I snorted all three lines of false happiness up my fucking nose.

I tipped my head back and pinched my nostrils together as the blow set a cold fire to my brain.

That's better.

Now I really didn't give a shit what she thought of me.

Now I could leap off the roof and fly to the other side of the bay and not give a shit.

"Fuck," I said, pressing my finger into the remaining residue and rubbing it against my gums.

"That recreational, or you got a problem?"

"Look who can suddenly talk again." I rolled my eyes and took off my shirt, throwing it on top of my bag. "Does it look like I'm having a fucking good time to you?" I snapped. "It ain't a problem either, at least not right this second." I thought about what I'd just said and as my high got better and better I agreed even more with my earlier statement. "Actually, right this second, I don't have a problem in the world," I sang, enjoying the few moments before I crashed when I could fool myself into thinking that everything was okay.

"No, you just feel like you don't," she corrected.

"I know, but I just don't give a fuck." I turned toward the door.

"Can...can I have some?" she asked. I paused mid-step.

"What?" I asked, turning around. Thia sat up.

"You said you don't care now. I don't want to care either," she said, tears welling up in her eyes.

"No," I said without having to think about it.

"Why not!?" she asked angrily, tossing the blanket off her lap and standing up off the bed. She walked toward me, her limp from earlier almost unnoticeable, her braless tits bouncing against the thin material of her tank top as she stalked toward me. "Why do you get to erase your problems and I don't. Chop told me you aren't in the MC anymore, so you snort cocaine to make it go away right? To pretend? Well, I want to pretend too."

Chop had obviously done more than work her over at the MC. Apparently he'd taken the time to run his cocksucking mouth as well.

"No," I said again, although she had a point. Then I remembered what Ray said and suddenly wished I hadn't just used the last of my stash.

"It's okay for you to forget, but I'm not allowed a few minutes to not feel like the world is crumbling around me? Like I'm not all alone? Like I'm not trapped? Like I won't wind up either dead or rotting in some prison?"

I didn't want to tell her that if she did go to prison that the MC would likely send an ol' lady or a friend of the club to kill her in there.

Prison was like summer camp for the Beach Bastards.

Summer camp with a side of homicide.

Thia was close to me now, so close I could see the agony in

her eyes and the freckles across her forehead. I could smell whatever girly soap Ray had given her to use, some sort of vanilla mixed stuff. Her hair was still damp, falling in heavy waves around her shoulders. She was a tiny thing, only coming up to my chest. Her thighs and calves were muscular and surprisingly lean and long for such a little thing. When she stood up on her tiptoes in challenge and was about to say something else I had the sudden urge to bite the sensitive skin between her neck and shoulder. "What did he do to you?" I asked, using a much softer tone than I had been. "Chop. Tell me what he did."

"Why?" she asked.

"I don't know," I answered honestly.

And just like that, with that one question, she began to wilt away again. She lowered herself off her toes and took a step back. Her shoulders fell. She got back in bed, again lifting the covers to her chin. "Nothing," she lied, turning onto her side, her back to me, effectively shutting me out. "Nothing that matters."

"I tell you what," I said. "I'll make you a deal. You tell me what happened and I'll help you forget for a while," I said, and I meant it, just not in the way she was thinking. I wasn't above bribery.

Actually, I was fucking amazing at bribery.

Hot damn this was good blow.

"We've already established that you don't care," she said, throwing my words from earlier back in my face.

I stomped to the edge of the bed and flipped her onto her back. She tried to swat me away but I caught her wrists and held them still. "You need to take those bloody shorts off, but something has you keeping them on. They're wet, so I know you didn't even take them off in the fucking shower. So why don't you tell me what the fuck happened at the MC, before I strip you naked, haul you over my shoulder, and throw you in the fucking bay."

"You wouldn't," she said, her eyes finally containing the fear I was used to seeing in the eyes of someone I was threatening, yet had been oddly missing from her except for the brief moment she'd first woken up in the bathroom.

"Fucking. Try. Me," I warned, loving that I was finally getting the reaction out of her I wanted. Vacant and distant was bullshit that pissed me off. Anger. Anger I could work with.

A wayward tear dripped down the side of her face and her shoulders shook silently.

What the fuck?

"Do what you have to do," she whimpered, the nothingness from earlier firmly back in place. "I don't want to talk about it. Any of it." I let go of her wrists and she rolled over again. "Please, Bear. Leave me alone. I just want to sleep."

Never in my life had a chick made me so angry. Following through on my threat wouldn't work on her like this.

I grabbed a bottle of whiskey from my bag and hit the light switch on the way out.

Dude, she's hot when she's angry, Preppy chirped in my head.

"Shut up," I muttered. He was right, but I wouldn't exactly call her hot. Without makeup or without even having brushed her hair in a while, she was devastatingly sexy, and that didn't even begin to cover it.

Cock achingly fuckable was a little closer.

I adjusted myself and settled on the couch for a long fucking night of avoiding sleep with my buddy Jack Daniels.

A VIOLENT SCREAM shot through the door. "Fuck you!"

I picked my gun off the table and ran to the door, throwing it open, ready to kill any motherfucker who was bold enough to come at me in the middle of the fucking night. Thia was on the bed, screaming like she was being attacked, but the room was empty. Her eyes were closed and her back bowed off the bed with each new outburst. The back of her head hit the wall above the mattress with a thud but it didn't even slow her down.

"Fuck you! Fuck you! I hate you! You can't fucking do this to me! You can't! I won't fucking let you!" she raged. I didn't know what to do, but I did know if she kept up her thrashing against the wall she was going to fucking hurt herself. I knelt down on the mattress and picked her up into my arms, crushing her to my chest, but she didn't stop. She slammed her closed fists against the sides of my face, my chest, anything she could make contact with again and again. She clawed her nails into my skin, raking them across my shoulder blades.

"Stop!" I growled, holding her arms down at her side. "Wake the fuck up!"

"Fuck you! Fuck you! Fuck this!" she screamed, still wailing away on me, her little fists feeling more like a vibration against my chest than a beating.

"Ti, it's me, wake the fuck up!" I said even louder. "Goddamnit, girl you're going to fucking hurt yourself. Wake the fucking fuck up!"

She stilled, but I continued to hold onto her. It took several minutes but I felt the moment the fight left her body as she sagged against me. She hadn't moved, hadn't said a word in so long I'd thought she might have fallen asleep until she spoke against my skin, her breath brushing over my nipple. "I killed my mom."

"I know," I said, unsure of what else I was supposed to say. "Come with me," I said and for once she actually listened, sliding off the bed and following me outside into the night. I walked over to the bonfire, the very place where Eli and his men laughed as they tortured me. I was going to take her down to the dock but decided against it, because if she pissed me off again I didn't know if I'd be able to resist carrying out my earlier threat and tossing her ass into the bay. For at least a little while the shitty flashbacks that followed me around like a possessed puppy dog nipping at the heels of my memory would have to take a backseat to the girl with the pink hair.

"Sit," I ordered, pointing to a white plastic lawn chair. Thia sat and watched me as I lit the end of a small piece of straw. When it glowed brightly I gently set it on the inside edge of the fire pit and set two small cut logs on top of it.

"Why the fire?" she asked.

"The fire is for a little light and..." Thia smacked her arm, and when she pulled her hand away she revealed the crushed up body of a big mosquito.

"And a little keeping the blood suckers away." She wiped the bug off her arm as the smoke started to billow into the sky from the pit. "That should take care of it."

I sat on the edge of the brick bonfire, facing Thia in her chair. She pulled her legs up into the chair and under her little white tank top, stretching the material over her knees, killing any chance I had of staring at her tits.

I packed the little one-hitter and grabbed my lighter. "Watch," I said, as I set the weed aglow, keeping my thumb over the hole on the side until it was time to inhale all the smoke I'd just created. I exhaled and held the lighter and bowl out to her. "It's not blow, but it will take the edge off."

Thia turned the lighter over in her hand and examined the

bowl like it was an artifact from a museum, running her fingers over the smooth blue glass. She attempted to light it but dropped the lighter when the only thing she managed to light was her fingertips. "Here," I said, picking up the lighter from the grass I held the flame over the bowl as she did what I'd showed her, taking her thumb off the hole and taking a shallow drag, releasing the smoke on a cough.

"I didn't kill my dad though," she said when her coughing subsided. "My mom did. I came home and she was sitting there in my brother's old room. She had my dad's pistol on her lap," she said, continuing her confession.

As much as I thought Thia could have been working for Chop it never occurred to me that she maliciously killed her parents, but I stilled at the mention of a brother, wondering if she was about to tell me there was a third body out there somewhere, but she filled in the blanks before I could draw my own conclusions. "My brother died when we were kids. We weren't that far apart in age. We were playing on the porch. There was always spiders out there. Groves give off a lot of moisture and spiders love a good wet heat and a little nook or crevice to hide in. The porch had all that. We saw a spider climb into my dad's work boot by the door, I was going to stomp on it, but my brother wanted to check it out. He reached into my father's boot..." She trailed off. "They took him to the hospital but it was too late. Brown widow. Not always fatal in adults, but in kids..."

"You don't have to tell me," I said, not wanting to send her back into a state of shock that her story might trigger. "I know what it's like to not want to relive the horrible shit over and over again."

Thia continued anyway. Looking up at the smoke from the fire as she spoke. "My mom started to slip away. Growing more distant every day. Most days went by and she didn't even talk to me. Business started to go to shit. They were always fighting. Then one night I came home and," she sniffled, "there was no more fighting.

"My dad was already dead. I made a run for it, but I tripped. She wanted to send us all to the same place. Said we were all going to be together. I convinced her that we should go at the same time. I switched guns with her, giving her one I knew always coughed on the first pull. She was so determined. There was no arguing, no getting out. I could have shot her in the arm, in the leg, but I couldn't be guaranteed she'd drop the gun, or that she'd stop firing. The look of determination in her eyes told me that shot or not she'd keep on coming. I couldn't let that happen. I thought about my dad. About him always telling me to be his strong girl. So I did what I had to do to be his strong girl, and I aimed at her chest and I fired.

"I'm going to remember this as the worst time in my entire life. The very worst." She shook her head. "There is nothing I can do to change that. Girls my age are playing sports, going to dances and parties, kissing boys. And that's never been me. I've had a full-time job at the grove and a part-time job at the Stop-n-Go. I've done nothing over the last few years except work my ass off and watch my family fall apart. Just when I thought it couldn't get any worse...now all this." She waved around to the house and to me and let out an awkward laugh. She took another hit off the bowl, passing it back to me. Her coughing much less than it was on her first try.

"Ti, how old are you?" I asked, clearing my throat as I ventured into territory I knew I shouldn't. She was a pistol, even if she was a sad one, but there was a wave of innocence about her that had me both feeling bad for her and salivating for a taste of her.

This is for her, not you. I told myself. It was only a partial lie.

"Seventeen," she said, sniffling. "Eighteen soon."

"You ever been kissed?" I asked, and her eyes met mine. "And not a peck on the cheek or a brief smack of the lips, but a real fucking kiss. One that leaves you without air in your lungs and your thighs pressing together in search of more?" I said, my voice coming out deep and strained. My cock coming alive at the thought of tracing my tongue along her plump lips.

"Why?" she whispered, and as soon as the words left her mouth I knew there would be no coming back from what I was about to do.

I pushed off the fire pit and pulled her up off the chair, pressing her tits into my chest and my straining cock against her stomach. I tipped her chin up and looked into her confused emerald greens. She followed my thumb with her eyes as I traced her bottom lip. There were too many lines marring her face, questioning what it was I was up to. I knew she would try to pull away at any second, try to stop me. But it was too late for that.

I was beyond stopping.

Just one taste.

"Answer the question," I pressed.

"No," she said with a slight shake of her head, and before she could try to argue, I leaned down and pressed my lips to hers.

I was already going to hell.

Might as well enjoy the ride there.

Chapter Fourteen

THIA

Bear is kissing me.

Out of pure shock I pushed against his granite chest, severing our connection. It felt cold where his lips had just been, yet warm and tingly between my thighs.

A real kiss.

"I don't need your pity," I said, touching my lips as if I needed to make sure what just happened was real.

Bear leaned in again, this time running his nose across my jaw. I closed my eyes and his words vibrated behind my ear, straight to a place deep inside me that tingled to life. "This may still be the worst time of your life, Ti. But when you remember all the shit that went down you can remember your first kiss too, and maybe it will take some of the sting you'll feel away. Let me do that for you. Let me help you." Bear cupped my face in his hands and again pressed his lips against mine. He grabbed my wrists and wound them around his neck before snaking his arms around my waist, his fingers biting into my hips.

Everything about the kiss was soft. Gentle. Nothing like I'd ever thought kissing Bear would be like. The feel of his beard against my face made me want to reach out and pull it. It was softer than I thought it would be.

HE was softer than I thought he would be.

He opened his mouth to me, just slightly, just enough to gently suck my lower lip into his mouth and his tongue across the seam. I let out an involuntary soft moan, immediately embarrassed by the noise. Bear pulled back and ran his hand over his beard. "Sorry I didn't mean to..." I started but then I realized that he'd done it. The entire time he'd been kissing me, even though it was just a few seconds, I hadn't thought about the MC or my parents.

It was thirty seconds of bliss.

I wanted more.

"If you keep making noises like that, Ti," Bear groaned, his chest rising and falling rapidly. I sucked my bottom lip into my own mouth, tasting where Bear's tongue had just been. "I can't promise that this is just going to stop at a kiss."

"You said if I told you what happened at the MC, then you could make me forget," I reminded him. "I want to take you up on that," I said, knowing what I wanted but unsure if Bear would be willing to give it to me.

"No blow, Thia. I already told you..."

"No." I interrupted him. "Make me forget, just like this," I said. Growing bold I reached out and touched his lips with my fingers. Bear groaned and surprised me when he sucked my fingertips into his mouth. My nipples hardened as if they'd been touched by a cold breeze. Bear pulled me flush against his hard body and groaned, the deep vibration resonating with parts of my body I didn't know could feel things. "I don't want drugs. I want you to be my drug. Make me forget, Bear. Please." I begged. "Take it all away."

Bear looked down and for a minute I was sure that he was about to tell me that he regretted kissing me and couldn't do what I was asking him. He was a biker. What they did wasn't a secret around the county. I know he was used to experienced women, club whores. Why would he want to kiss me? "Tell me why you are still wearing these and I'll kiss you again," he said, tugging at the waistband of my shorts.

"I don't know how you are going to react. Everything seems to make you mad," I said honestly.

"I can't promise you I won't be angry, but I can promise you that I won't be angry at you," Bear said. "You understand that, Ti?" He searched my eyes. "None of this is your fucking fault. You get that?"

I nodded. "I'm afraid," I admitted. I hate being afraid. Growing up I was the fearless one. The one who took care of everyone else. "It's like saying the words out loud is me acknowledging that this nightmare is real, and I don't want it to be real. I don't want any of it. And the worst part is that I feel so weak and this isn't me. I'm not a weak girl. I've always been the strong one."

"Tell me and I'll kiss you again. Maybe it will make you forget, maybe it won't. Maybe it will help give you back a little bit of that strength." Bear chuckled, rocking into me with the hardness between his legs that almost had me jumping back until he said, "Or maybe it will just add some more torture to my rock hard cock."

Before he made it seem as though his erection was just a natural reaction. Now he was making it clear.

He wanted me.

The lightness in his voice, a tone I hadn't heard him take in the last twenty-four hours helped to loosen the tight cogs around my brain and I reluctantly told him the truth. "I keep them on because I don't want to see the bruises. I don't want to be reminded of what he did." My voice cracked with my admission. I hated the weakness in my voice. "I'm not ready to face it just yet."

Bear's nostrils flared, but when he caught me staring at his lips he reached out and grabbed my face, leaning down he pressed another kiss to my lips. This time harder and he was right, he was angry, but he fed the anger into his kiss, into every nip, suck, and dance of his tongue that I lost myself in his lips, in him, and within a few seconds there was nothing around us. No fire, no bay, no ghosts of terrible things.

There was just the two of us and our angry hungry lips.

"More," Bear said, pulling away, kissing the corner of my mouth where it had just started to scab over. He trailed his lips to my collarbone softly brushing his lips over every inch of skin, leaving a trail of fire in his wake I didn't even know was possible. He paused. "Tell me more," he said as I leaned in and he leaned back. I frowned at the lack of contact.

"I was in a room with Chop. You look like him you know," I started. "Not exactly, but in a way I could tell right away that he was your father."

"I've heard that before," he muttered. "But let's get one thing straight. He's been my old man since I was born, but he's never ever been a fucking father to me."

"I can't imagine he was," I said.

"Keep talking," he ordered softly, trailing kisses down my arms and then over the few inches of bare skin between my tank top and shorts. I looked for my thoughts but couldn't find them with his lips trailing their way toward a part of me that was throbbing with a need that was unlike anything I'd ever felt.

"Room with Chop," Bear prompted.

"Right. Um... the prospect had already given him the ring. Your ring. He was mad. He threatened me. He...he hit me." I sucked in a breath remembering when he'd thrown me to the floor. Bear must have felt my tension and hesitation because he stood back up and captured my mouth in another kiss. Each one more mind-numbingly perfect than the last. He opened his mouth to me and his tongue found mine. I couldn't resist the urge to lightly suck on the tip of his tongue. He moaned into my mouth and the kiss deepened and grew heavier and faster. I tried to mimic his tongue's movements but there was no rhythm, no pace except frantic need.

Sparks ignited in my very core, making me feel empty. I rubbed my thighs together, needing to feel something more. Friction. Anything. Just something more.

Bear hooked his fingers into the waistband of my shorts and pulled them down my thighs. "Wait!" I said, reaching for the elastic.

Bear grabbed my wrist when I tried to yank my shorts back up. "Ti, let me help you," he said, looking back up to me and in that moment I saw the Bear from the Stop-N-Go seven years ago, the Bear I trusted. I released my grip on my shorts and he pulled them down to my feet and I stepped out of them.

I closed my eyes, waiting for whatever it was he was going to do next, but opened them again when I heard him say. "Stay here." Bear jogged back to the apartment, appearing less than a minute later with a damp washcloth in one hand. He knelt down in front of me. "I don't..." I started, but I had no idea what I was going to say.

"I'm not going to fuck you," Bear said. And when he leaned in and swirled his tongue around my belly button in a move that had me bending my knees involuntarily, literally weakening from his touch. I swore I heard him mutter. "Yet."

"Keep going," he prompted again, sliding lower down my stomach, licking and nipping everything on his way, however he avoided my breasts entirely, leaving my shirt completely intact. He slipped his fingers into my underwear and I braced myself for what he was going to find. Most of my injuries were dull throbs, but everything he'd done to me down there throbbed like it was hours ago, not days.

"He bit my nipple. Drew blood. Then he flipped me over onto my stomach," I said, reliving the way his teeth had felt as they bit down into my flesh over my shirt.

"Did he fuck you?" Bear asked, lifting up his head so he could witness my answer.

"He said he was going to wreck my body, tear me apart and send you back the pieces," I whispered.

Bear growled and pulled off my panties. "What are you going to..." I started, but stopped when Bear pressed the cool washcloth between my legs.

"Did he touch you here," Bear said, dragging the washcloth through my folds and across my opening, cleaning me of the dried blood.

Of Chop.

I nodded. "With his finger, he scraped me. Inside. With his nails." Bear dipped his head between my legs and dragged his tongue across my clit and through my folds, pushing it up into my opening and pulling back out again. I started to shake and for the first time in days it wasn't because I was going into shock.

Or maybe I was.

Trembling because of one long lick of his hot wet tongue across my core and I wasn't sure how much longer I could remain standing. The heat from the fire and the heat radiating within me was too much. It was too hot. It was too...oh my god, he did it again.

"Holy fuck," Bear growled. Leaning in again he asked, "Did he touch you here?" Right against my clit as ran the cloth between my legs again, but this time he nudged my thighs apart and reached further, pushing the cloth between my ass cheeks and I winced at the contact.

Bears eyes shot up to mine.

"Just with his thumb and then he tried to use his... he was going to...but he didn't get far. There was an explosion and then I was in a car or something with a guy named Gus. But it hurt. It hurt so bad," I admitted. "It was like he was using a power drill on the base of my spine." Bear lowered himself, his big hands braced on the inside of my thighs, spreading my legs wider to make room for him. I pushed against him, feeling suddenly ashamed and embarrassed, but he didn't let me.

"Ti, let me see. Spread your legs for me. Open up and let me see what he did to you. Let me take from you what he did and make it better." Reluctantly, I opened my knees and Bear sucked in a gasp.

"You're bruised up. But it's healing," Bear said, shocking me when again his tongue took the same trail the cloth had taken, first dipping into my folds. I thought he would stop when he got further but he didn't, he trailed his tongue between my cheeks and lapped over the sensitive bundle of injured nerves, cleaning me in a way the cloth couldn't.

"Bear, you don't have..." I said, trying to pull him up by the hair. He swatted my hand away and pressed a kiss over the tight and damaged bundle of nerves.

Everything inside me clenched and the sensation took me by such surprise that I clamped my thighs around Bear's head, releasing him when he chuckled into my core. I groaned and then clamped my hand over my mouth.

"Did you tell me everything, Ti?" he asked against my clit before sucking it into his mouth. My hips jumped toward him but he held me firmly in place.

"Yes," I answered, breathlessly.

Bear stood up suddenly and I fell back into the chair in surprise. "Then we're done here," he said, wiping his mouth on the back of his hand, his voice raspy and scratchy. He doused the bonfire with water from a red beach bucket and shot me a look of complete disgust before heading across the grass, back toward the garage.

He left me in the dark, alone, half naked, humming in the places his tongue had been, and wondering what the fuck just happened.

He hadn't healed me at all. He hadn't made me forget.

No, if anything, he'd just broken me more.

Chapter Fifteen
THIA

Mosquitos the size of small birds buzzed around my ears like small vultures circling the air above its intended prey. I don't know how long I sat out there, but by the time I figured out how to move and trudged back to the garage, Bear wasn't there.

He didn't come back that night, or the next morning. It was for the better, anyway. The door knob had been replaced at some point but it wasn't locked anymore. I wasn't a prisoner. He wasn't keeping me there anymore.

He was telling me to leave.

He WANTED me to leave.

He didn't have to tell me twice.

I hated Bear. And not just because he left me in the dark without a backwards glance but because I didn't want to hate him. I didn't want to like him either, but like an idiot I let down my guard and invited myself to be his joke once more.

What happened the night before was never happening again. My life might have been some cruel joke, but I wouldn't let myself be made into one at his expense.

I took a shower. A real shower without the barrier of my shorts. The soap stung as the water rinsed it down my body and into my crevices, but it didn't last long and after a minute I was able to wash and dry without feeling like I was suffocating.

I wiped the steam off the mirror, my stomach flipped when I heard the door to the apartment open.

He'd come back.

I hated myself for hoping it was him.

He didn't deserve my hope.

"Thia?" A female voice called out, slowly opening the bedroom door. "Oh, there you are." Ray appeared with a bright smile. "I brought you some fresh clothes," she said, setting another shirt and pair of shorts on the bed.

"Thank you," I said, moving toward the stack. "I really haven't had much of a chance to tell you how much I appreciate…"

"Don't worry about it. Trust me, I know it's not easy to be the new kid around here," she said, her voice full of sincerity. "I had someone to help me back then, and now I'm just glad that I'm here to help you." She looked at the floor and then to the ceiling like she was suddenly trying to fight back tears. "Anyway," she said, shaking away whatever had crossed her mind, "I was just wondering if you wanted to come up to the house for a bit? Have some lunch? I see that you really haven't eaten most of the food I've been bringing you, so maybe you just need a new setting for a while? A little reset?" I stood there without answering because I didn't really know what to say. I needed to come up with a plan, not have a lunch date, but I also didn't want to disappoint her. "Maybe you can help me not strangle the kids?"

Searching my brain for reasons why that wouldn't be a

good idea, her words suddenly registered with me. "Kids?" The girl didn't look old enough to have one kid never mind kids with an 's' on the end. I'd seen her almost every single day in one way or another for brief periods of time, but this was the first time I felt like the fog had cleared long enough to actually be able to think about her as more than the bringer of clothes and food.

Ray's hair was so light blonde it was almost white. It was long too, hanging straight over her shoulders, ending just under her breasts. Her one shoulder was covered with colorful, yet feminine tattoos that turned into a quarter sleeve. While Bear's tattoos gave him an even harder edge, they seemed to do the opposite for Ray, the light pinks and blues made her look soft. More feminine. She was definitely young, maybe my age or a little older, but had an odd air of maturity about her that made me think that she could be nineteen or she could be thirty. "Get dressed, you're coming. They love terrorizing newbies," she said, patting the pile of clothes.

I held onto my towel, wrapping it even tighter under my arms. "I'm not really a kid person," I lied. I'd always loved kids and I was practically a mom to Jesse, but she didn't need to know that.

Ray winked like she could see right through me and I knew there was no way she was letting me out of lunch. "Good because neither am I," she said, throwing me a shirt off the pile. "But within the last year I've acquired three of them, so hurry, before the two oldest ones knock the house off its pillars."

Ray was in the living room when I emerged from the bedroom. She looked me up and down and tossed a pair of brown flip-flops onto the ground in front of me and I shimmied my feet into them. They fit perfectly, and so did the shorts. Although the black tank top she'd given me was a little tight over my boobs, but it was clean and comfortable and I was grateful to have clean clothes. "How do you get your hair that color?" Ray asked as I followed her out of the garage and into the wet heat. She crossed the lawn the same way Bear had the night before when he'd taken me to the fire pit.

My traitorous skin tingled, the hair standing on end when I remembered how he first pressed his lips to mine. When he washed me gently, when he used his tongue...

"You in there?" Ray said, nudging my shoulder.

"Yeah, sorry. Just zoned out," I admitted. "I don't do anything to get my hair this color. When I was born my dad said it was fire engine red but as I grew up the blonde started to take over. From the age of five to twelve it was practically pink, I'm just glad it's faded a little bit. Kids at school didn't think it was so awesome," I answered.

"Yeah, kids can be assholes," Ray said. "I'm so glad those clothes fit you. At least someone can get some use out of them right now. I tried squeezing my ass into those shorts this morning, but it was a no-go situation, they were so tight I think I damaged my lady parts trying to button them," she said with a sigh.

Ray was seriously beautiful and in the light of the sun her bright blue eyes looked like huge glaciers. If she'd gained weight, it was probably for the best, because she wasn't overweight by any stretch of the imagination and I found myself envying her curves.

The main house was a three-story stilt home that at night looked dark and menacing, but in the light of day was anything but. It was old and in need of some repair, but it was beautiful, sitting proudly in the center of a large grassy piece of property like a manatee emerging from the surface of the river.

The smell of paint grew stronger as we passed THE fire pit that I avoided looking at entirely. "We're having the house painted, what do you think? I'm having trouble choosing a color." She pointed to where a ladder was leaning up against the side of the house. A pretty dove grey color had been painted into a large square against the faded siding with several other smaller squares around it, all in varying shades of grey's. Some more blue, some with a lavender tint. "I did that this morning, but I keep going back and forth. I think these kids are rotting my brain." The second she opened the back door the screams and squeals of kids assaulted us.

It sounded like home.

When I still had one.

"Mama! Mama tell Sammy to stop!" Squealed a cute little girl with blonde pigtails who jumped into Ray's arms, nearly knocking her back into the wall.

"Sammy stop chasing your sister." Ray warned the little curly haired boy who ran circles around her feet all the way to the kitchen.

Big windows lined the far wall next to the front door. The kitchen, living room, and dining area existing in all one big, light and open space. "Come in, come in, it's a work in progress in here too, but we just finished putting in new wood floors. Sammy dropping his paints was the end of the old carpet, but it was for the best, it had already lasted ten years past its shaggy expiration," Ray said, setting the little girl down on the floor. She took off again, her little feet running midair before her feet even hit the ground. Immediately Sammy started his chase all over again screaming, "Maaaaaaxxxxxxxy come here," after her as they took off down the hall in a tornado of yips and yells and laughter.

"Don't wake the baby!" Ray called after them in a whisper yell that was impossible for them to hear across the house.

Just when I was wondering if Ray had left the kids in the house by themselves when she had come to the apartment I heard a throat clear and spotted a little old woman with white hair sitting at the dinette set in the center of the kitchen. Next to her was a pitcher of some sort of green drink and an empty glass filled with ice which she was lazily tracing her index finger around the rim. A digital monitor was leaning against the wall, and on the screen was a tiny sleeping baby wrapped in a pink blanket.

That's why Ray was being so critical of her weight.

She'd just had a baby.

"Grace, I swear to god if you let them eat all the popsicles again, I'm sending them home with you," Ray said, opening the lid to the trash can.

"I admit to nothing," Grace said, licking her thumb and turning the page of her newspaper. Ray reached into the garbage can and picked out a box of popsicles, rolling her eyes as she shook the empty box before tossing it back into the can.

"Are all these kids yours?" I asked and upon hearing my voice Grace finally looked up.

"Yep, the whole lot of them," Ray said, plopping down onto the chair across from Grace and pointed to the seat next to her. "It's a long story but, technically Max is King's, and Sammy is mine, but we're all a family now. Nicole Grace was born last month." She might have been complaining about the kids but the way she looked down the hall where the little girl and boy had just disappeared down made me think that Ray was more than happy with her current family situation.

"Am I off duty now?" Grace asked, grabbing the handle of the green pitcher and looking to Ray like she was asking her permission.

"Go ahead," Ray said with a roll of her eyes.

Grace smiled and poured herself a glass. She took a long sip making an exaggerated 'aaaaaaahhhhh' sound. "That's better." Shifting to her side with her legs crossed and an elbow propped up on the table she turned to me. "Mojito?" she asked, raising her glass and shaking it, clinking the ice from side to side.

"No thank you, ma'am," I said.

"Oh hush now, you can call me Grace, and it's fine with me that you don't want one because more for me," she said downing half of her drink. "So you're the girl..."

"Her name is Thia," Ray interrupted. "Thia, this is Grace."

"Thia is such a beautiful name, Abel told me it's short for Cynthia, is that right?"

"Yes," I said. The name Abel sounding oddly familiar, although I didn't know who Grace was referring to.

"Welcome, welcome. I am so happy to meet you. I wanted to come pluck you out of that dark garage, but I was warned to give you some space and that you'd come out when you were ready, and HERE. YOU. ARE." Grace reached over and with a strength I didn't think the frail older woman had, plucked me from my seat and pulled me in for a hug that threatened to crush my lungs. "It's a pleasure to finally meet you."

"Likewise," I said out of the side of my mouth, my cheek pressed up against her clavicle as she smushed me to her boney chest.

Ray chuckled. Grace pulled back and set me back down onto the chair. She sat and recrossed her legs, taking another sip of her drink. "Thank you for bringing my boy home," Grace said.

"Your boy?" I asked.

"Abel," Grace said.

"Who?"

"Bear," Ray said.

Abel.

Bear was Abel. I'd known that. He'd told me that when we first met but I'd always thought of him as Bear and almost completely forgot that he'd told me his real name.

Abel.

"I didn't bring him home. I needed his help and, I didn't know where else to go..." I said, unsure of how much I should be telling her. "It's a very long story."

One I didn't want to talk about. Not then.

Not ever.

Grace waved me off. "No need to explain. You're here now and so is my boy and that's all that matters."

"Are you Bear's mom?" I asked.

"No, but I'm the closest thing he's got to it. Someone has got to look after these boys. Before Ray here came along all they had was me and I did my best to make sure they knew that my home was their home," Grace said. Ray twisted a silver ring on her left hand and I wondered if it was an engagement ring or a wedding band. "And now that you're here I won't have to worry so much about Abel."

"I'm sorry, but I'm not staying," I said. "I'm leaving. Really soon, actually."

They didn't have to know how soon.

Grace tossed the newspaper she had been reading onto the table in front of me and I caught it before it slid right off the table. The headline on the front page was the same as the one from Bear's phone a few days earlier. Except this time there was a picture of a girl under the headline.

A picture of me.

"Well, it doesn't look to me like you're going anywhere, anytime soon." Grace sighed and leaned back like it had been settled, and I was staying regardless of my argument to the contrary. Which I noticed was a pattern with Grace. Ignoring anything she didn't want to believe was true and settling for her own skewed version of what was going on.

"I'm so happy my boys have found you girls," Grace said, despite my argument that Bear and I were not together. I wanted to argue but Ray shot me a look like she was telling me that I was fighting a losing battle. "I've loved Abel like he was my own since the very day Brantley brought him over to the house."

"Brantley?" I asked.

"King," Ray corrected. "My King. My fiancé."

"Abel had ridden his motorcycle right up on my lawn after a downpour, leaving deep valleys all the way up to my plant beds, then he left a grease stain the size of North Carolina on my love seat." She cupped her glass with both of her hands and looked into the ice like it was replaying the day she'd met Bear right there in her drink. "He was too young to be driving that damn thing, told him so myself, but by the next time he came to the house he was a natural. That boy was born to be on a motorcycle. The man and the machine."

I'd only seen him on a bike once and it was driving away from the gas station and even though I was just a kid at the time I knew exactly what Grace was talking about when she said he was born to be on a bike.

"He was a funny one too," Grace said.

"Funny?" I asked. Bear was a lot of things. Rude. Crude.

Sexy as hell. INFURIATING. But funny was a side I hadn't seen.

"Very. Used to tell me a new joke over my mama's meatloaf on Thursday nights. The most ridiculous jokes that he probably heard around the club. Most of them the filthy kind you couldn't repeat louder than a whisper and couldn't say within ten miles of a church, that's for sure." She shook her head. "As he got older, slowly but surely, the light in that boy's eyes grew dimmer and dimmer, by the time he rode off a few months back, there was nothing left in them. Broke my damn heart." Grace wiped a tear that spilled from her eye. "He deserves better than to walk around this world alone and with his own broken heart."

Ray stood up when the baby stirred on the monitor. "I'll be right back," she excused herself, and headed down the hall, emerging a few minutes later with a tiny little baby wrapped in a pink blanket.

"Isn't my grandbaby beautiful?" Grace asked proudly.

"Yes, she really is," I agreed. She was a tiny little thing with a headful of chestnut curls. She yawned and opened her eyes, and I had a strong urge to want to hold her, but I didn't want to ask. Ray didn't know me very well and I'm pretty sure there was some sort of Mom rule out there about how long you have to know someone before they let you hold their babies.

Ray must have seen my warring expression, because she asked, "Would you like to hold her?" Before I could answer she gently placed the baby in my waiting arms. Her itty bitty hands and feet were wrinkly, her cheeks so chubby they pushed up into her huge eyes making them appear much smaller than they really were and slightly slanted.

"Not a kid person huh?" Ray asked, leaning against the counter, calling me out on my earlier lie.

"When it's your turn I think Abel will be a really great father." Grace chimed in. "Just like my Brantley is."

"Grace," I said, unable to take my eyes off the tiny little one in my arms, "I'm not just denying it for the sake of denying it. Bear and I aren't together. I'm a problem for him, not any sort of solution."

"Grace used to tell me the same thing and I used to deny it too. But it turns out I was wrong," Ray said, leaning forward on her elbows.

Grace brushed her finger across the baby's cheek, the contrast of old and wrinkled hands against plump and innocent skin was a beautiful sight that made my heart sing a little.

Just a little zap like a mini heart reviving machine.

"What's her name?" I asked.

"Nicole Grace, but we're going to call her Nikki," Ray said, looking proudly over the baby in my arms. Grace beamed at the mention of her name as part of the baby's name.

"I saw Abel this morning for the first time since he's been back," Grace locked eyes with me. "He still looks angry as hell, but I can tell that something is shifting and I just know the light will be coming back soon. Mark my words, my Abel will be back for good. So I'm gonna say right now that you're wrong too, you just haven't realized it yet." She smiled at the baby and then up at me. The wrinkles around her eyes changing shape as her lips curled upward in a knowing smile. "I'm not a well woman, Thia. I'm feeling good now, but my time on this earth is limited."

"I'm so sorry..." I started, but Grace cut me off.

"Oh hush now. Don't be sorry. Just don't hurt my boy and I won't have to spend my remaining time alive hunting you down and making you pay." She leaned back in her chair and I glanced up to Ray to see if maybe I'd misunderstood the meaning behind Grace's words but Ray just stood there hiding a tight-lipped smile. "Now who wants lunch?" Grace asked, popping out of her chair and heading over to the refrigerator.

Ray stood on her tiptoes and opened a cabinet, taking out some plates and setting the table, while I just sat there, baby in my arms, with my mouth agape. "What the hell just happened?" I whispered to Ray.

She shrugged. "Congratulations, you've been threatened by Grace."

"What does that even mean?" I whispered, not wanting Grace to hear me and not wanting to wake the little girl who had drifted off to sleep in my arms.

"In a way," Ray said, setting a plate down in front of me, "it means welcome to the family."

Grace had brought over some sort of cheesy potato casserole and a big leafy salad. Although Ray had been bringing me food for the last few days it was the first meal that I actually remember tasting.

And it tasted fantastic.

Grace fell asleep shortly after lunch on the couch and the kids went down for a nap after refusing to eat anything but salad dressing and chocolate milk. "Thanks for dragging me up here. It actually felt pretty good to be in the land of the living again," I said as Ray walked me to the back door. "It's nice to know that no matter how much horrible stuff happens in life that the world still manages to keep turning."

"Listen Thia, I know you're going through a lot, and I know it's really hard, but you have to remember that you're not the only person who has lost family, and you're certainly not the only person here who has gone through some seriously horrible shit. I don't know what Chop did to you at the MC, and wondering about it makes my skin crawl, but you have to know that you're not the only one in this house who has been through something awful like that."

"You?" I knew there was more to Ray and her story then the beautiful young mom before me.

"Yeah, and I'll tell you the entire tale some day, but it's actually not me I'm talking about."

"Grace?" I looked over to where she was sleeping on the couch. Her deep snores growing louder and louder with each inhale. "Who would hurt Grace?"

Ray shook her head. "No, not Grace."

"Then who?" I hoped to God she wasn't going to say one of the kids.

Ray looked out the door toward the garage and then back to me. "Bear."

It was the last person I expected her to say, but after she said it, it made sense. Why he hated that I'd been hurt. Why he wanted to heal me. Why he hated me all at the same time.

Why he wanted me gone.

I was more than just a burden. I was a reminder. No wonder he walked away from me last night. He was dealing with his own shit.

He didn't need to deal with mine too.

If I wasn't sure before, I was definitely sure now.

The second I could figure out how, I would be gone.

Consequences be damned.

Chapter Sixteen
BEAR

"You got any weed?" I asked Ray who was on the couch in the living room.

"I don't know, Bear, do you know how to knock?" Ray asked, shooting daggers at me with her eyes.

"Never knocked before."

"I wasn't breastfeeding before," Ray said, and that's when I noticed the little bundle of pink pressed up against Ray's bare tit. I'd never seen anyone breastfeed a baby before. Not in person at least. I always thought it would be something gross, but I was wrong. Baby attached to it or not, a bare tit is still a bare tit and although I knew my feelings for Ray had never been anything real, she was still fucking beautiful...and her tit was still out.

"You got any weed?" I asked again, trying not to look at her tit but in the process managing to only look at her tit.

She grabbed a small blanket from over the couch and slung it over her shoulder. "You can look now."

"Don't think I ever stopped," I admitted. "But do you? It's kind of important." It was actually very important. I'd fucked up. I kissed Thia. I pressed my tongue into her pussy and in all my life I can honestly say that I'd never tasted anything so fucking amazing.

But then I got up and left her sitting there probably wondering what the fuck she'd done wrong when she'd done nothing wrong. It was the opposite. She'd done everything right.

Too fucking right.

She was so responsive and I knew that if I spent any more time with my mouth on her or touching her in any way that she would have come.

It was the mere thought of her coming around my tongue that set me off and made me start to lose control. Shit, it was probably that first fucking kiss. Her innocent tongue finding its way to mine.

My cock was so hard it fucking hurt and I was seconds away from taking her right there at the edge of the fire pit. If it wasn't for a crackling of the fire, a reminder of what I'd been through in that very same spot bringing me back to reality there was no doubt that I would have done just that.

The weed was my peace offering to her. My way to show her that I really did want to make her forget in a way that didn't involve me plowing through the barrier of her virgin pussy with my cock. I also had something else to tell her. Something that kept me on track with my original plan to get back on the fucking road.

"You think I can smoke weed while breastfeeding?" Ray asked, calling me back to the present.

"I take it from the way you're looking at me like I'm a fuck up that the answer to that is a big resounding motherfucking no?" I asked.

"You would be right," Ray said. "King is in his studio, he

keeps everything locked up pretty tight these days with the kids around, but he probably has something." She shifted the baby and her shirt before sliding the cover off. "Now was that so hard?" I liked arguing with Ray almost as much as I liked arguing with Ti.

HA HA you just admitted you like fighting with her. You have a crush you big fucking pussy!

I rolled my eyes at Preppy's mental commentary.

King was in his new studio, on the other side of the garage from the apartment, just as Ray had said he would be. He was hunched over an angled desk, his pencil moving quickly over the page. I leaned over to check out what he was drawing, it was an old school style dragon, breathing flames and it was one of the most detailed sketches I'd ever seen him do. Dramatic. Bold. "Nice digs," I said, looking around his new studio. His old one was just a small room in the house, outfitted in neon and posters. This one was cleaner, more grown up. More sterile. Pictures of previous tattoos he'd done hung in frames on the wall, a KING'S TATTOO sign with a skull wearing a crown hung over the door.

"Thanks. Feels good to have a workspace again since the kids take up every inch of the house and then some. Never knew kids had so much shit," he said, smudging a line with his pinky, wiping the top of the page with the side of his hand.

"You always surprise me, brother. This is next level shit right here," I said, pointing to his dragon.

"You'll never fucking guess who it's for," King said, spinning around on his stool.

"Who?"

"Ray's dad."

"No fucking shit. Senator asshole is getting tatted up? What happened to the good old days when we were planning his quick and timely demise?" I asked as I continued to look around the wall at the different types of tattoos he'd done.

"Things change. He's got all sorts of scars where he took the bullet in his chest and his shoulder. Wants a dragon to cover up part of it, reminds him of the old Jet Li movies he likes or some shit like that."

"If I had any room left I'd have you put that on me. Shit's totally fucking tits man," I said. "Speaking of tits, I just saw Ray up at the house and I was wondering if you've got any weed."

"Why the fuck did that sentence start with SPEAKING OF TITS?" King asked, tacking his sketch onto a board beside the window and glaring at me like I just told him I fingered her in his bed.

"'Cause your girl was up there feeding your kid. She was in the living room. Calm down dude, it's not like I saw nip or anything."

"You're starting to sound like Preppy," King said. "And the only reason why you're not dead right now is because you are about to tell me that you covered your eyes, turned your ass around and walked right out the fucking door when you realized she had her tit out."

"Sure. Sounds good. That's exactly what happened," I said sarcastically. "But seriously you got any weed? I'm out and I need it for something."

"Like getting high?" King asked.

Smartass.

"Yes, motherfucker, like getting high. But it's not for me, it's for Ti. She asked me why I was doing blow and I told her to check out of reality for a bit and she surprised me by begging me for it so she could forget too, I damn near gave in."

I neglected to tell him that I also needed it to apologize for tonguing her down without finishing. For promising to help her forget and instead running away right when I was getting to the good part.

"Why didn't you let her? Never seen you stop a girl from a good time before," King said.

"I didn't have any left, but it didn't feel right anyway. She's not some club whore."

"You finally decided she's not out to get you?" King asked.

"I guess not."

"You figure out what to do with her yet?"

"Plan hasn't changed. And I made a call which should help."

"What kind of call?" King asked, eyeing me warily.

"Bethany Fletcher," I admitted.

"Wow."

"Can't call club lawyers, they don't work for me any more. Figure if I can get Ti off the hook for shooting her parents then I can sneak her out of here and drop her off far enough away where the MC won't ever look for her."

"I still can't believe you called Bethany," King said.

"When you're at war with the devil sometimes you gotta dial up a demon," I said.

"Hope you know what you're doing."

"I do."

I had no fucking clue.

King walked over to the wall where a big painting of a melting clock hung from the ceiling to the floor. He shifted the painting, revealing a hidden safe. He turned the dial and when he opened it there was another safe inside, this one requiring a code.

"You want me to wait while you dig a key out from the backyard to open safe number three?" I asked.

"Fuck off," King said. "Got kids running around here now. Things are different. Can't have shit everywhere like we used to."

It was hard to imagine King, a man who did what he wanted his entire life without giving two shits if it was right or wrong, sneaking off at night to get high in the garage after the kids went night night.

"My mom did everything and everyone in front of me," he continued. "I don't want that for my kids. Want them not knowing about the bad shit. Want them believing in Santa Claus, the Easter Bunny, and the goddamn tooth fairy until they're fucking forty."

"Why?" I asked, not understanding what he was trying to get at.

"'Cause they're kids. Want them to just be kids. Play with toy guns and not have to worry about using the real deal before they're old enough to drive. I want their biggest worry to be about whether we're having pizza or hot dogs for dinner. You and me? We didn't get the chance to be kids. It was stolen from us by our shit parents, and instead of a childhood we were given a big plate of harsh fucking reality. Not gonna do that to them. I won't."

Since I'd gotten back to Logan's Beach I was under the assumption that King had gotten soft, but I was wrong. Wanting to protect his kids didn't make him soft. It made him even more fucking crazy, just in a different way.

Because he had a different purpose.

"You'll get it one day. You'll have your own to worry about, and then you'll realize that the psycho you thought you were, the one no one was stupid enough to fuck with, should be very fucking afraid of the psycho you will become to protect your family."

"Right now I can't see past tomorrow, never mind that far into the future. My days are numbered anyway. The MC is gunning for me the second I step out onto their turf. May not live long enough to knock someone up."

King tossed me a small ziplock bag and I shoved it into my back pocket. He closed the safe and leaned against his desk, crossing his arms over his chest. "I'm sorry, I didn't realize you'd turned into a big fucking pussy while you were gone."

"Fuck you," I spat.

"The old Bear would have phrased that shit differently. Tell me something, man. You still want it? The gavel? Because a few months ago you said you didn't want it yet you're wandering around here like you're a lost fucking puppy dog."

"Now the answer is 'I don't know,'" I said honestly. "Been asking myself the same fucking thing."

"Ain't gonna find your answer at the bottom of a bottle of Jack."

"Oh yeah, since when did you become my fucking mama?"

"Since an old friend asked me if I remembered who I was and I realized I'd lost touch. Thought you might like the same kind of reminder," King said, throwing my words back at me that I'd told him months ago. "Do you want to know what that old friend would have just said?"

"Sure," I said, because I did want to know.

"The old Bear wouldn't have said that the MC was gunning for him the second he stepped on their turf, the old Bear wouldn't have said shit, but he would have reigned down hellfire on them until it wasn't their fucking turf anymore," King said.

"How the fuck am I supposed to do that? I'm just me. All of my brothers besides one, take their orders from Chop. I'm only one soldier when they have dozens. Going into the MC would be fucking suicide and shit's fucked up but I'm not ready to go out just yet."

"That's funny, because a second ago it sounded like you were giving up."

"I'm not, just doing what I gotta do to get through life, man."

"That's even more funny," King said, lighting a cigarette.

"What is?" I asked, growing annoyed with my friend.

"That you think what you're doing is living," King pointed out.

"Shit is so easy to say coming from someone who's gone civilian."

"I'll soldier for you," King said. I was just about to light a cigarette but his words made me pause, the flame flickering inches away from my smoke, swaying in the air while I took in the gravity of what he'd just said.

"No," I said finally. "You've got Ray and the kids. If she found out you were gonna soldier for me so we could take back the MC she would fucking kill you before they had a chance to."

"See? That's how I know that you don't know shit," King said, pointing up to the house through the window. "Ray and my kids are my everything, but she knows and accepts me for who I am and what I need to do. When the time comes, and you see your way clear of all the bullshit you're insisting in stewing in, I'm in. I'll soldier. No fucking questions."

King had finally lost his goddamned mind. "No. And I'm not saying it just to say it man. I couldn't let you. If Ray doesn't kill you, she would most definitely kill me."

"Oh yeah?" King said, sitting back down at his desk and turning his back to me. He picked up his pencil and began another sketch. "Then why did she suggest it?"

I was mulling King's idea to take back the MC over in my mind. Wondering if it was a real possibility. With every step I took toward the apartment it sank its teeth into my brain and by the time I opened the door it took hold, but the thought didn't last long because as soon as I opened the door I felt it in the air. I knew before I even peered into the bedroom. I knew before I ran back up to the house to ask Ray if she'd seen her. I knew before I spotted my ring on the coffee table still attached to the chain.

Thia was gone.

Chapter Seventeen
THIA

The venom of a brown widow spider is six times more powerful than the venom of its cousin, the black widow. But unlike its darker relative, the brown widow's first response to a threat is to retreat, rarely biting unless direct contact is made. Attacking is its last option.

A last resort.

Kind of like me.

I had more in common with the spider that killed my little brother than I did with Bear.

Sheriff Donaldson wasn't ever in his office until after three pm. The town of Jessep may have been big in land mass but we were small in population, so small in fact that our town sheriff only worked part time.

Jessep was one of the oldest towns in Florida and being old meant a lot of its laws had been written a long time ago. One of its charms is that those laws hadn't ever been revised, leaving all sorts of backwards southern rules on the books.

Under Jessep law, men were not permitted to wear women's clothing, but it didn't stop there. More specifically, the punishment for those men caught wearing satin strapless gowns would be much more severe than those caught wearing knee-length skirts.

Showering naked was also a big no-no. Oral sex, even between married couples, was strictly forbidden as well.

It was illegal to sing in a public place while wearing a swimsuit. The rule makers may not have liked singing at all because it was also illegal to sing to a goat.

Even on the goat's birthday.

It was illegal for a single woman to parachute on Sundays.

I peddled back into my backwards hometown on a bicycle I'd found in the garage, an old blue beach cruiser with a tattered orange flag attached to the back of the seat. I'd rode all the way back to Jessep without stopping, my need to put distance between me and Bear and my desire to face what I had coming to me head on propelled me forward, faster and faster I'd pedaled until I'd finally slowed when I turned down the road with the Welcome to Jessep sign, Population 64. I'd meant to go straight to the sheriff's office. I hadn't meant to go to the house but before I'd realized it, I was still on the bike with my feet on the ground staring at the yellow crime scene tape that had detached on one side and was now floating in the wind.

I walked slowly up the path, taking the bike with me. I didn't plan on getting off or walking up to the porch or sitting in the old rocking chair inhaling the smell of rotting citrus.

But I did.

The afternoon rains had turned my mother's blood on the side of the house from fresh red to pale brown. Anyone who didn't know what happened there would have just thought it was a mud stain.

But I knew what happened here.

What I didn't know was what was going to happen next.

That's when I saw it.

The spider.

I stood on the rickety porch holding an old straw broom with a broken handle. I watched as it turned over a small black bug using a few of its many long and striped legs. It was lingering under the fascia, minding its own business, wrapping up his lunch, while I stood only feet away and planned its imminent demise.

The sun was beginning to set, one of the only hours of the day when the weather was tolerable and right before the summer rain settled in for its evening cry above Jessep.

I understood how it felt to want to be left alone and for a brief moment I contemplated sparing the spider the death sentence, but quickly changed my mind.

One just like it killed Jesse.

It had to die.

It seems I was good at killing things.

I set up our old rusty ladder and climbed up to the top, positioning the end of the broom handle over the innocent spider who had no idea what was coming. "Sorry little guy," I whispered, right before I crushed him into the corner. Over and over again I hit and hit and hit him, crushing him into oblivion. I killed that spider over and over again and kept killing it until my hands were bleeding from the splintered broom handle and tears ran down my face, long after what was left of the spider fell from the end of the broom and into the grass.

"Miss Andrews?" a man asked. I gripped the top of the ladder with both hands to maintain my balance, and dropped the broom. It fell onto the uneven porch and rolled off the side into the grass.

A very tall man stood on the dirt drive holding a manila folder and a handkerchief that he kept using to wipe the sweat off his red face. He was wearing a wrinkled grey suit and a sideways smile.

"I'm sorry Miss. I didn't mean to startle you," he said in a proper southern accent. If his clothes weren't a dead giveaway for not being a local, his accent would have done the trick. "I'm looking for a Miss Andrews?" the man asked again, holding up the file to shield his eyes from the sun as he watched me climb down from the ladder.

"Who wants to know?" I asked, turning around to wipe my eyes, picking up the broken broom handle from the grass and tossing it back onto the porch.

"My name is Ben Coleman and I'm here on behalf of The Sun..." I didn't need to hear him finish his sentence to know why he was there. The Sunnlandio Corporation were vultures and assisted in my mother's downhill descent into crazy before falling off the side and taking my dad with her.

Ben Coleman didn't seem to notice the crime scene tape floating in the wind. He stood on the driveway on a Tuesday night, wearing a wrinkled grey suit and dripping so much sweat it looked as if he'd been caught in the rain storm that I could see in the distance but hadn't yet come.

Ben approached and extended his hand to me. I folded up the ladder and walked right past him toward the shed on the side of the house. "You can leave Mr. Coleman, I know why you are here and I want nothing to do with it." I set the ladder in the shed and shut the door.

I could smell the approaching rain before I could see it. I used to make fun of my dad for saying he could smell the rain, but as I got older I could feel the shift in the air and I learned to recognize the sweet pungent zip of fresh oxygen before the clouds rolled in, turning off the stars and changing the night sky from black to grey. "Miss Andrews, I just need to go over this with you. We have the groves best interest at heart." Ben said, holding out the folder toward me.

I laughed. "Did you have my parents' best interest at heart when your company cancelled the contract the grove had with Sunnlandio since the 60's? Because I would ask them if they felt like you had their best interest at heart but I can't. And judging from the look on your face you know why I can't. So for whatever reason you are here, go sell it to someone else. I'm not interested and on top of that I don't have time. I have a meeting with the sheriff."

The wind picked up, zipping around the house, blowing my hair into my face. Ben's suit jacket blew open as he continued to follow me on my way to the front of the house.

That's when I spotted his gun.

Either he was the kind of businessman that was used to southerners shooting at him or he was no businessman at all.

The rain was already drenching the open field next to the house, it was only a matter of seconds before it found its way over. "Cut the shit, Mr. Coleman. If that's even your name. What is it that you want?"

"I need you to come look at this file. Tell me what you think. It's an offer to buy the grove. A generous one at that." He held out the manila file.

"Get off this property right now and take that with you," I warned.

"You're going to make me have to play hardball with you, Miss Andrews. I was willing to make you a proper offer, but you leave me no choice. Since you weren't yet eighteen when your parents died and they had no living will on record this property isn't yours and it won't be yours until it goes through an expensive and rather lengthy court process. And I hate to state the obvious but without a contract with a distributor like Sunnlandio the grove isn't worth anything anyway. There is also the little matter of you potentially going away for a very long time and I assume that's what your little meeting with the sheriff is about. But we at Sunnlandio would rather we take care of this now and we rather put the money up front than wait for the judge to deed us the property."

That's when the gravity of the situation hit me, what evil lurked in suits and ties and concealed their misdeeds in folders and briefcases. "That's why you did it? That's why you cancelled my parents' contracts isn't it? To devalue the land then screw them over with some bullshit offer?"

"Miss Andrews, I don't make those decisions, but I will admit that the law is on our side here. We're just trying to streamline the process by having you sign off."

"I'm not even eighteen yet, I can't sign anything," I said.

"Your birthday wasn't two days ago on July the twelfth?" Mr. Coleman asked, flipping open his file and reading off the date before closing it again.

I missed my own birthday?

The wall of rain came, soaking everything in its path, including the man in the suit who stood his ground, smiling as his hair flattened to the top of his head. "I am going to court tomorrow to file the offer with the probate judge and demand that the grove be properly appraised. You can either sign off on this now or ready yourself for a battle that you're not going to win. A battle you can't afford."

The law is on our side.

The law is on our side.

I saw red. So much red that I wished that a lightning bolt would come out of the sky and strike this suit wearing creep right off the driveway. Ben set the folder on the porch and flashed me that smug smile again and a salute of all things before heading back down the driveway. "Mr. Coleman?" I asked sweetly. He turned back around. "Yes, Miss Andrews?" he asked, shouting above the sound of the pouring rain.

"Did you just say that the law is on your side?" I asked, tilting my head to the side.

"Yes. That's right."

"Well then," I dialed in the code on the lock on the heavy porch box and the hinges sprung open. I removed what I needed off the hooks connected to the underside of the lid. Unlike the older one I'd risked my life with when my mother and I played Russian Roulette, this one worked on the first pull every single time. "Did you know that here in Jessep, anyone can shoot someone on their property for no reason at all?"

"You wouldn't," he said, not with fear in his voice. With challenge. He held his hand over his jacket, but he knew he didn't have time to go for his gun.

One step is all it took.

He took one step forward, calling my bluff.

I pulled the trigger.

"Welcome to Jessep, Mr. Coleman."

Chapter Eighteen
BEAR

An echoing CRACK pierced through the night, so loud I heard it above the roar of my bike, rippling the air around me like I was stuck in a wave. Something small but fast zipped by my ear like a scream, so close I felt the heat trail on the side of my neck.

A bullet.

Crack. Echo. Crack. Echo.

There were two bikes on my tail. Two bikes I recognized. Two bikes I helped build.

Bastards.

I knew there was a possibility that the second I left Logan's Beach on my bike these fuckers could be trailing me. The problem was that I was too wrapped up in finding Thia before they did that I hopped on and sped off without even telling King where I was heading.

Fuck, maybe they already did.

My chest stung like I'd already been hit with a bullet.

The Beach Bastards might have been lawless, but they

weren't soulless, one of the codes we lived by was 'Always look a man in the eye when you are about to take his life.'

The club must have gone even more to shit than I'd originally imagined because the two pussies behind me, firing at my back, had chosen to ignore that particular code.

CRACK.

I felt the heat against the skin of my neck as the bullet whizzed by.

I passed the Welcome To Jessep sign and tried to shake the fuckers following me by taking a sharp right.

No such luck.

Bullets might have been flying, Thia might have been in danger or already dead, but when I picked up speed and leaned forward pushing the machine between my legs to its limits I was reminded of another time, another cloudless night when going fast wasn't fast enough.

I'm five years old and I'm in the passenger seat of a car I've never been in before. My mom is driving.

She's mumbling to herself and biting her nails.

When she picked me up from school I'd gotten into her red convertible, but she passed the street we always turn on, the one that takes us to the clubhouse. The only stop we'd made was when we'd traded her car for this one behind the Stop-n-Go.

The little Toyota we are riding in smells like the time I got sick after drinking Tank's special soda he'd left on the pool table. The only special thing about his soda was the amount of puke it made me spray all over the floor of my dad's office.

Dr. Pepper is way better.

Mom lights a cigarette and rolls open her window, but just a crack. The car fills with the smoke she breathes out, but it doesn't bother me because I'm used to it. Everyone in the club smokes. I saw a commercial on TV once that said that smoking makes you stop growing, and I want to be real tall like my old man, so I've decided I'm gonna wait until I grow a lot taller before I start smoking.

It's dark outside, but since we are on the highway, every time we pass a street light the inside of the car goes bright and then dark, like someone is flipping a light switch on and off. I don't count how many times the switch gets turned on, but it's a lot. I stop when I get to a hundred because that's the highest number I know.

Every time a motorcycle passes, Mom grips the steering wheel really tight and holds her breath until it speeds by. She keeps checking the mirrors and wiping the hair out of her eyes. She's got bubbles of sweat on the top of her face and when the car lights up the next time, I notice she's got tears leaking from her eyes.

"What's wrong, cunt?" I ask.

Mom rolls her eyes and shoots me an angry look. "Just because your father calls me that, doesn't mean it's a nice thing to say to someone. You just stick with calling me Mom, okay?"

"Cunt doesn't mean beautiful girl?" I ask, confused because Tripod is the one who told me what it meant, and he is the VP of my old man's club, so he knows a whole lot.

"No honey, it doesn't mean that. It's a bad word so don't ever say it again, okay?" She ruffles my hair with her hand and goes back to checking the mirrors.

When I get back to the clubhouse I'm going to ask Tripod about that word again. My old man says that girls sometimes don't understand things the way boys do, so Mom is probably just confused.

"How can a word be bad?" I ask.

"It just can, Abel," she says with a huff. Mom has the same look on her face she gets before she sends me to time-out, but at least her eyes aren't leaking anymore.

I don't like it when her eyes leak.

I also don't like it when her nose leaks blood after she argues with Chop, my old man.

"Mama, what's wrong?" I ask her again.

She shakes her head at me and smiles. "Nothing baby. Nothing's wrong. In fact everything is great."

"But I want to go back to the clubhouse," I whine.

"No!" Mom yells, slamming her fist against the wheel. She takes a deep breath and another drag of her cigarette, stubbing it out in the ashtray. She reaches over and grabs my knee. I giggle because it's my ticklish spot. "Abel, we are going somewhere you are going to love. It's even better than the clubhouse. I promise." She removes her hand and lights another cigarette.

I shrug and start to get excited, mostly because I think my mom might be taking me to Disney World. I have never been there, but it's the only place I could think of that could be better than the clubhouse.

I go back to stretching the arms of my Stretch Armstrong and tie them behind his back the way I saw the cops do when they took Uncle Gator away yesterday. Cops aren't friends of the club, so I didn't tell my old man how cool I thought the lights and sirens were. He said Uncle Gator won't be home anytime soon, but that we can visit him next month in a place called Up-State.

I hear a familiar rumble and I turn to look behind us. "Hey Mom, Dad's here," I say, but she only looks ahead and nods. Her eyes start leaking again. Motorcycles surround the car and my mom slows down but doesn't stop. I recognize Tank and his bike when he pulls up close next to us. Even with his helmet and yellow tinted goggles I can tell he's angry by the lines around his mouth. He's shouting something, but I can't hear him over the other bikes. My mom hears him because she shakes her head 'no' like she's answering him.

I see Tank kick out his boot and the next thing I know the back window explodes into the car and the glass flies everywhere. Even though I duck behind the seat it's too late. I catch a piece in the corner of my eye and it feels like a deep burning scratch. My mom screams and the next thing I know I feel the car veer to the right, the tires bumping over uneven ground before coming to a stop.

I take my hand off of my eye and try to open it but the second I do it shuts automatically and I'm sure that the glass piece might still be in my eye. Mom grabs my face and inspects my eye. The bikes have all come to a stop around the car and now I see Chop. He gets off his bike and throws his helmet to the ground. My mom picks a small shard of glass from my eye that's stained with red. "I love you, Abel. Now and forever. Just remember that." She whispers as Chop tears her door open and drags her out of the car by her hair. She screams and kicks but Chop doesn't stop dragging her until they are covered by the trees on the side of the highway.

I may not be able to see them, but I can still hear them. "Do you not know how to fucking listen!" Chop shouts. "I told you that if you ever set foot in Logan's Beach or near my fucking kid again, that I'd cut your tits off and hang them on the fence of the clubhouse! Did I look like I was fucking joking, cunt!"

I've heard them yell at each other before but something about this times seems different. "Come on, buddy." Tank tells me, leading me out of the car and back to his bike.

"Why the fuck did you think you could steal my kid and live to fucking tell about it!" He shouts. He must have hit her because I hear my mother scream again. The leaves on the trees shake and I can't take my attention away from where I know they are. Tank continues to lead me to his bike but I'm walking backwards.

"I had to try!" I hear my mother shout. "I had to try to give him a life where he wouldn't end up..." she pauses.

"Say it, bitch. You know how this works. This ends the same way no matter what so you better get it out now...while you have the chance," Chop says. I hear a click.

"I wanted to take him away from here so he wouldn't end up

like you!" My mom shouts and as soon as the last word leaves her mouth there is a popping sound.

And then nothing.

Tank puts me on the back of his bike and starts it up, the others that are with us do the same. Biggie, one of the younger guys, jumps into the Toyota and speeds off. Pager, one of the oldest in the Bastards, is waiting at the edge of the brush when Chop appears with blood splattered across his cheek, his gun still in his hand. He tosses the gun to Pager who wraps it in a rag.

Tank signals something with his hand to Chop, who sees him because he nods in response, but his eyes are locked on mine. He breaks our connection to wipe the blood from his cheek with his bare hand.

I wasn't ever scared of him. Not when he beat my mom. Not when he beat me for any number of things I'd done that he didn't like. Not when he brought me on his airboat and forced me to watch as he shot a man and dumped his body in the Everglades.

It's this very moment when a shiver of fear snakes down my spine and for the very first time I'm afraid of my father. He looks down at his now red-coated palm. Shivers dance down my spine when his eyes again find mine...

And he smiles.

Heat exploded in my back, radiating through my shoulder, followed by the mind-numbing pain as the bullet connected with bone, tearing through the front of my shoulder. I'd been shot before, but it's not a feeling you can get used to. Tiny grenades tearing through your skin and muscles then exploding once it's sunk deep enough inside of you. Every nerve in my spine jumped and my arms contorted, steering the bike sideways, causing it to swerve all over the road. "FUUUU-UUUUCCCCKKKKK!" I screamed through my teeth while white-knuckling the handlebars, righting my bike just seconds before my front tire was about to dip into the ditch lining the side of the road. Grass and dirt fanned out from under my tires, mud rained down on top of me as my tires again took purchase of the road.

With bullets still whizzing around my head it took everything I had to keep the bike straight and keep up my speed. Just a few small ticks on the speedometer in the downward direction and I was a dead man.

I may not have been wearing a cut, but I wasn't some bitch, I was running toward Thia, not running for my life.

I slammed on the brakes, spinning my bike around to face the bitches who were coming at me full speed. Tonk and Cash. Two brothers I'd personally recruited as prospects.

Ungrateful motherfuckers.

Two brothers who were also about to learn the hard way that just because I wasn't wearing my cut didn't mean that I was weak.

Or that I forgot how to pull a motherfucking trigger.

My bike continued to spin as I lifted my hands off the handlebars and pulled both guns from my shoulder holsters. Pain ripped through my back at my sudden movement, but my aim was steady.

I enjoyed the look of shock on those motherfucker's faces as they barreled toward me and I began firing. Cash went down first, his bike turning on its side as I put two in his chest. Tonk followed, flipping over his handlebars after I put one through his right cheek.

My bike spun out of control, but it looked like it was the world around me spinning instead of me. Orange groves circled me and so did the smell of something rotting. I careened off the side of the road, smashing into the ditch I'd managed to avoid only minutes earlier. I sailed over my bike, flying through the air, smiling.

I might have been going out, but at least I was going out knowing that I took those two motherfuckers with me.

My last thought before I hit the ground was of a girl with pink hair.

Chapter Nineteen
THIA

Mr. Coleman had wobbled away on his own accord and I ran into the orange grove before he could remember he had a gun of his own. I was disgusted with what I'd done, and even more disgusted with the fact that I didn't regret it.

When my lungs burned and I couldn't run any more I dropped down to my knees. "I'm so sorry, Dad. I'm so sorry I couldn't save all this for you. For us. But most of all I'm so sorry I couldn't save you," I said into the trees. The leaves around me rustled with the wind, every so often I heard the THUD of a falling orange.

I briefly contemplated burning it all to the ground, going as far as picking a leaf off a nearby tree to test how dry it was and how fast it would burn when the ground beneath me rattled, little bits of foliage and loose chunks of dirt jumped around my knees.

I'd lived in Florida my entire life, and we'd never had an earthquake before.

Was an earthquake even possible?

A rumbling sound started in the distance and I stood up in a panic, preparing myself for the earth to shift. The rumble grew louder and louder and my heart beat faster and faster, every muscle in my body tensed as the seconds ticked by, slowly filling the silence.

It was a sound you felt before you heard. A rumble that grew louder and vibrated in your bones.

An earthquake on two wheels.

A motorcycle. And from the sound of it, maybe more than one.

Bear.

He'd come for me.

Don't be stupid, Thia. Millions of people ride motorcycles besides him, it's not him.

But it could be the MC.

And then...BOOM.

An explosion so loud my hair blew into the wind like a bomb had gone off.

A burst of bright orange light flew into the night followed by the contrast of billowing grey smoke against the cloudless black sky.

I was running toward the explosion before I could talk myself out of it, reaching the road in less than a minute.

The mangled wreckage of metal was strewn about both sides of the road. I wasn't sure if it was one bike or two until I saw two bodies strewn across the road, lying at lifeless unnatural angles. I ran to the first body and my heart started to race out of control. The man's arms covered in so much blood I couldn't make out any of his features or tattoos.

In a panic I knelt down and used all my strength to try and turn the man over but he didn't budge. Then I pictured the face of the man I didn't want it to be and I needed to know if it was him. I tried again, using all the strength I didn't know I had. I wasn't successful at turning him completely over, but had managed to get him on his side. The second I saw the rounded face and short brown hair I breathed a sigh of relief.

When I came upon the wreckage I was positive it was a crash, an accident. I was sure that there were two dead bodies lying in the road who'd died on impact.

I was wrong.

I ran to the next man who was lying face up, with his head turned to the side, his eyes and mouth were wide open.

A bullet hole in his cheek.

I gasped. Standing up, I backed up into the grove from where I came, like for some reason I had to keep my eyes on the wreckage and the bodies or they would pop back up and come after me.

That's when I realized that my panic that one of the bodies would be Bear was for no reason. Both the dead men were wearing Beach Bastard cuts.

They'd come for me.

Bear hadn't.

I knew he wouldn't, but I still couldn't help but feel disappointed and afraid all at the same time.

There could be more of them on their way.

Slowly I backed up until the trees had almost swallowed me entirely. Crickets chirped all around me. Frogs croaked and the bug zapper on the front porch could be heard zapping all the way from the porch, which was a good half mile away. Further and further I stepped until I backed right up into something big and hard that definitely wasn't a tree. Chills shot up my spine as a hand came around my waist and another covered my mouth, muffling my scream.

"Ti, stop, it's me," Bear growled in my ear as I struggled

against him.

I stilled.

He had come for me.

Bear loosened his grip and I spun around in his arms. The moon was big and bright, acting like a spotlight right above our heads. He was shirtless and covered in dirt. His normally blond hair and beard were streaked with dark mud. His jeans were torn at the knee. "How busy is this road?" he asked suddenly.

"Not busy. There is one other farm, but it's back up the other way. We stop on a dead end."

"Anyone scheduled to come up this way? Mailman, deliveries of any kind. I need you to think."

"No, nothing. Mail goes to the box in town and the grove has been out of business for a while."

Drip.

Drip.

Drip.

There were no hoses anywhere, no running water since the water company turned off the supply when we couldn't pay the bill and the rain had already passed.

THUD. Bear spun around. "What the fuck was that?" he asked.

"Oranges. They sound like that when they fall from the trees," I said. With his back turned to me I saw the source of the dripping.

It was coming from Bear.

Blood.

Streams of bright blood that appeared black under the light of the moon dripped from the back of his shoulder, merging onto his belt, then falling onto the soft ground. "You're hurt," I said, pointing out the obvious.

Bear turned back around, his eyes darkened and glowed like blue flames. "I don't give a fuck about my shoulder, Ti. What I give a fuck about right now is you taking off when I told you it wasn't safe." Bear looked down at me like I'd crossed him in a way I didn't understand. "Maybe you didn't believe me when I said the MC would be coming for you." He nodded to the bodies in the road. "You believe me now?" he asked, his nostrils flaring.

I took a step back and he took a step forward, not allowing me the distance I wanted to put between us. "Why did you come?"

"What the fuck did I just say? I came because you didn't listen. I came because it's not safe and if I hadn't come you'd either be dead right now or wishing you were dead once they got through with you," Bear said. And for the very first time, I was afraid of him. Not because I thought he would hurt me, but because I'd never seen him so angry.

"I don't understand you," I said.

"You don't have to understand me," he growled, and as if he was proving his point he crashed his lips over mine.

I wanted to push him away. I wanted to tell him no. But after thinking he could have been one of those dead men in the road, my body wouldn't let me. My brain wanted to scream at him, punch him, but when his tongue ran along the seam of my mouth seeking entrance my traitorous lips opened for him, groaning when his tongue found mine, pressing myself up against his dirty body. He cupped his hands around my face and kissed me like he was screaming at me, punishing me for disobeying him, for being in his life, for not being in his life.

I took his punishment and gave it back to him, telling him all the things with our kiss that I didn't understand myself. The coolness of his rings pressed against the skin of my back underneath the hem of my shirt.

Bear pulled back, breathing heavily, staring through me like he could see right into my soul. "You just have to fucking listen to me, but as much as I want to have a conversation with you right now where you tell me what a shit person I am and I tell you that you're the most anger inducing girl I'd ever laid eyes on. And much as I want to keep my mouth on you, we have another couple of problems I'm gonna need you to help me take care of first before they become bigger problems." Bear wrapped a muddied hand around my neck and closed the distance between us.

"What?" I asked, trembling under the weight of his stare, somehow forgetting about the dead men lying only feet away from us.

"You know how to sew?"

"That's an odd question."

"Not that odd seeing as I'm bleeding out," Bear said, releasing me and grabbing onto his shoulder. "It's clean through, just needs some putting back together."

"Shit. Here," I said, ripping off my shirt I stood up on my toes to press it to the back of his shoulder blade.

"Fuck," Bear groaned. I let up on the pressure, thinking I'd hurt him. "Maybe you should let me bleed out. Might be worth it," he said, licking his lips. I followed his gaze to my naked breasts. My nipples hardened under his stare.

"Fuck, Ti, you may not have pulled the fucking trigger, but I got a feeling you're going to kill me yet." His hands settled on my ass, while I tried to stop the bleeding, his fingers kneading into my flesh as I concentrated my efforts on his wound.

"What's the other thing we have to do?" I asked, feeling the blush burning my cheeks and neck, grateful for the cover of night to hide my embarrassment over being so obviously turned on.

"Cleanup."

Chapter Twenty
THIA

"I can't go in there," I said, stopping just short of the front porch steps, my arms crossed over my bare chest.

"Needle and thread," Bear said, wincing, still holding my bloodied shirt over his shoulder. "Where would I find it?" he asked and I was relieved he wasn't going to force me inside.

"Sewing room off the kitchen, right on the left. Mama kept that stuff in a tackle box in the drawer next to her Singer."

Bear disappeared into the house, emerging a few minutes later with my mom's entire tackle box. "No lights," Bear said, tucking his lighter, which he had been using to guide his way through the dark house, into the pocket of his jeans. Of course there were no lights. The bill was past due before my parents' deaths, and the dead don't pay the electric bill. Most of the time, in our house, neither did the living.

He tossed me a blue tank top that he'd gotten from my room and I hurried to cover myself with it. "Thank you," I said. Bear's response was a small grunt.

I opened the toolbox on the porch and picked out a flashlight. I clicked the button and thankfully it came to life.

"You've been here all day and you haven't gone in yet?" Bear asked, sitting on the top step with his back to me. I shined the light down as Bear picked out what he needed from the tackle box.

"I didn't plan on coming here at all."

"Then why come back here?" he asked, pouring vodka from a bottle that I didn't notice he'd come out with onto the thread. He handed the bottle to me. "Pour this on the back of my shoulder."

I grabbed the bottle and using the flashlight I was finally able to get a good look at Bear's wound. He was right it was clean through, but it was much deeper than I'd thought. "Shit," I said, dropping the flashlight. "Just pour it on, Ti and tell me why you're here if that wasn't your plan."

I shined the light on his wound and for some reason found myself closing my eyes as I tipped the bottle over and poured the alcohol directly into his wound. Every muscle in Bear's body tensed. "Ti, speak. Now," Bear said through gritted teeth. He grabbed the bottle from my hand and poured the rest over the hole in the front of his shoulder, bracing his hand on the ledge of the front step he tore off a chunk of the old rotted wood. When he was done he tossed the wood into the yard and set down the bottle, handing me the needle and thread.

"Sheriff Donaldson isn't in until the afternoon. I was going to go see him, but then I ended up here and I got...distracted." Distracted was a good term for Ben Coleman and his audacity to even step foot onto the grove.

"You were going to confess?" Bear asked, the anger seeping back into his voice. He crossed his arms over his thighs and leaned forward so I could have better access to his wound. I set the flashlight on the banister and using the only stitch I remembered that my mama had taught me I pulled Bear's skin as close together as possible and tried to pretend it wasn't his flesh and muscle I was putting back together, but a thick quilt or tough leather.

"Yeah, I thought it would be best to lay it all out, take whatever I had coming to me. My friend Buck is the deputy, figured maybe they'd cut me some slack. It's not like if I go to prison anyone would miss me. The world would still turn. Nobody would even know I was gone."

"I would."

"Yeah, you would know I was gone, but you'd be happy to be rid of me," I said bitterly.

"Ti..." Bear started. I stopped breathing, waiting to hear what he had to say. "Aaaahhhh," he grunted as I dug the needle in deeper than I'd anticipated.

"Sorry," I whispered, thinking that maybe I should remember that I was sewing a person after all.

"I got a lawyer for you," Bear said, surprising me. "Last one I wanted to call, but she'll do right by you."

"You did what?"

"I got a lawyer, a bitch of a woman. If the devil wore fancy suits and wore red lipstick it would be Bethany Fletcher. She's good though. Right now she's sorting through all this shit. Making calls and digging in a little deeper into your case. Right now you're only wanted for questioning, you're not under arrest. You bolted before I had a chance to tell you."

"You repaired the door, but you left it unlocked. I figured you were telling me to go," I said honestly.

"I was telling you that you weren't a fucking prisoner," he corrected. "I thought you'd fucking listen and do what you're told. I see now that was a mistake and don't worry I won't make it again. I should have listened to King and cuffed you to the fucking bed." His entire body stiffened and my needle stilled, unable to make progress into his muscle.

I ignored his threat to cuff me, and focused on my task. "I know it's hard, but try not to tense up, it will just make the pain worse."

"Oh yeah?" Bear asked, sounding amused. "Where did you learn that?" His muscles relaxed slightly and the needle moved in and out with more ease making quicker work of putting him back together.

I smiled, recalling the memory. "Dr. Hartman told me that when he fixed up my knee. My brother Jesse and my friend Buck and I were practicing casting the new reels we'd gotten for Christmas one year. Well, they weren't brand new, but they were new to us."

"You got water this far inland?" Bear asked.

"Oh yeah, we got a pond in the middle of the grove, deep one too. Every once in a while Mr. Miller used to stock it with stuff he caught on one of his trips to the lake. But that day we weren't practicing at the pond. We were on dry land, just out back in the clearing. We set up hola-hoops on the ground for targets and weighted down our lines. It was good practice too, but looking back I guess we didn't need the hooks. I walked a little too close behind Buck when he was about to cast and caught a hook to the knee." I stretched out my leg onto the front step so Bear could see the long scar that ran from the top of my knee to the bottom. "He didn't realize he hooked me and kept going, tore the skin and the hook right out of my knee. Twelve stitches," I said, pulling my leg back.

Bear held out his left hand and pointed to a scar between his thumb and index finger. "Same injury. Different friend. We were probably about sixteen and in this little dingy doing some inshore fishing. If we caught a few red fish sometimes we sold them to one of the restaurants on the other side of the causeway for a few bucks. Sometimes they were just good eating. But the only thing we caught that day was a buzz and about an inch of skin off my hand."

"I'm done on this side," I said, biting off the thread and tying it off in a series of unbreakable knots. I rethreaded the needle and knelt on the step to the side of Bear. It was an awkward position that had me almost teetering off the edge and he noticed, because he grabbed my forearms and spread his legs, pulling me in between and resting my elbows on his thighs, he released my arms and his hands came around to rest on the small of my back.

"Better," he said, looking right into my eyes. I was all too aware of his gaze as I started to close off the wound, which was smaller in the front than it was in the back. He watched me as I worked, the edge of his beard brushed against my skin, his breath warm against my neck sending tingles between my thighs.

I needed to concentrate on my stitching before I hurt him again. "There was a picture in the apartment of you when you were younger. You and King with another boy wearing a bow tie. Was that Preppy?"

Bear leaned forward, resting his nose in the crook of my neck and nodded, his lips and beard setting my skin on fire.

So much for concentrating.

I cleared my throat. "Does he live in Logan's Beach?" I asked, as I finished the last stitch. The thread was short after stitching both the front and back of his shoulder. I had to close my mouth around the thread, my lips flush against his skin as I cut it with my teeth, resisting the urge to taste him with my tongue, before tying it off like I'd done on the other side. I blew on his skin to ease some of the pain and Bear stood up, catching me before I tumbled down the steps and setting me back onto my feet.

"He's dead," Bear said, picking up the bottle of vodka and pouring it over both sides of his wound, hissing between his teeth.

That was the end of our personal conversation, after which Bear turned all business. By the time he'd asked how deep the pond in the middle of the grove was and tested the tractor on the side of the house to see if it was running, I was starting to figure out what he'd meant by 'cleanup.'

After I watched him tie the bodies of his former brothers to what was left of their bikes and sink them into the pond…I had an even better idea.

"Sun's up soon," Bear said, looking off into the distance to where the pink had just started to invade the night sky. He pulled out his phone and pushed a few buttons, his lips moving silently as he read something over, shoving his phone back into his pocket when he was done. He hopped down from the tractor and came around to my side, about to help me down.

I rolled my eyes. I'd been jumping on and off that tractor since I was in diapers. Bear stalked toward me, backlit by the rising sun he was dirty, sweaty and muddy to all hell but he was surrounded with a halo of light like he was an angel from hell. "Bethany messaged me. She arranged for you to be questioned by the sheriff at her office in Coral Pines. He wanted to do it tomorrow, but she managed to push him off for another forty eight hours because she wants to meet with you first and go over some things."

"What kind of things?" I asked.

"Your story," Bear said. "She wants to make sure you say the right thing and that you know how to answer his questions."

"What right thing?" I asked, following him around to the side of the house where he unraveled the hose. "I killed my mom after she killed my dad. That's all there is to it."

He let out a frustrated sigh and held up the end of the hose with the nozzle, searching for the spigot.

I stomped over to where the hose bib was hidden by a thorny bush and turned on the water.

"When are you going to learn to stop questioning me and fucking listen? Your story," he said, closing the distance between us, "will be whatever Bethany tells you it is."

"When are you going to learn that I don't like being told

what to do?" I crossed my arms over my chest and Bear adjusted the nozzle, testing the spray in the grass.

His eyes burned with anger, a warning not to continue to argue with him. Fine. I won't argue.

But that didn't mean I was agreeing with him either.

"You said the sheriff isn't in office until the afternoon?" he asked.

"Yeah not until two or three," I said. "Buck might be around, but that's it for Jessep, just the two of them."

"Good. My bike's not in the worst shape, but I need a couple of parts. We can make a quick run at first light and head back to Logan's Beach." My stomach chose that moment to let out an embarrassingly loud growl.

How long had it been since I'd eaten? Then I remembered, not since lunch with Grace and Ray.

"And we have to get you some food," Bear added. My cheeks reddened.

"Wait, you want me to come back with you? Why?"

"You ask too many questions," Bear growled, unbuckling his jeans he gave me no warning before pushing them down to the grass and stepping out of them. He turned the hose on himself, rinsing off the events of the night.

I turned around because I wasn't sure what else to do or where else to look. "I ask, because I want to know," I said with a huff, the image of Bear's naked ass burned into my mind. My nipples hardened and something inside of me clenched. I didn't need to go back to Logan's Beach with him, I needed to check myself into a mental facility for teenagers who can't keep their hormones in check. "Why did you come after me? Why did you want to make sure the MC didn't kill me?" And because I couldn't resist and because my mouth was running away with me, "And why did you kiss me?"

I waited for him to answer me but nothing. I heard the spray of the hose turn off and was about to turn around to see if he walked away when I felt his heat against my back. His wet heat.

His naked wet heat.

He pulled me up against him, his strong chest on my back and rock hard thighs against my ass. With one hand splayed under the hem of my shirt against my bare stomach he breathed into my ear, "Stop asking so many questions," he said, the tip of his tongue barely making contact with my skin but sending a flush of wetness between my legs.

"Just answer me why," I said. It came out as a whisper.

As a beg.

Bear chuckled and it vibrated against my neck. I leaned into him, my lower back coming into contact with his growing erection.

"Do you really want to know?" he asked, tracing the underside of my breast with his calloused thumb. "Do you really want to know why I kissed you? Why I kissed your sweet pussy? Do you want to know that I can still taste you on my tongue right now and I'm fucking salivating for more? Do you want to know that you were tight around my tongue and I imagined the entire time that it was my cock you were squeezing with your virgin cunt?" he asked, rocking against me.

"Yes," I begged. "Yes, I want to know."

"Because, I fucking wanted to," he said and my stomach damn near flipped out of my body. He punctuated his words by nipping at my neck before pushing me forward and turning the hose on me.

The cold stream dousing the fire of lust that had started to build in my belly.

"Son of a bitch," I screamed, running toward the spray of the water, intent on killing him and adding him to the bodies at the bottom of the pond.

He tossed me the hose and I caught it by the neck. "Clean up."

"You could have just said that," I spat.

"Now where would be the fun in that?" He bent down and picked up his jeans off the ground, shrugging them back on. I covered my eyes with my hands but couldn't help peeking through my fingers to catch another glimpse of his round and tight ass.

"I'm sorry, I wasn't aware this was fun," Bear said. "You can take your hand down now and stop pretending you weren't looking."

"I wasn't looking!" I lied. Bear chuckled to himself disappearing back up the steps to the house as I finished hosing off, wishing that the water was colder.

Much, much colder.

Chapter Twenty-One
THIA

"I can go into town by myself," I said, climbing up into the driver's seat of my dad's old Ford.

Bear had grabbed me some dry clothes from the house, but couldn't find the keys. After a few minutes of pulling wires out from under the steering wheel he managed to get it to start by twisting some wires together. "Just tell me what you need and I'll get it." I went to close the creaky door but Bear held out his hand and caught it.

"I'm not letting you go alone," Bear said. "We got time before the MC figures out that Tonk and Cash are not of this world anymore. Tonk's phone was busted but I sent a few texts from Cash's to Chop before they went for their late night swim. Bought us some time."

"Okay, so we have time. That means it's safe. You don't have to come with me," I argued, again trying to pull the door shut and again he stopped me.

"You afraid to be seen with me or something? Afraid what the townsfolk are gonna think?" he teased.

"No, it's not that."

"Ah, so you think the big bad biker is going to scare the natives," Bear said, stepping up into the truck. I had no choice but to scoot over to the passenger side to avoid being crushed underneath him.

The truth was that I couldn't seem to think around him. A few minutes to myself might be able to clear some of the Bear induced haze that had been following me around, but there was no way in hell I was about to tell him that, so I came up with something that was still true, although a little less important on my scale of reasons for not taking him into town with me.

I threw my hands into the air, letting my frustration show. "I think you don't seem to own a shirt and Emma May at the Stop-N-Shop is going to take one look at you and have heart attack number three."

The corner of Bear's mouth turned upward in a crooked smirk that made little lines appear at the corner of his eyes. He slowly leaned over me, closer and closer. I leaned away, plastering myself against the seat like I was trying to force myself to be one with it. "You think I'm hot, Ti?" His cool breath fluttered against my neck. "You jealous? Afraid I'm gonna make some little old lady's panties just as wet as I make yours?"

"What...what are you doing?" I asked breathlessly when he reached across my lap.

"I drive kind of...wild," Bear said, pulling the old lap belt across my waist and clicking it into the rusted buckle.

I breathed a sigh of relief and disappointment when he sat back up straight and started up the truck. He lifted up off the seat and pulled out something that had been hanging from the back of one of his pockets.

A shirt.

He pulled it over his head.

More like a tight black tank top.

If anything it did more to enhance the defined muscles of his chest and the ones on his stomach that trailed down to the V that pointed down into his low slung jeans. "See? You were wrong, I do own a shirt," Bear said with a wink. With one long arm across the back of the bench seat, his fingers brushed my shoulder as he turned the truck around and headed down the driveway.

"Like that helps," I muttered.

"Didn't catch that," Bear said, although I had a feeling he had.

"I'm perfectly capable of driving," I said.

"I'm sure you are, but you're with me right now, and as long as you're with me, I drive."

I turned my head toward my window and rolled my eyes.

I watched the orange grove pass us by as we made our way down the road and past the spot where Bear had raked over the dirt to erase any and all traces of the crash from the night before. Oranges were stacked high under the trees. The sickening sweet smell that had been permeating the air for weeks before THE NIGHT that changed everything had turned into something that smelled like takeout left in a refrigerator for a week too long.

"Why does it smell like something died out here?" Bear asked.

I shot him an obvious look. "Maybe because something did?" I replied sarcastically.

"Not what I meant, Ti. You know it. I mean, why are the oranges rotting?"

"When Sunnlandio pulled their contract it became pointless."

"Why?" Bear asked, looking genuinely concerned. He lit a

cigarette using the old push-in lighter on the dash. He rolled down the window and leaned out with his elbow on the ledge, his hair blowing in the breeze.

I shrugged and tried not to launch into the evils of the Sunnlandio Corporation. "Short story is that they discovered it was cheaper to import from Mexico."

"But why let the oranges rot?"

"Harvesting costs a lot of money," I explained. "And when you don't have buyers lined up it becomes as much of a waste as the oranges to attempt a harvest. Chain supermarkets and big juice companies already have their own contracts or their own groves, or like Sunnlandio, they've switched over to importing. It's cheaper to let them rot which sucks because it's such a waste. Can't even donate them because that still means that someone has to pick and deliver them."

"You've been doing this all on your own?" Bear asked, taking a drag of his cigarette. I'd told him what had happened with the grove before but being face to face with thousands of rotting oranges made the situation even more real. Even more disturbing.

"Most of it. Dad had his hands full with Mom. I did what I could. Farms all across America are in the same boat. Whether it's oranges or another crop. Letting it all rot right off the trees because they can't afford to pick them. People are starving all around the country and I'm sitting in the middle of tons and tons of dead fruit." I shook my head.

"How the fuck old are you again?" Bear asked suddenly. When he'd asked me previously I'd said seventeen but that was before Mr. Coleman so nicely reminded me that I'd missed my birthday.

"Eighteen," I said for the first time. Bear raised his

eyebrows like the math didn't compute. "I had a birthday, recently. VERY recently."

"I can't believe you've been doing all this shit on your own." Bear ashed his cigarette out the window. "Where I come from most eighteen year olds can't string two sentences together, especially the girls that hung around the club, and you're out here running a fucking orange grove."

I laughed. "You make it sound like an accomplishment. When in reality I haven't accomplished anything. Just the opposite. Maybe if I knew more, did more, I could have saved it." I sighed. "There isn't anything impressive about that."

"How have you been living? Your family?"

"I got a job at the Stop-N-Shop a few nights a week."

"THE Stop-n-Shop?" Bear asked.

"Yeah, the very place that started it all," I sang, staring out the window as we passed row after row of my failure.

"I also used to drive over to Corbin to clean motel rooms on the weekends," I said. "After I paid the grove's expenses it was enough for us to get by...sometimes."

"You realize that's crazy right? You have two jobs to support your other job?" Bear asked.

"Turn here," I said, pointing to the slightly wider road hidden behind an overgrown bush. Bear turned the wheel and the truck jumped and swayed from side to side as it navigated the bumpier cut through the road that led into town. "And don't call me crazy," I added, crossing my arms over my chest.

"I take back ever thinking that you were mature for eighteen, because right now you're pouting like a little kid," Bear said as we passed the first sign that we'd reached the edge of town, Margie's Used Appliance Warehouse which was more junk yard than warehouse.

"Am not," I argued, looking straight ahead. "You can park

there." I pointed to the empty street in front of the Stop-N-Shop.

"Logan's Beach isn't exactly a big city, but this place is like a ghost town." Bear turned off the truck and got out. I did the same and when I hopped down he'd already met me on my side.

"Yeah, ever since they closed the exit of the highway the only people left here are farmers, and more and more of those are disappearing, abandoning their farms and moving where the work is." I shielded my eyes from the sun and looked around. Two trucks and a John Deere were parked across the street in front of Mickey's Bait Shop and Bar. Two bicycles were tied up on the post in front of the Tick-Tock Cafe. "Looks pretty busy to me," I added.

Bear looked around again like he was missing something. "The hardware store has an auto section," I said, heading into the store. "Mostly parts for fixing trucks, but you might luck out and find what you need there," I said, pointing over to Handy Hardware and Feed Store.

"Catch," Bear said, tossing something at me that I caught before it hit the ground.

"Why?" I asked, staring down at the silver skull with the diamond eye that had been in my possession for a large part of my life. "It's not mine."

"Just hang onto it for me. I'll call you when I'm done," Bear said. "Be quick and keep your eyes open just in case."

I rolled my eyes, squeezing my palm around the ring. I put the chain back around my neck and its familiar weight was more comforting than any hug could ever be. I nodded, heading toward the door. "Ti, I need your number." Bear pulled a cell phone out of his front pocket.

"I don't have a phone."

"If you don't have a phone then why did you just agree that I should call you when I'm done?"

"The old fashion way." I cupped my hands around my mouth and shouted, "THEEEEEEEYYYYYAAAAAAAA!" I pushed open the glass doors and left Bear laughing in the middle of the road.

Bear

"You lost?" The guy behind the counter at the hardware store asked. He wore overalls without a shirt underneath, the jean material stretching over his protruding stomach.

Lost? Maybe slowly finding my way.

He looked me over, his eyes stopping on the tattoo on my good shoulder. The skull symbol of the Beach Bastards. "I don't want no trouble," the man said, holding up his hands like I was robbing him.

"Put your hands down, man. I'm not looking for trouble today," I said.

"Don't look like you're avoiding trouble," he said pointing to my freshly stitched up injury.

"That ain't none of your concern, but I meant it when I said I wasn't looking for trouble."

I had trouble. Plenty of it in the form of a pink haired girl with so much attitude it made me crazy.

And hard.

Crazy fucking hard.

The man nodded. "Been awhile since The Bastards have been through these parts. I just want to let you know that nothing's changed. I'm still waving my white flag. I'm still inactive."

"Inactive?" I asked. He turned around and pointed to the huge wolf symbol on his back, clearly recognizable to me as the symbol of the WOLF WARRIORS even though parts of it were covered up with the straps from his overalls. Chop had started a fight with the Warriors years ago about gun running from Miami, I didn't know the specifics of the fight, all I knew is that Chop said we were at war so we were at war, and I'd put my share of WOLF WARRIORS to ground.

"They called me Bones back in the day, but now I just go by Ted." The man turned back around.

"You don't have anything to worry about. I'm kind of between MC's myself at the moment," I joked, pulling at the collar of the shirt I was going to take off the second I got back in the truck, because while wearing my cut used to be like wrapping myself in soft leather, the simple tank felt like it was strangling me.

Ted nodded, visibly relaxing when he finally got it through his head that what I wasn't looking to stir up a decades old war between old men over something I didn't give a shit about.

"What can I do you for?" he asked with a smile, flipping off Biker Bones and flipping on Toolman Ted.

I looked around the small store but didn't see anything I could use at first glance in the tiny three shelves of auto parts. "I don't suppose you got a bike section in here. I'm in need of some parts." I glanced out the door and spotted Thia in the store across the street, filling a red basket.

Ted shook his head. "Ain't got no bike parts on the shelves

but I might be able to do you one better." He ducked under the counter and walked over to a door that was covered with keys on little hooks. I didn't even realize it was a door until he turned the knob and opened it. Ted stepped aside and waved me over. I almost fell over after seeing what was on the other side.

It was a graveyard.

A bike graveyard.

"The Misses don't want me to have nothing to do with bikes since I left the Warriors, so she made me move all this from the house. She thinks I threw it all away." Hundreds of feet of bikes in different stages of rust and rot. Parts hung from the ceiling and off the walls. A small footpath had been cleared on the floor but other than that it was pieces and parts stacked on top of one another.

"I'm not a soldier anymore, but I never lost my love of the machine that made me want to ride in the first place," Ted said, slapping me on the back. Rival MC or not, Ted, the guy from the hardware store that dressed like he was applying for one of those BIG FAT REDNECK shows, was probably the only person on the earth who understood what I was going through.

"This room makes my fucking dick hard, Ted," I said with a straight face.

Ted laughed and walked back over to the counter. "Sort through and find what you need. We'll sort out price when I see what you come out with."

It only took me fifteen minutes to find what I needed in Ted's bike junkyard. I paid him and said my good-byes.

I dumped the parts in the bed of the truck and wiped my greasy palms off on my jeans. I looked around for Thia, but didn't spot her through the glass doors of the store. I took one step in that direction when a shrill scream pierced the air.

    I reached inside the cab of the truck and grabbed my guns, running top speed toward the scream.

    Toward Thia.

Chapter Twenty-Two
THIA

"Get your hands off me, Buck!" I shouted. I thrashed wildly, kicking and punching him anywhere I thought I could do damage on his freakishly giant frame. My little arms and legs were no match for the Sasquatch who'd hoisted me across his shoulders like a sack of dry cement, but I thought maybe, at the very least, I could get him to stop and listen to me. "Let me down!" I ordered again.

No such luck.

Despite my best efforts, Buck still managed to make progress into the little room I was trying my hardest not to let him put me in. "Nooooooo!" I protested, reaching out to grab onto the door frame with every ounce of fight I had in me. I held on so tightly I felt as if my fingertips were going to pop off and go bouncing around the room like the shiny metal balls in a pinball game.

With one last guttural growl Buck took one more step into the room and my fingers slipped from the door frame. Before I could even be upset about losing my grip, he'd already removed me from his shoulders and tossed me into the tiny metal cell, slamming the door shut. I landed on my side on the cold concrete, but didn't stay there long, springing up from the floor. I held on to the bars as Buck hastily turned the ancient looking key in the lock, the metal of the key made a high pitched shriek as it scraped against the metal of the bars, making my jaw ache and my ears feel like they were about to bleed. "I got an appointment with the sheriff for my questioning. You can't hold me here!"

"Don't you think I know that? I'm the deputy for Christ's sake. We will come back around to what happened with your parents, but this ain't about that. This is about a certain Mr. Coleman," Buck said, resting his hands on his gun belt.

Shit.

"You and I both know I was well within my legal rights, and besides, it's not like I really hurt him," I argued.

"How many times do I have to tell you to call me Deputy Douglas when I'm clocked in? Oh, and here is something you may not have thought about, NEWSFLASH, this time we aren't ten years old and you didn't get caught spray painting the Griffin's new John Deere pink. You SHOT a guy, Thia! What do you expect me to do? Look the other way while he's up at Dr. Sanderson's getting his leg put back together?" Buck plopped himself down in front of my cell on a wooden crate labeled with the Blue Mountain green bean logo, dust from the crate puffed into the air and billowed around him.

He waved it away, focusing his attention on his new prisoner.

Me.

The back room of the Stop-N-Shop doubled as the sheriff's station. Shelves lined every available inch of wall space. Several lines of discolored paint marked the place on one of the walls where a few rows of shelving had been removed to make room for the old wooden school desk where Buck and Sheriff Donaldson were supposed to write their reports.

As a past employee of the Stop-N-Shop I knew for a fact that the box of Alphabettio's soup on the shelf above the desk contained an old black and white TV that saw a lot more action than any paperwork ever had.

It's not like anything happened in Jessep anyway.

The cell itself had a retractable cot that hung down on a chain and was only large enough for two small people, or one large one.

If I hadn't stocked shelves for Emma May, I would've gone through life not knowing that our little blip of a town had any sort of sheriff's station at all.

Or the cell I found myself locked inside.

"I shot him, but only in the leg!" I shouted, stomping my foot like a toddler. "He barely even screamed."

Buck rolled his eyes and removed his wide brimmed sheriff's hat, revealing his receding hair line that made him look twenty years older than his nineteen years, and a red mark around his forehead from where the hat had been squeezing his head too tightly. He wiped the sweat off his face with a handkerchief. "Either your head is getting bigger than it already is, Bucky, or that hat has shrunk. Either way, it needs a coming to Jesus, or at least a resizing before the brains you might have left in there get squeezed out through your ears."

"Deputy DOUGLAS!" Buck corrected again. This time slower, enunciating all the syllables in dramatic fashion. He sighed. "You sound real sorry about all this," he said sarcastically.

I wasn't. Not one bit.

The only thing I would change about what happened would be next time I'd take into account the slight wind from the impending storm, something I usually considered when shooting cans off the fence post, but had oddly forgotten when my target became the living, breathing, human kind. "The only thing I'm sorry about was that my aim was off." I huffed. I was being a brat, but I didn't care. I've been 'adulting' since I was fourteen. As far as I was concerned, being locked in a cell by someone who I used to share bath times with, was a perfectly good occasion to cash in some of my unused bratty time.

"Thia, you've won every shooting competition over three counties since we were kids. You nailed him square in the thigh. I'd call that pretty dead on," Buck said, leaning forward and pinching the bridge of his nose. It wasn't the first headache I'd caused him over the years.

"I wasn't aiming for his leg, I was aiming for his balls!" I shouted, crossing my arms over my chest and leaning back against the bars. I blew out a breath of frustration.

"You can't just go around shooting people," Buck said, like I was a child that needed to be scolded and taught a lesson.

That's not necessarily true I thought, my mind wandering to the pond in the middle of the grove that now held more than algae and old fishing lures.

I hated being talked down to. It had been a long time since Buck and I were real friends and a lifetime ago since he knew what I was going through or anything about my life that gave him any sort of authority to judge me or talk down to me like I was a kid. I flashed Buck my best fake southern smile. "You know as well as I do that county law states I can shoot anyone on my property for whatever damn reason I want. That law is the one of the only good things about living in this backwards town. So LET. ME. OUT."

"I'm pretty sure the law doesn't say that," Buck said, putting his hat back on his head and standing up.

"I know it's not those exact words, but you know what I mean, don't act like you don't know what I'm talking about. Everyone around here knows that one. In the eyes of whatever hillbillies wrote that law, and whatever other hillbillies kept it on the books, I didn't do anything wrong." Instead of unlocking the cell, Buck turned and headed for the door.

"Where are you going?" I asked in a panic. "You can't keep me in here!"

Buck shook his head. "I may not be taking you to see the judge in the morning, because as much as I hate to admit it, the law is law and you're right, I can't arrest you."

"Okay so unlock this cell," I said, reaching for Buck through the bars, putting on my very best pouty-save-me-face.

"But I am going to hold you until your appointment to see the sheriff, make sure you don't go anywhere until we can get what happened up at your parents' house squared away." Buck sighed. "Why didn't you call me? I could have helped. I could have done something, but instead you ran. Where did you go?"

"I just went away. I went to..." As I tried to come up with something I absent-mindedly ran my hand over Bear's ring.

"You went to HIM didn't you?" he asked and I looked down to where he was staring and took my hand off the ring like he'd caught me doing something seedy.

"Buck," I started to explain and then I realized why Buck was really holding me in that cell.

"You know Thia it hurts that you didn't come to me, but it hurts even more that you turned to a complete stranger. Spend some time in there to sit and think, might do you some good." With a tip of his hat, and the same sideways smile he used to flash me right before he sent a dodgeball sailing into my ribs, Buck was gone.

"This is bullshit!" I shouted at the closed door. "We're not in kindergarten anymore, Buck. You can't just put me in time out," I said, pounding my hands against the bars. My hands vibrated, stinging from the impact of sensitive flesh and bone against hard metal. I bent over and rubbed them together to ease the sting. When I stood up to shake them out, it sank in that Buck really wasn't coming back.

"Shit!" I said, and without thinking I hit the bar again, my right hand turning into one gigantic funny bone.

The entire situation was far from fucking funny.

What really wasn't funny was the biker who was probably tearing the town apart looking for me and what he would do to Buck if he stood in his way. "Buck!" I called again, this time not because he needed to release me but because I needed to warn him.

But it was too late.

There was a commotion on the other side of the door, followed by a bang. "Where is she, asshole?" barked a familiar deep voice.

Oh shit.

The door opened and a frightened looking Buck appeared in the doorway. His eyes wide and his palms up in surrender. Behind him, with a gun firmly pressed between his shoulder blades, was Bear. "You okay, Ti?" Bear asked through his teeth with his nose scrunched up in a snarl.

"I'm fine. Bear, This is Buck. The deputy sheriff. He's the friend I told you about. Well, I thought he was a friend until he tossed me in here," I said, wrapping my hands around the cold metal bars.

"How many times do I have to keep reminding you that

you SHOT someone?" Buck yelled back. Bear nudged him with his gun and he tripped forward, grabbing onto the cell bars to keep from falling. Buck turned to look at Bear. "You got a concealed weapons permit for that thing?"

"Does it look like I'm concealing anything, motherfucker?" Bear seethed. Gesturing with his chin to the double holster he wore around his arms that he hadn't had on earlier. He must have had his holster in the truck but I hadn't seen him put it in there.

Buck raised his hands and slid to the ground on his butt, his back against the bars. "Listen, I'm just doing my job."

"No you're not, Buck. Yes, I shot him. But he was on my land and didn't leave when I asked him to. The law is the law. You've got no right to keep me here because you think I need a time out! I get that you're hurt but you've got to let me go."

"If she didn't break any laws I suggest you let her out of that cage right the fuck now before I break one that you won't live long enough to arrest me for," Bear warned.

Buck's hands shook as he took the key from his pocket and unlocked the cell door. Bear reached forward and grabbed me by the elbow, dragging me out of the cell and then from the room. Leaving Buck on the floor inside the room he slammed the door and locked it from the outside.

Bear's steps were long and it took me three of mine just to keep up with him. His grip tightened around my arm as he dragged me toward the truck. I was about to ask him what's wrong but something told me I didn't want to know the answer. He opened the passenger door and didn't wait for me to climb in. Grabbing onto my waist he tossed me into the cab and slammed the door.

"You were screaming," Bear said through his teeth, getting in on the driver's side and starting up the truck.

"Yeah, because Buck was being a dick," I said. "He's just hurt and trying to prove a point."

"I should go back and kill that motherfucker right now for laying his hands on you," Bear said, rubbing the back of his neck with one hand while the other was white knuckling the steering wheel. He spun us out onto the road and within seconds we were clear of town.

"He wasn't going to hurt me," I assured him. I was growing worried over the fact that he wouldn't look at me. I grew more worried when he turned completely silent, the rattling of rocks bouncing off the undercarriage sounded like bullets in the quiet.

"You got history with that guy? He your boyfriend or something?" Bear asked.

"Buck? No! He used to be my friend. My only friend. Now he's just an asshole who works for the sheriff."

His jaw was set in a hard line, a muscle by his temple jumped and his throat was tight with tension. Bear suddenly pulled over to the side of the road and put the truck in park. He lunged at me, my back still smashed up against the passenger door he set his hands above my head on the window and glared down at me. "He laid his hands on you. You screamed. He didn't stop. I would kill him without blinking. I almost did." Bear's eyes darkened, gleaming with intensity. "If he ever touches you again I am going to do just that. You got me? Fully expect me to break his fucking wrists or end his fucking life, but I get to choose which. Not you. Is that understood?" I nodded, not because I agreed with him, but because I knew he meant every word. "Good girl. This shit between us? I got no clue what it is, but it's something. That's why I gave you my ring back. You know it too, and that's why you didn't hesitate to put it back on." At the mention of it, I felt for the skull ring beneath my shirt. "But, Ti, I'm dead serious when I tell you that if you need someone shot, it's me who does the fucking shooting." He ran his nose along the line of my jaw. "Is that fucking clear?" he asked, pulling away, cupping my jaw in his hand, searching my eyes for the answer.

"Yes," I whispered, lost in what it was that I was agreeing to because my thoughts were mostly on the fact that Bear was only inches away from my face.

From my lips.

Which was where his eyes went when my tongue darted out to wet them.

"Good, now fucking kiss me," Bear said, crushing his lips to mine.

Chapter Twenty-Three
THIA

Bear's lips on mine wasn't just something amazing. It was an event. It was downright magical.

Which is why it needed to stop.

All of it needed to stop.

I pulled back, but he didn't move, hovering over me, breathing hard. His lips glistened from our kiss, his hair fell into his face. His muscles bulged as he braced himself on the window above my head. His sapphire blue eyes mirroring the raw lust I knew he had to see in my own because it was so overwhelming I felt like I was about to bust out of my own skin. "You can't do this again. I won't let you. If you plan on kissing me and walking away just so you can prove some sort of point about how much of a joke I am, then stop now because I won't be toyed with."

Bear growled. "Is that what you think happened when I left you by the fire pit? That I was playing some fucking game?"

"Yes."

"The only game I was playing was good guy, which I admit

is extremely hard to play and I don't fully understand all the rules."

"Good guy? You walked away because you were playing the role of the good guy? What does that even mean?"

"It means that I walked away because you were battered and bruised and me kissing you, tasting you, was a mistake."

"Oh."

"Not in the way you think, Ti. It was a mistake because I was seconds away from bending you over the fire pit and ramming my cock into your tight little perfect pussy. I walked away because it was the right thing to do, which is new for me. I thought I was supposed to feel good about making the right decision but I didn't, I regretted not taking you. I fucking ached that night." I reached up and pushed his hair out of his face that had fallen into his eyes and he leaned into the palm of my hand. "I'm still fucking aching."

"Don't lie to me."

"And you don't get to say shit you don't know what the fuck you're talking about. Because let me tell you something, Ti. If I didn't give a shit about you, I would have stayed after that kiss, after I tasted you. I would have fucked your virgin pussy until you couldn't walk straight, see straight, fucking think straight. I would have made you see God if I thought such shit existed. But I did care. I do care. So I left you the fuck alone and walked away."

"So what now?" I asked, overwhelmed by his confession.

"I'm done leaving you alone." Bear tangled his hands in the back of my hair and tugged my lips down onto his. "I want you. Still fucking want you, more than I've ever wanted anything. Been a dead man walking with a price on my head and I'm walking around with a fucking hard on all day thinking about being inside of you. That first night when I saw you in that bed hanging onto my ring like you were drowning and it was your life preserver, I just knew."

"Knew what?" I asked as Bear dipped down to run his lips across mine.

"That you were mine. And looking back, even to that day when we first met. You were mine then. Not in the way my cock wants to claim you now, but in a way that made me care and I don't care about a lot of people Ti, but that first day? I cared about you. So no, I'm not going to just kiss you and leave." He lifted the back of his tank top over his head and tossed it to the floor. "Because I'm not stopping at kissing. I'm not stopping until you're mine in every fucking way. I'll try not to hurt you, but this is happening right fucking now. I'm warning you that I want you so much, my version of gentle still might be really fucking hard." Bear's lips again met mine and his tongue danced with my own. My heart hammered in my chest and I was so wet between my legs, my inner thighs slid against one another as I tried to find some sort of friction, which was going to be impossible given Bear's large frame in the tiny cab of the truck.

Or so I thought.

Bear sat up and pulled me onto his lap so that I was straddling him, his enormous erection prodded against the very spot I needed him most. I threw my head back and moaned, not caring what I sounded like. I ground against him. "Fuck," he growled and I did it again, loving the reaction I could coax from him.

I vaguely heard the door opening and then suddenly I was airborne. Bear's hands were on my ass as he carried me to the bed of the truck and pulled down the tailgate. He pushed me down onto my back, the cold metal biting into my bare skin. He rocked into me, pushing his hardness against my core creating a wave of tightening in my lower belly.

"I'm not gonna promise you shit I know I can't give you," Bear said, his hand snaking up my shirt and splaying out over my stomach. "So you need to tell me to stop. Right now. Before it's too damn late, and I can't hold back. This is your last chance to get away, little girl." Bear warned, speaking into and around my mouth as our kiss turned into a frantic possession of each other's lips.

Bear

I was selfish. I was an asshole.

I needed to fuck her more than I needed to breathe.

I waited for her to tell me no. To tell me to go the fuck to hell. To tell me she realized that letting me inside her was a big mistake and would only bring heartache and pain.

The stupid bitch did none of those things.

"Yes," she moaned, closing her eyes and arching her back into me, pushing her tits into my chest and my inner monster came alive, wanting more than to just fuck her. I wanted to possess her. Own her.

CLAIM her.

I leaned down close to her ear and whispered. "You stupid, stupid girl."

"What does that make you?" she whispered back.

"Me?" I chuckled, running my hand down the side of her shirt, pushing it up and brushing the outside of her tit with my fingertips, "I'm the guy who's about to fuck the stupid, stupid girl."

Thia

He was right.

I was a stupid girl, because when he latched his mouth onto my nipple I damn near bucked myself right out of the truck and all rational thoughts left the building, or the truck, or the whatever. "You ever been touched like this?" Bear asked, hooking his fingers inside of my panties. I shook my head, barely able to catch my breath. "How about like this?" he asked, finding my folds and running his fingertips through my wetness and over my clit.

I was on fire. Every nerve ending in my body was firing, alive and active and every single one of them wanted Bear to make me his once and for all.

Every promise that dripped from his mouth made me feel like for the first time in weeks that I was alive, and not just the one person living in the land of the dead, but a real live person with needs and wants. It just so happened that both my needs and wants were on the same page.

Bear.

His lips assaulted my mouth then moved to my neck, he

continued to rock against me, my insides clenching and unclenching, my core tightening, my senses on complete overdrive and all I could see in my tunnel vision was Bear and when he pushed a finger inside of me I let out a groan that could be heard three counties over.

"You're so fucking tight, baby. By the fire pit when you were about to come on my tongue I felt how tight you were, but right now, with just one finger..." He pushed in further and moaned. "Your pussy is going to strangle my fucking cock."

Bear pushed up my shirt, exposing one of my breasts to him. "Perfect tits," he mumbled, dipping his tongue to the tip of my already stiff peak. How did I not know that nipples could do this? I felt like they had a direct line to my core and every single time Bear stroked his talented tongue over my flesh it was as if he was stroking my clit. He hooked his finger inside of me and sucked my nipple into his mouth.

Holy shit.

"Yes," I said. "Yes, please. More."

"You're gonna get more alright. A lot fucking more." Bear pushed inside me deep, dragging his finger along the front of my inner wall when he pulled out and then back up again. Faster and faster until I was shamelessly riding his hand. The in and the out was a sweet torture. He sucked on my nipple as his hand worked me until the clenching in my lower stomach turned almost painful.

He grabbed the back of my neck and kissed me like he was fucking me with not just his fingers but his tongue. We were at war, a war of passion and lust, and anger and hate and every feeling I'd had toward the confusing man since I was ten years old. The pressure mounted and when he added his thumb to stroke my clit I screamed into his mouth as an explosion of pleasure went off like a bomb in my core, spreading throughout the rest of my body in waves upon waves of pure ecstasy like I never even knew existed.

I was still seeing stars when Bear picked me up and set me on his lap again so I was straddling him, my legs spread wide over his pulsing hardness making my insides quiver as if I hadn't just had a mind and body blowing orgasm. "You coming is the single most fucking beautiful thing I've ever seen," Bear said, pushing a stray hair out of my face and tucking it behind my ears. With one hand he lifted up my shirt and tossed it into the bed of the truck.

"I need to get these off of you right fucking now. I need you baby. I need to be inside of you," Bear said, his voice strained and raspy, shivers danced up my spine. He pulled down on the waistband of my shorts with one hand and I lifted my hips so he could remove them and my panties in one pull.

We were face to face, skin to skin. He knew all my secrets. He knew exactly who I was and every time I'd wanted to run and hide from him he hadn't let me. I was fully exposed to Bear inside and out and although I'd never been naked around anyone since I was a kid I felt more comfortable in that truck bed with Bear than I had fully clothed with anyone else in my entire life.

Bear's eyes were heavily lidded with lust as he took a step back to look me over with appreciation and pure animalistic need. He undid the buckle and the button on his jeans. With one hand on my throat he again pushed me until my back was against the cool metal of the truck bed, his hand dragging down my chest between my breasts, his thumb again finding my clit and a primal moan escaped my mouth sounding nothing like my normal voice. I could smell the rust from the motorcycle parts just above my head, the ridges from the truck bed captured my shoulder blades making it hard for me to move my arms.

It wasn't romantic.

It wasn't flowery.

But it also wasn't lies.

It was just us.

Bear grabbed my feet and as he climbed on top of me he ran his hands up the inside of my legs, spreading them to make room for him between my thighs. And that's when I saw him. All of him. His thick and heavy cock bounced slightly with his movements, the tip glistening with moisture. His finger had felt huge and filling inside of me, there was no way he was going to fit but I trusted him and I didn't care. He could rip me in two and I still didn't care because it wasn't what he could do to my body that I was worried about.

It was what he could do to my heart.

He stopped mid climb and bracing himself with his hands on the underside of my knees he dipped his head down and ran his tongue along my folds, stiffening his tongue and pushing it as far inside of me as he could. He pulled back and licked his lips. "Never tasted anything better than you," he said and with his hands on the very inside of my thighs, his fingers kneading into my sensitive flesh he spread my legs as far as they could go.

He kissed me. Hard and eager just like his erection which he slid up and down my wetness until I was writhing underneath him, the need that had been sated minutes earlier was now back and a hundred times more powerful than before. He reached between us and grabbed the base of his shaft, lining it up with my entrance. His skin was soft and hot and the contact was almost too much. The anticipation of him inside of me had me raking my nails along his back. He groaned and growled and swore in my ear before surging forward, stretching my opening to the point of pain, filling me with him.

"Holy fuck, Ti. Wider, open up for me," he said like he too was in some sort of pain. He pushed my knees apart until I was as open as I could possibly be and Bear didn't waste any time pushing forward in one hard thrust.

He really was ripping me open. It hurt. It really fucking hurt.

I really didn't fucking care.

I couldn't be any more full. Body and heart. Both happy. Both at peace.

Both in pain.

"Fuck. I knew it would be fucking amazing, baby. But Jesus Christ, your virgin pussy really is strangling me," Bear groaned, the cords of his neck tense and tight as he pushed until he was as far inside of me as our bodies would allow. "Never doubt that this has always belonged to me. YOU have always belonged to me," he said, staring into my eyes which were watering from the pain and something else that was bubbling up from deep inside of me. Fear. Relief.

Love?

I couldn't think on that one long because Bear started to move, pulling out of me and pushing back in, burying himself to the hilt all over again. The feeling of physical pain was still there, but morphed into a kind of pleasurable pain. Each time he thrust into me he went all the way in, making me gasp. When he pulled out he dragged his cock along every sensitive bundle of nerves inside of me, making me moan. Harder and harder, faster and faster he thrust in and pulled out until my vision blurred and my insides clenched around him in rhythm with his movements. I was lost in the white hot pleasure. I was lost in the moment.

I was lost in Bear.

I knew right then and there that there would be no coming back from it.

"I feel you tightening around me, Ti. I know you're close. Been thinking about making you come around my cock since that first night back in the apartment." He thrust inside me, hard. Reaching between us he used the pad of his thumb to rub light but furious circles around my clit. I was almost there. Almost over the edge. "You are so fucking beautiful," Bear said, coming down over me and pressing his lips to mine.

That's when I lost it.

That's when I came.

His thumb.

His cock.

His lips.

Him.

I came until I thought my insides were going to flip onto the outside. I came until it hurt so bad I thought I was going to pass out. I came and came and the waves of pleasure only increased with each pulse of my release. He kissed me and fucked me and claimed me until there was only one truth between us which Bear pointed out when he said, "Never doubt that this pussy has always belonged to me. YOU have always belonged to me."

He kissed me again then ordered. "Wrap your arms around me." I did what he said and wrapped my arms around his neck. He put his hands on the back of my thighs, lifting me slightly off the bed of the truck, angling me so he could thrust even deeper. Faster and faster he pushed in and out until we were a clattering of lips and teeth and until he tipped his head back and opened his mouth releasing a guttural roar that made me think I was going to come all over again. With one final crazed thrust, he held himself still deep inside of me, pulsing long and hard, filling me with warmth and satisfaction, love and confusion.

Filling me with him.

"Ti," Bear groaned, breathing hard.

He had done what he'd set out to do.

He'd claimed me.

Body and soul.

Out there in the bed of that rusted truck on the side of the road, with only the smell of the rotting oranges and the warm breeze as our witnesses, in that moment there was no more hiding, no more denying the truth.

Bear was right.

I'd always been his.

Mine.

Bear

Thia

We were naked, panting and in a mound of tangled limbs. My arms rested on some sort of part Bear had bought for the motorcycle. He was face forward between my breasts.

Still inside me.

He lifted his face and looked up at me. He held up his ring, which had fallen off to the side. "I still can't believe you kept it all these years."

"Never took it off," I said. Then I wished I hadn't said it, realizing how pathetic it made me sound. "I mean..."

"You never took it off?" Bear asked, his eyes so bright blue they rivaled the color of the cloudless sky.

"No," I answered honestly. "Told my parents that I found it, not like they really cared where I got it, they had enough other stuff to worry about. Buck is the only person who knew the truth behind it. I think that's why he was all pissed off back there. Mad I ran to you instead of him for help."

"And tell me something. Be honest," Bear said. A lump was forming in my throat as he played with the ring, turning it over and over in his hand. "You really shot a guy?" he said with a laugh.

"Yeah, it was stupid but he was from Sunnlandio. He tried to buy the grove and since they had canceled the contracts it was worthless."

"It was a fucking set up."

"Basically. Guess I should have thought first, shot later, but I was so mad."

"So you can shoot?" Bear asked, kissing his way around my belly button, his facial hair tickling my skin.

"Yeah. My dad taught me. Won a few competitions when I was younger. Farmer's Daughters of America."

"Sounds like a redneck dating site."

"It does, doesn't it?" I asked with a laugh.

"It's so fucking hot that you can shoot," Bear said, sliding out of me and down my body. My core tightened like it didn't want to let him go. "So fucking hot," Bear said again, this time over my clit.

His jeans buzzed and with a groan he reached over me and into the pocket. He pulled out a phone and looked at the screen. He frowned. "We gotta go." The playfulness from a moment earlier was gone. His hard jaw set in a straight line once again. He tossed me my clothes. "Get dressed," he ordered. "Now."

"What's going on? Who was on your phone?" I asked, pulling on my shirt and scooting to the end of the truck bed to shimmy on my shorts.

"More Bastards are on their way."

"They text you that?" I asked, confused. Bear pulled on his jeans and hopped down from the truck. He lifted me off the tailgate and pushed it shut.

"No, they told Cash that," he said, tossing me the phone he took from Cash's body to keep tabs on the MC. I looked down at the screen.

BE THERE SOON.

We took off for Logan's Beach in my father's truck without going back for Bear's bike, which he'd hidden in the back shed under an old tarp. Bear didn't say a word. He smoked a cigarette and kept checking the rearview mirrors. He'd called King to tell him we were on the way and he was waiting for us outside the garage by the time we got back. "I'll be back, go into the apartment and for fucks sake, listen to me and stay there," Bear ordered, but when I looked into his eyes I saw more than an order. I saw a plea.

"Fine," I said, a little sharper than I wanted. I went into the apartment and King and Bear left the garage, closing the door behind him.

Ray brought me some food but quickly left because the kids were up at the house all alone. I flipped channels on the TV and scanned the pages of an old Guns and Ammo magazine from 2007.

I showered and put on one of Bear's t-shirts, tucking myself in bed. There was no way I was going to sleep without knowing where he was. I wanted to leave, to find out where he was, but I also wanted to keep my promise.

So I stayed.

It was well after midnight when I heard the door to the bedroom creak open and shut. I couldn't see him in the pitch blackness and I didn't know what to say. What to ask. The mattress dipped when Bear sat on the edge of the bed. I heard him kick off his boots then the clanking of his belt buckle as he removed his jeans. A cool breeze licked my back as he lifted up the blankets but was quickly replaced by Bear's heat as he came up behind me, surprising me when he reached out and grabbed my waist, dragging me up against his chest. He was naked. His erection twitching the second it came into contact with my bare ass. He rested his chin on the top of my head, his hand splayed out under my shirt on the skin of my lower stomach.

"Where did you go?" I whispered.

"Trying to sort shit out. Things have kind of changed. Plans needed to change," Bear said, hearing him acknowledge what had happened between us earlier made me able to relax into his hold.

"Do you have a new plan?"

"Not yet," Bear said with a sigh.

"Anything I can do to help?"

"This. This helps," he said into the back of my neck and I arched backward into his now hard erection. "You okay?" he asked, snaking his hand down between my legs. "Here, I mean. I got a little crazy before and forgot to ask you."

"I'm fine," I said. And I was. I was a little sore, but nothing that could outweigh the magnitude of what had happened between us.

"Good, 'cause I need inside you, Ti." Bear ran his tongue down the back of my neck and my lips parted when he sucked the tip of my earlobe into his mouth. He pushed one long finger inside of me. "Fuck, your pussy is so fucking wet for me already," Bear said, stroking my clit.

I moaned. "Gonna make this fast and hard," he murmured against my skin. He lifted up my leg and pushed inside of me, stretching and filling me in two hard long thrusts. He started pumping into me before my body was ready for him and the bite of pain made each stroke torturously erotic.

"Never felt nothing like this, Ti. Wanna fuck you and smack the living shit out of you all at the same time. Don't know what this is, but it makes me want to keep you filled with my cock all day long and dripping with my cum. I want to mark you. I want to fucking own you." He grunted as his thrusts became harder, more frantic, more erratic.

Just more.

"What the fuck are you doing to me?" he asked on a ragged exhale.

Sparks played behind my eyes and Bear must have sensed I was close because he reached over and circled my clit with two fingers until I came undone around him. "Fuck, so fucking good," he groaned, finding his release inside of me, pulling me so close into him that I thought he was going to crack one of my ribs.

I wouldn't have wanted it any other way.

Chapter Twenty-Four
BEAR

I was telling the truth when I told Ti that I had no fucking clue what the plan was moving forward. Shit had changed so quickly. With her, and if I was being honest, with myself.

I wanted to talk to King the night before, but he had clients coming and going all night so I sat on the dock by myself with an untouched bottle of Jack on the ground next to me, trying to figure out my next move, and in the hours I spent down there all I figured out was that I didn't know shit.

Not yet anyway.

My new plan was simple. We'd meet with Bethany, the lawyer, and go from there.

We'd deal with the law first.

The lawless second.

"Where the fuck do you think you're going?" I barked as Ti walked out of the garage and right past where I was crouched down on the driveway trying to put my bike back together again. King had sent a tow truck to get it from the shed at Ti's house and thankfully it came back without raising suspicions. I wiped the sweat on my forehead with the rag from my back pocket and lit the cigarette that had been dangling from my lips. I drank in Ti's long muscular legs and my fucking cock jumped to attention like it always did when she was around.

God damn she was beautiful.

And she was mine.

"I was looking for you." She crossed her arms across her chest, pressing out her braless tits against the fabric of the t-shirt I'd given her to wear the night before. "I woke up and you were gone. You know it's okay to be nice. You don't have to snap at me all the time."

"I didn't sleep much," I said, standing up and taking a drag of my smoke. I felt bad for snapping at her but the truth was when I saw her leaving I had a flashback of her trying to run away and I immediately got heated.

"I can't sleep with your tight ass pressed against my cock. You need something?" I asked, taking another deep drag off my smoke and letting the nicotine invade my brain. Truth was also that it had been days since I'd hit the hard stuff and the headache I was sporting made it seem like the world was yelling at me.

She looked down to the gravel. "Yes. No. I mean...yes?"

"Ti, spit it out," I said, looking down at her rapidly healing face. The bruises around her eye were barely visible. Each minute that passed she looked more and more fuckable, and now that I'd actually had her, all I wanted was more.

I used to think that I wanted to go out in a blaze of bullets and glory. Now I think that I'd like to go out balls deep inside my girl.

MY girl.

"Can we just...for today, can we just, pretend?" she asked, rocking back on her heels and biting her lip.

"Pretend? Pretend what?" I took a drag of my smoke and

slipped my other hand into my back pocket, leaning up against the side of the garage.

"Let's pretend that I'm just Thia Andrews, a girl whose parents aren't..." She looked away and sniffled, shaking her head. "And you're just Bear, and you're not pissed off at the world." She smiled and cocked her head to the side. "Not today anyway."

I searched her face for the punch line, but there were no signs of a joke.

She drew a circle in the gravel with her flip flop. "Today I want to be a normal girl and you can be a normal boy and we are going to do whatever normal people do so we don't get stuck thinking on all the bad shit that's been happening." She closed the distance between us and came to stand under me, looking up with pleading pale green eyes. "Please, Bear. Please. Just give me today. Be normal with me. Just for today."

The idea was ludicrous, I didn't even know what normal was. Normal was what I'd been battling since I'd left the club. I didn't know how the fuck to do normal. I opened my mouth to tell her just that, but the hurt in her eyes when she saw the rejection coming broke me.

She shook her head and turned around. "Never mind. I knew you wouldn't..."

I reached out and grabbed her wrist, pulling her back to me. "Go put some clothes on," I said. "Be back out here in twenty minutes." I sounded like an asshole again, giving orders to a girl who only wanted to hang out like a normal kid, but after years of actually being an asshole, it was a hard habit to break.

"Really?" she asked, bouncing on the balls of her feet and smiling from ear to ear. The girl didn't have a stitch of makeup on, there wasn't a false thing about her and yet she was prettier than any supermodel I'd ever seen on the cover of any magazine and not to mention the absolute most amazing fucking pussy I'd ever had the pleasure of sticking my cock in.

I really need to start thinking about something else...

"Twenty minutes," I repeated, coughing when my traitor of a heart actually skipped a fucking beat.

Who are you? A fucking preteen girl?

With her new brilliant smile plastered on her face, she spun around and skipped back into the dark garage toward the apartment.

I stomped out my cigarette on my boot and headed up to the main house. "Wait!" Ti called. I turned around to find her back outside again. "Where are you going?" she asked.

I pointed up to the main house. "You want to be normal today, right?"

"Yeah?"

I started walking again, calling back to Ti, "Then I gotta go figure out what the fuck it is that normal people do."

Ray had looked at me like I'd sprouted an extra head when I asked her where she thought I should take Ti. "Bear, I'm nineteen, technically widowed, and engaged with three kids. That's not normal no matter how you look at it," she'd said.

She had a point.

I couldn't take Ti anywhere remote so I decided on the Rosinus State Park. It was public enough that if the MC did know where we were they still wouldn't make a move.

"Here, wear this," I said, handing her a plain black baseball cap.

"What? Is this supposed to be some sort of disguise?" she asked.

"Just put it on," I said, watching her thread her hair through the opening at the back.

"Can you recognize me?" she asked sarcastically.

"Smart ass."

"Okay so where is your brilliant disguise?" she asked.

I pulled the black v-neck t-shirt over my head. "Viola."

"A shirt? Your disguise is a shirt?"

"Yep."

"The funny thing is I can actually see how that could work," Ti said, looking me up and down.

"Really?"

"Nope!" She opened the door and bolted out of the truck, jumping up on top of the nearest picnic table, her tits bouncing as she danced around.

The park was small, no more than five acres with a beach type area, except instead of sand it was covered with pine needles that butted up against a huge lake. Tall pine trees lined the edge of the water, every tenth tree or so had been removed to make room for a picnic table or bench. There were

Chapter Twenty-Five

people around but not too many to make it crowded, just enough to make witnesses.

Ti held out her arms and took a deep breath, inhaling the fresh air. She looked down at me as I approached and my chest tightened.

"This place is perfect," she said, flashing me another brilliant smile. She hopped down onto the bench part of the table and walked to the edge, leaping off dramatically before landing on her feet in the dirt like she was a gymnast, raising her arms above her head and taking a step back like she was in the Olympics.

"Seven," I said, holding up a fake scorecard.

"Bullshit, biker-boy," she scoffed. "That was at least an eleven. Seven? Please!" She jumped back up onto another bench and pointed her index finger in the air. "Let's go to the tapes!" she announced, queuing up her imaginary replay.

"Sorry," I said, sucking air in between my teeth and bobbing my head from side to side. I stood below her, my face just inches away from the top of her thighs. "The judges have reviewed the tape, and they all agree. Although it would have been a two..." I said, turning her around by her legs so that she was facing away from me. "But you got the extra points because I really dig your ass being at eye level." I turned my head to the side and rested my cheek on her ass like it was a pillow that I wanted to take a nap on.

Because it was.

I wasn't able to linger on the phenomenally sexy image of my face pressed against her naked ass for too long because she reached back and swatted at my head with her hat like I was a bee buzzing around her legs. "Bear!" she screeched playfully, jumping back down from the bench and then running around it, holding onto her butt like we were in a

Chapter Twenty-Five

locker room and she was protecting it from an impending towel swat.

"Just watching you jump around is exhausting," I said, reaching into my jeans and pulling out my cigarettes. I lit one and waved the smoke away from my face.

"Mama used to call me her little jumping bean because they could never get me to sit still," she admitted, finally sitting down on top of the picnic table.

"Fitting," I said, feeling like I was able to relax now that the jumping bean had stopped jumping.

I took a drag of my cigarette and blew out the smoke. It had taken me forever to figure out where to take Ti. So long now that the sun had just started to set into the horizon. I liked the night. I liked the dark. Smoking in the dark always held more appeal for me than smoking during the day. Maybe it had something to do with being able to see the smoke against the dark background of the night sky. Or maybe it was being able to see the glowing ember from the end of the cigarette or the bright yellow flame when I fired up my lighter. Smoking was familiar to me. It felt good.

It also reminded me of home.

I'd be shit at making one of those anti-smoking public service announcements.

Ti leaned back on the table, closing her eyes like she was soaking up rays that had long disappeared with the setting of the sun.

"I feel like you know so much about me," she said, although I didn't think that was true. I don't think I'd tapped into even half of what made Thia Andrews tick. "But I don't know that much about you."

"You know more than anyone else," I said, and that really was true, but for the exception of King and maybe Grace. In

Chapter Twenty-Five

the short time I'd spent with her, she learned more about me than the men back at the club.

Men who were supposed to be my brothers.

Most of whom I'd known since the day I was born.

I leaned back on my elbows, the same way Ti had, soaking in the same imaginary rays. An eerie sense of calm washed over me. I wanted to burn the feeling into my memory, because I knew it wouldn't last. After the meeting with Bethany tomorrow plans needed to be made.

Decisions needed to be made.

Quickly.

My phone rang. "It's Bethany," I told Ti, holding the phone up to my ear. "Yeah," I answered.

"We have a problem," Bethany said. I looked over to Ti who thankfully hadn't heard her. I stood up and walked away casually.

"Go ahead," I said as calmly as I could muster.

"She's no longer wanted for questioning," Bethany snapped.

"That's great," I said, looking back over to Ti who smiled.

"No, she's no longer wanted for questioning because there is a warrant out for her arrest."

Fuck.

"They finished analyzing the gun and they called in some fancy CSI from Atlanta. There is only three sets of prints in that entire house and only two sets of prints on both guns. The mother's and Thia's and since the mom is dead..."

"How do we proceed from here?"

"She turns herself in. I try to call in as many favors as possible and in the meantime I'll put together a self-defense strategy in case it moves to trial."

"Is there an alternative?" I asked, wandering around

Chapter Twenty-Five

looking at the trees like I was actually interested in the same fucking pine trees that had been growing in that park since before I was born.

"I have another idea," Bethany said, "But you may not like it. In fact, you're not going to like it at all." I didn't have to like it. Ti was dead if she got locked up. Might as well drive her over to the MC and dump her off at the gate.

Wasn't going to happen.

"Shoot," I said.

"How attached are you to this girl?"

"What?" I asked.

"I need to know if this is a fling or a fuck or if you knocked her up or I need to know if this is the real deal, trust me. It's important."

I looked over to Thia and didn't have to search long for the answer. She had picked up a dandelion and was waving it in the wind, spitting them out when the breeze blew the little white petals directly into her mouth.

"Real deal."

I let Bethany say her piece then hung up the phone and walked back over to Ti. I promised her a normal day and I was going to give it to her no matter what. We still had today.

Not tomorrow.

But we had today.

"What did the lawyer lady say?" Ti asked as I came to sit beside her.

"Just making sure we would be on time tomorrow. She's kind of a stickler for details," I said, which was the truth, I just didn't add the part about the cops that would be there waiting with a warrant.

I thought about running. Taking Ti on the back of my bike and heading out of state as fast as my bike could take us. The

Chapter Twenty-Five

alternative Bethany offered wasn't much of an alternative at all.

The choice I had to make was an easy one.

It would also be an ending to something that hadn't yet had a chance to begin.

"I guess that's a good thing for a lawyer to be."

"Guess so," I said.

"So as I was saying," she said, breaking me out of my thoughts. "I don't even know what your favorite color is—" She stopped mid sentence to look me over, taking in my shirt, boots, and jeans, which were all black. "Okay, never mind, so your favorite color is black, but what is your favorite movie? Favorite holiday?"

I chuckled and shook my head.

"Okay fine, but besides being a big bad biker dude who has issues with his pop, and has eyes that could melt the lock off a chastity belt, I don't know much about you and you know everything about me, so give it up. Spill the beans, Bear. Rake the dirt. Dish out the good stuff." Ti ordered, nudging me with her sharp little elbow. She pulled her legs up onto the table and hugged her knees to her chest.

"Melt the lock off a chastity belt, huh?" I asked, raising my eyebrow at her suggestively.

She rolled her eyes. "It figures that's the only part that registered with you. It's only an expression."

"Uh huh, one I've never heard," I teased, feeling a little bad when her face started to redden. I cleared my throat. "But then again I've never heard half the shit that comes out of your mouth."

She shrugged. "You're not the first person to tell me that. My dad used to say that all the time."

"Okay, Ti. You win," I said, changing the subject. "But

Chapter Twenty-Five

favorite movie is a tough one, what category are we talking about?"

"All of them," she said with a smile. "Start with drama."

I raised an eyebrow at her. "The lady is demanding."

"Yes she is," she said. "I bet it's Scarface. Is it Scarface?"

I laughed. "Ask anyone else in the club and I think that's the answer they'd give you. But I like the classics. Watched a lot of old westerns growing up. I don't have one particular favorite, but anything with Clint Eastwood, and the older the better."

"Westerns? Westerns? I was positive you were going to say The Godfather or Scarface."

"What the fuck is wrong with Westerns? Westerns are the shit."

"Oh yeah, tell me, why are westerns THE SHIT?" Ti said, air quoting around THE SHIT.

"Because back in the old west, the men were real men. They took charge of the situation. They handled their business by earning respect and gunning down anyone who stood in their way. Cowboys were the first guys to have the balls to be lawless and say fuck-all to society." I held my cigarette between my lips and pulled up my shirt, pointing to one of the tattoos on my ribcage. "This was one of my very first tattoos."

Thia gasped. "Clint Eastwood? You have a Clint Eastwood tattoo?" She covered her mouth with her hand. "I mean I've seen you without your shirt on and I knew that was a portrait but I didn't realize it was actually Clint Eastwood."

I pulled my shirt back down and took a drag of my cigarette. "Laugh all you want, Ti. C.E. was Chuck Norris before there was a Chuck Norris."

"Oh my god please don't tell me you have a Chuck Norris

tattoo," she said, grabbing her stomach and continuing to laugh at my expense.

I loved that sound.

I would remember that sound.

"What's wrong with a Chuck Norris tattoo?" I deadpanned.

"Oh, I didn't mean. He's ummm..." I burst out laughing as she tried to backtrack.

I could have let her struggle a little while longer, she looked adorable when she was all flustered, but I was having trouble keeping a straight face. "I'm just fucking with you," I finally said.

She let out a sigh of relief. "Oh thank god. I didn't know how I was going to get out of that one."

"Okay, so now you know my favorite, so what's yours? Same category."

Thia smiled so big and brightly I thought her mouth was about to swallow her face. "I have two."

"And...?" I pressed.

"Scarface and The Godfather."

I laughed more that day than I had in the last twenty-some-odd years, all because of the girl with the crazy pink hair.

The girl I'd fallen in love with.

Fuck.

"You're different, Ti," I said, when we'd both recovered enough to speak again. "But I've known that since the day I met you."

"You mean the day your friend held a gun on me," she corrected.

"Yes, I mean the day the little kid version of you almost took out a biker seven times your size," I said.

Chapter Twenty-Five

"Well, serves him right. He shouldn't have been trying to rob a kid," she argued.

"Technically, he was trying to rob a store, not a kid," I countered.

She shot me a look that said 'oh please.' "So you're saying that if it was Emma May at the counter it would've somehow ended things better? Because I can tell you right now, it wouldn't have been a lick better for Skid or Skud or Skuzz or whatever his name was, because Emma May is a shoot-first, don't-care-about-asking-questions kind of old lady. Just ask her first husband." She scratched her chin and wrinkled her nose. "Or her fourth…"

The way Thia talked with her hands, reminded me of a character you would find in a comic book.

One with really, really nice tits.

"See what I mean?" I pointed out. "I've never heard anyone say the kind of shit you say. You're just…different."

"Different," she said the word slowly like she was examining it, turning it over on her tongue. She twirled a strand of her hair around in her fingers. "Isn't different just a nicer word for bat-shit-crazy?" she asked, her face serious.

She looked down at her feet.

I reached over and lifted up her chin so she could look at me.

So she could SEE me.

"No, I said different and that's exactly what I meant. In my world that's a good thing. No, that's a fucking GREAT thing. You ain't like other girls, certainly nothing like the BBB's." When Ti wrinkled her nose in confusion I filled her in. "Beach Bastard Bitches, club whores," I clarified. "When I'm positive you're going to react one way to something, you keep surprising me by doing the complete opposite and I'm a hard

Chapter Twenty-Five

man to surprise," I said, stubbing out my cigarette on the bottom of my boot.

"I bet you tell all the girls they're different. Bet that line's worked a thousand times." Ti pulled her chin away and stared down at the table, picking at the old red paint that had bubbled up on the surface. There was a hint of jealousy that crept into her question, and if it had come out of anyone else's mouth I'd probably already ended the conversation and left the second she asked it. But it didn't come from anyone else.

It came from Thia.

It was...cute.

I could have lied to her and said she was the only girl I'd ever said that to, but there was already a lingering lie between us, or rather an omission of truth on my part, and I didn't want to add to the growing pile. "There was a girl, just one other. She was different, but not in the same way you were. I thought she could be different for me too," I admitted out loud for the first time, remembering the sting of pain I felt when I saw King and Ray fucking up against the pillar under the house the night I tried to make her mine, and failed.

"What happened? Why did it end?" she asked, looking up from where she'd just picked off a huge chip of paint, exposing a bright blue strip underneath the red.

"My best friend knocked her up. They're getting hitched," I said, and then I waited. But it didn't come. The regret. The bitterness that usually followed all thoughts of my best friend being with the girl I thought I'd let get away.

Nothing.

"You mean King and...Ray? You and Ray?"

"No, me and Ray nothing. Never even started. It was an idea in my head. An idea that got snuffed out quickly. I never

Chapter Twenty-Five

cared about a woman in my entire life and kind of confused my feelings for something it wasn't."

"I'm sorry," Ti said and I genuinely believed she was sorry, any bitterness or jealousy was gone from her voice.

I shook my head. "Don't be. I'm happy for them."

I really meant it.

"Ti, are you jealous?" I teased, although I knew she wasn't. I nudged her a little too hard and she almost fell off the table, but recovered quickly, using her hands to regain her balance.

I'd officially lost my god damned mind. Not only was I flirting but I'd resorted to pushing her around like a school kid with a crush.

"No, I'm not jealous," she argued. "I shouldn't have even asked. It's none of my business. Besides, you don't need to tell a girl that they are different to get them into bed, you probably just smile and say 'Darlin' and the panties start dropping," Ti said, crossing and uncrossing her legs that made me want to spread them apart and sink my face down into her tight heat.

I put my hand on top of hers to ease her rambling, but when our hands met I didn't expect the volt of static energy that sparked between us from a simple touch. Ti looked up at me and her jaw dropped open.

She'd felt it too.

I tried to take away my hand but I just couldn't.

Better yet, I didn't want to.

I clasped my hand around her much smaller one and yanked her onto my lap, she shrieked in surprise. I almost forgot what I was about to say when I noticed that my lips were lined up perfectly with that little indented spot where her neck and shoulder met. She struggled to get off of me, but I held her tight and leaned into the spot as close as I could without actually touching her. "You're right, you know. I've

Chapter Twenty-Five

never in my life said anything to a chick that wasn't true to get her in my bed," I said right against her skin.

Ti shuddered. "What would you say to them?" she asked, tilting her head to grant me more access to her neck. Her question took me by surprise.

"You want examples?" I asked with a small laugh. "Okay, I'll tell you." I grabbed a hold of her neck with one hand and held her tightly at the waist with the other. She smelled like some sort of girly shit that was making my dick even harder than it already was from her wiggling around on my lap. Every little movement of her struggle sent another surge of blood to my cock. The conversation we were having was doing very little to ease the strain behind my zipper. I knew then I'd have her dripping wet and leaking my cum before we made our way back out to the truck.

I ran my nose along her shoulder and up her neck toward her ear where I officially went crazy, because I whispered to her the words I really had said to women, before fucking them senseless, against the sensitive spot behind her ear. "I would just tell them the truth. What I wanted from them. What I wanted to do to them." And then the words fell from my lips. "Take off your clothes and get on your fucking knees."

"What?" Ti asked nervously, if not a bit breathlessly.

"That's what I'd say when I want to fuck." I moved her hair away from the back of her neck, brushing my lips and my words over her sensitive skin that was coming alive with goosebumps as I made my way from one ear to the other. "I'd tell them to fuck me. Suck me. Ride my cock. Bend over and lift up your skirt. Make me come." She gasped and I knew my words were having an affect on her, especially when her movements became less of the struggling kind and more of the rubbing against me for relief kind.

Chapter Twenty-Five

"Keep going. Tell me more. What else?" she asked, closing her eyes, letting her head fall to the side.

Seeing Ti turned on was beyond beautiful.

It was fucking glorious.

I grabbed her by the waist, spinning her around on my lap to face me. Her legs wrapped around me like I hoped they would.

She opened her eyes and then her mouth to say something about our sudden change in position, but I ran the tip of my index finger across her collarbone, following up the touch with a feather light trace of my lips, letting out a breath I didn't know I had been holding when she again closed her eyes and began slowly rocking back and forth on my lap, causing me to hiss between my teeth at the sensation. I didn't want her to snap out of whatever the hazy reality was we were existing in, because in that reality, Ti had her legs wrapped around me and was grinding her pussy on my cock, and was turned on so badly by my crude words and simple touches that I could feel the space between her legs grow hotter and wetter as we continued on with whatever the fuck it is we were doing, and if I had my way, we would never stop doing.

We were fully clothed.

We were in a public place.

Yet the small space we were sharing smelled like sex.

Like pussy.

Ti's pussy.

I groaned into her hair and my cock stiffened to the point of pain, but it wasn't enough to make me stop.

I never wanted to fucking stop.

"Spread your legs," I continued, my voice coming out strained and rough. Every inch of me ached to rip her shorts off right there on the picnic table and bury my cock so deep

Chapter Twenty-Five

inside her she'd be able to feel it in her throat. "Show me your pussy." I knew full well I was talking to her now, not repeating shit I'd said in the past.

Her lips parted and she turned her face upward toward the sky, her grinding became more fluid. Up and down she slowly dragged herself against me and even through my jeans and her shorts I felt the heat from her pussy up against my rigid cock.

It was the thought of how it would feel to be doing the very same thing, with Ti, without clothes in the way, that had me on the verge of blowing my load right then and there. I took a fist-full of her hair and I used it like reins, pulling her in as close as possible while I continued to talk against her prickled skin. "I'm going to make you come so hard, it's going to fucking hurt." She leaned back, pushing her tits out toward me. I tightened my grip on her waist.

She moaned again and this time my hips involuntarily jerked upward at the sound, my cock slamming against her with such force that pain radiated down my shaft. It was completely worth it, because the sound that came out of Ti's mouth was downright animalistic. It was more of a roar than a moan, something so primal coming from somewhere so deep inside her it exploded in the form of a sound that had me shaking under the tremendous amount of need that kept building and building.

My little fucking cock tease.

I was blinded to everything around us and all I could see, all I could feel, all I could think about was fucking my girl again. "I want you," I breathed. "I want to fuck you. So fucking hard."

She put her hand over her mouth when she realized how loud she'd gotten, but I pulled it away. "No one can hear you," I said, looking around to where the only other people in the

Chapter Twenty-Five

park were a couple of teenagers at least ten tables away. "You can be as loud as you want. Besides, I like it when you scream." The sun had just set but truth be told it could have been daylight with a thousand-people standing around watching and I would have only stopped when the cops came to drag us away.

Bad train of thought.

"I want to taste you again. I'm going to make you scream my name until you go hoarse. And when you think it's not physically possible for you to come again or you're going to break...I'm going to make you come again...and I'm going to break you."

Or I would fucking die trying.

"Bear," Ti moaned, writhing against me. I was going to come if she didn't stop, but when I opened my mouth to tell her to stop nothing came out.

I was so swept away in how she felt against my cock it took me a few seconds to register the rustling of the nearby brush.

I saw the barrels of their guns before I saw who was holding them.

I growled against her ear, "Pretend time's over, baby."

Chapter Twenty-Five
BEAR

I knew the moment Thia registered we weren't alone because her legs tensed around my waist. I turned around to face the threat and reached behind me, pushing her knees back together, keeping as much of her hidden behind me that I could. "Stay quiet," I ordered.

I reached in the waistband of my pants for my gun, but I'd barely brushed the handle when the first gunman emerged from the bushes wearing a Bastards cut.

"I don't fucking think so, Bear," Mono said, with a big fat grin on his big fat face. "Hands off the fucking gun or I start firing now and chances are if I do that, that pretty little thang behind you is gonna be just as full of bullet holes as you're gonna be." He came to a stop about ten feet in front of us.

I released my gun and grabbed my lighter instead. "Just grabbing my smokes, man," I said, lighting another cigarette. "You can tell Harris to come out of the fucking bushes," I said pointing to the brush. "I know the Irish Twins never travel alone and besides, I can see the motherfucker's shining bald ass head from here." Ti's knees shook against my back and I push back against her to ease her nerves, but her shaking only intensified.

Harris emerged from the brush with the same stupid grin on his red bearded face and joined his pseudo brother, his pistol raised as he approached.

"Chop put you dumb fucks on me? I thought he'd at least send someone with some fucking brains, but he sends the fucking twins to do his dirty work?"

Mono and Harris joined the MC around the same time I was patched in. The name 'Irish Twins' has nothing to do with them looking alike because they weren't related and aside from their bald heads and red beards they couldn't have looked more different. Mono was around six feet and stocky, while Harris stood around six five, but was much leaner. It was their personalities that were identical, from the ear bleeding music they were always blasting from their rooms at the club, to the dark and bitter beer that they chugged for breakfast.

Mono spit his dip onto the ground and smiled, his teeth coated in black tar. "You weren't all that hard to find you know, you could have tried harder to run."

I scoffed and took a drag of my cigarette. "I've been in town for weeks. I was right under your nose the entire time, you stupid fucks."

Harris chimed in. "Easier to take you out when King isn't up your ass, although I'd love to take that pussy out as civilian collateral damage."

"Only a handful of places you could go. Even had eyes on that fucking old lady you liked so much."

Grace.

"Surprised you two fucking morons even found me," I said. "You two can't find your fucking cocks half the time. There is no way you tracked me on your own." Mono sneered and came forward until we were almost chest to chest. There were two trackers the MC used and I hoped to God that it was Gus because if it was Rage there was no way I'd survive the next few minutes.

Rage never missed a target.

Never.

"You're about to die motherfucker," he spat. "If you shut your fucking mouth and take your death like a man then maybe we won't kill the pretty little thing behind you when we're done playing with her."

"You won't fucking touch her," I warned.

"Step to the side or you'll die watching Mono face fuck her before we put a knife in her throat," Harris said, moving to the side of the picnic table to get a look at Thia. He licked his lips and sucked on his upper teeth.

"No," I growled, but then I felt a tug in the back waistband of my pants.

No. You stupid fucking girl. Don't.

This is all my fault. Ti was going to die all because I lied to her when she was a kid. Because I had to keep her in my life once she crashed her way into it.

It was because of me that we were both going to die.

Mono and Harris didn't seem to notice what Ti was up to and she didn't seem to get my telepathic message so when I felt a final tug, freeing my gun I knew it was now or never. We would survive because we had to survive.

Because Ti had to survive.

No. Matter. Fucking. What.

"I'm moving I'm moving," I said. Taking one wide side step toward Harris, obstructing his view of Ti.

Ti fired.

I lunged for Harris. Luckily, I'd already had my hand on

his gun and was wrestling for it when it went off while aimed at the sky. I fell on top of him and the second I was able to get the gun from his hand I turned it on him, putting a bullet into his temple.

I turned back around and expected to see Mono laid out but he wasn't on the ground. He was standing up. Blood was pumping out of his shoulder. His good arm was wrapped around Thia, his knife at her throat. "What the fuck did you just do!" Mono roared, his knife bit into her skin and trickles of blood spilled down her neck.

"Let her go or I'll blow your fucking head off," I warned, turning my gun on him. It was a bluff and he knew it. I didn't have a clear shot. There was no way I could shoot him without risking hitting Ti as well.

Mono laughed low and evil. "I don't fucking care." He shrugged and locked eyes with me. "Eye for an eye and all." Mono tightened his grip on Ti and white knuckled his knife as he began to drag it across her throat. I lunged for them, but there was no way I was going to be able to reach them in time.

"Noooooooooooo!"

A shot rang out and Mono's eyes rolled back in his head and the side of his neck exploded. His stare went blank as he released Ti and fell sideways into the dirt.

"Ti!" I said, running for her and scooping her up off of the ground.

"I'm okay?" she asked like it was a question and not a statement. I examined where the blood was dripping from her neck. The slice was about a half of an inch wide. "It's not deep." I sighed in relief. Maybe a stitch or two.

Thank fucking God.

"Who shot him?" Ti asked pointing to Mono as I picked her up and held her tightly to my chest. Stepping over Mono's body I carried her back to the table and set her down to examine her for further injuries. "Who?" Thia asked again, scanning the brush for more Bastards.

I didn't need to look around, because I knew exactly who shot Mono.

"That would be me," a familiar voice said with a slight Spanish accent. I turned around to find myself face to face with Gus. "And you're fucking welcome."

Thia

It was the first time I'd seen Gus since he'd saved me from Chop that night. "Such a waste," he said, staring down at the two lifeless bodies of who Bear had called Mono and Harris. Gus had dragged one of them next to the other so that they were now lying side by side on their backs.

Bear continued to search my body for wounds that weren't there and I tried to catch my breath.

"Hi. I'm Gus," Gus said, never taking his eyes off the bodies. His tone was flat and even and he spoke in a volume a few notches down the volume dial than most people did.

"I remember you," I said and Gus simply nodded.

"I was hoping they used you to track and not Rage," Bear said after finally being satisfied that I wasn't bleeding from anywhere besides the small wound on my neck. He turned to me and pushed the hair off my face, resting his forehead on mine.

"That was a stupid move," he said.

"Bear," I started to argue.

"Let me finish," he interrupted. "It was a stupid move that I'm glad you fucking made or we'd both be dead right now." He pulled back and pulled a joint out of his pocket. He didn't light it instead he passed both the joint and lighter to Gus who reached behind him to take it from Bear, his eyes still glued on the bodies while he lit it and took a deep drag.

Gus knelt down next to the bikers and surprised me when he ran his index finger across Mono's bloody face, leaving a white trail down his cheek through the sticky red. He stood back up and held the bloody finger under his nose. Closing his eyes, he inhaled the blood like he was sniffing a fine wine.

"Shame," he repeated, opening his eyes. He used a rag from his back pocket to wipe the blood from his finger.

On the night Gus saved me from the MC he was just a shadow, no face, no body. A distant memory of an explosion and a ride in a van.

Gus was now a living breathing person with olive skin and dark hair just long enough on the top to brush forward. Tiny pointed bangs hung high on his forehead. His height fell somewhere in the middle of the height difference between my 5'4" and Bear's six foot something. He wasn't wearing a cut, just an untucked navy blue and white flannel shirt and light jeans with yellow work boots. He wasn't attractive, especially not in the same way Bear was. Gus's pudgy cheeks, which were coated with dark hair that was a few hours over a five o'clock shadow, would suggest he was heavier than his medium build. An ornate tattoo decorated his right temple. The whites of his eyes seemed brighter than most against the blackness of his large pupils, which bulged out of his head when he spoke.

I was acutely aware that he didn't blink often and found myself staring at his eyes trying to catch him in the act.

"They should've been on plastic with a dental bar in their mouths. I would have taken my time and started from the back. The back is a good place to start when pulling teeth. Molars are the most painful and the hardest to extract. They are also the bloodiest and when the blood drips down their throats they choke on it and choking increases the fear. You can smell it in the air." He shook his head and looked up at Bear. "It would have been beautiful."

"I'm sure it would have been, man," Bear said, leaning back against the table, obviously used to Gus's oddities.

"You owe me," Gus said, coming to stand in front of us

"Two." He added, holding up two fingers, his voice never rising or falling with his words.

"Two," Bear agreed. "With the shit-storm I have coming my way I don't think that will be a problem."

Gus turned to me and I held out my hand. "We were never properly introduced. I'm Thia," I said, clearing my throat to remove any remnant of nervousness from my voice. Gus looked down at my hand and jumped back like I was holding out a spider.

Bear put his hand on my forearm and gently pushed it down. "Gus doesn't shake hands," Bear said, as Gus shook his head frantically from side to side, his fists curled up into balls under his chin as he cowered away from me.

"You're afraid of ME? I just saw you kill a guy then rub your finger in his blood," I pointed out.

Gus unfolded his arms from himself when he saw I was no longer holding out my offending hand and stood up, smoothing down his already smooth shirt. "Blood is clean. Blood is beautiful. Blood is life and watching that life drain out and fade away is a gift I like to give myself as often as possible. Hands are dirty. So dirty. Like motel rooms." He rambled, gagging when he mentioned 'motel rooms,' turning his mouth into the crook of his elbow. He took a deep breath, fixing within himself whatever it was that I had broken by trying to shake his hand. "Did you know that most motel rooms are covered in feces and semen?" Gus asked out of nowhere. "And I'm not talking about the bed. Depending on the age of the motel and the number of available rooms and the amount of parking spaces, at one time or another every single surface had been covered by either semen or feces or both."

"Well hello to you too, Gus," Bear said with a laugh.

"It's true," Gus said, turning to Bear. "And it's not funny.

Now you owe me three." Gus took another drag of the joint and passed it back to Bear who held it between his lips and inhaled until the red ember on the tip dripped with ash.

He spoke as he exhaled. "I know it's not funny man. What's also not funny is that if it wasn't for Ti grabbing my gun and you showing up that we'd be a couple of corpses stacked on your pile right now."

"I keep my promises," Gus said, "You saved my life."

"Never doubted you, brother, but you didn't have to take off your cut for me. I would never have asked you that," Bear said, gesturing to Gus's cut-free attire.

"I didn't take it off for you. I took it off for me."

"Why?" I chimed in.

"Because I found out who the mole is."

"What mole?" I asked.

"The one who fed intel to Isaac and then to Eli. The one who tried to have me killed twice, but still can't seem to get the fucking job done," Bear informed me. "But it doesn't matter now, because Chop wants to kill me himself."

"Three times," Gus corrected.

"What?" Bear asked, his brows creasing with confusion.

"Three times," Gus said. "The first time was when he let Isaac into the club when he knew what Isaac's plans were. The second time was when he told Eli where you were. The third time was today, right now."

Bear sat there silently and took another drag of the joint, rubbing his temples with his thumb. "Fuuuuuuccck!" he roared, standing up on top of the table.

"I don't understand," I said. "What does you leaving the MC and the mole have anything to do with one another..." I stopped when the realization hit.

Bear looked down at me and nodded.

"The mole is…" I started, but stopped as it all sank in. Bear growled and finished my sentence.

"My fucking old man."

Gus nodded. "Chop. Chop is the mole."

So much for normal…

Chapter Twenty-Six
BEAR

"So, your old man was gunning for you long before you threw down your cut? Why?" King asked, lighting a joint and passing it to me. "That doesn't make any fucking sense."

"I know. There has got to be more to it. My old man's a son-of-a-bitch, but he's not fucking stupid. The problem is now that we can't get any more intel. Gus laid down his cut. He's out, which means I don't have anyone left on the inside." We were back in his tattoo studio and I'd just told him what had gone down at the park. Luckily, Gus was all too eager to handle the cleanup on his own, so we left him to it. "It's not like it fucking matters. If he wants me dead, he wants me dead, the reason isn't important anymore. The only real problem is that he's willing to go through Ti to get to me."

"But why Thia? You have other people he can get to. Me. Grace. Ray. Why choose her?"

"'Cause Chop's a cocksucker, but he's not fucking stupid either, he took one look at her and knew..." I paused. "He's following code, or at least he's making it appear to the brothers like he is, meanwhile he's been going behind their backs, planning to have me killed for fuck knows how long now."

"But that still doesn't make sense. How could going through Thia to get to you..." King started but stopped when I flashed him a knowing look. He answered his own question. "Girls in the club, old ladies, even the BBB's, they aren't considered civilians. She's fair game as far as he's concerned because he thought you'd claim her."

I leaned my head against the wall. "I have claimed her."

"Oh shit."

I stood up from the couch and pretended to be interested in the new sketch King had been working on to finish Ray's sleeve. It was all three of their kids' names woven into a mangrove tree on the bay.

"Never thought I'd see the fucking day, man."

"It was stupid. Twice now and I didn't wrap up either time."

King laughed and motioned for me to bring the joint back to him.

I shoved it into his hand. "What's so fucking funny?"

"Let me ask you something, man. Of all the girls you've ever fucked, how many times you forget to wrap it up with?"

"None. Not a single fucking one," I admitted.

"It's funny, cause that's how you know. Never thought about it with Ray. Never crossed my mind and honestly, if it had, I didn't give a fuck about the consequences. Anything to keep her linked with me was all right by me. I may not have known that at first, but I sure as shit know it now."

"Now you got three kids, man. Two of which are tearing the house apart block by block."

"Yeah, it's pretty fucking great. Still don't think to wrap up either," he said with a laugh.

"I'm not thinking about having kids right now. I'm thinking about how to keep this girl alive."

"Your girl."

"Yes, MY girl! There I said it, does that make you happy now?"

"It's a start," King said. "So, you think about what Bethany said to you? 'Cause if you are going to go through with it then you need to tell her. She should know what she's in for. There are things you need to go over with her. I've been there man. You don't want her going in blind."

I lit a cigarette. King was right, but I had no idea how to start the conversation with her. "I got something else in mind," I said.

"If you're thinking of doing something stupid, don't," King warned.

"Stupid was taking her into a public place and almost getting her killed. Stupid was making a promise to a ten-year-old I never intended to keep. Stupid is every fucking thing I've ever done in my life up until this point. I got to keep her safe." I stubbed out my smoke in the ashtray on the coffee table. "Nothing stupid about that."

THIA WAS up at the house to help Ray with the kids or dinner or something, to be honest I hadn't been paying attention because I was too focused on the fact that if it wasn't for Gus or Ti's quick thinking, she wouldn't be breathing right now. I was too busy thinking with my cock instead of worrying about keeping her safe.

You were thinking with your heart, dumbass. It's that other useful organ in your body. Preppy informed me.

I made a promise to myself that although all this shit started out as a lie, I would keep my promise to her. I would protect her, but I made another promise to myself too. I would not just protect her, but I wouldn't let her get sucked into my life. She was better than it.

Better than me.

I would keep her safe.

I just couldn't keep her for myself.

Thirty minutes and one text message later, a practiced hand was wrapped around my cock.

I'd drank straight from the bottle of Jack until I didn't care, which although I was hammered, still wasn't working. Because Ti was going to walk through door at any second and see what kind of man I really was. I was hoping I would be drunk enough not to see the look of hurt in her eyes. Not to register the look of disappointment on her face.

Why did I even care?

She knew I'd planned to leave from the moment we met. I never told her that had changed. I never promised her that I was going to stay.

Or that she was going to stay.

King was locked up for years. I made him promise that he would call in all the favors he still had on the inside because I could protect her for now, but wouldn't be able to when we weren't together anymore.

Fuck, why does this hurt so bad?

"Mmmmmmmmm..." she murmured, like I wasn't paying her to jerk me off. I wasn't even hard.

Every time I started to wake from whatever self-induced coma I'd put myself in, my newly conscious state always brought a wave of disappointment with it.

It's not that I wanted to die. I just wanted to live in a state of oblivion. Was that too much to ask? Oblivion didn't have thoughts of being a biker without a home. Oblivion didn't have confusing thoughts of Ray, although in recent days those had started to fade away.

Oblivion definitely didn't have HER.

And come tomorrow, I wouldn't either.

I wanted it to be her hand on my cock and I imagined it was, living in my imagination and in the lie for just a few more ignorant moments.

Jodi stroked me. Or was it Dee? Danni? Denise?

Regardless of the expertise being used to get me off I felt myself going softer and softer. I thought of pale pink lips and strawberry blonde hair, but every time she appeared behind my closed eyelids, she disappeared just as quickly.

I groaned in frustration. The girl getting me off took the noise as a sign of encouragement, picking up her pace. Jerking me harder. Long fake nails clicked together as she worked me.

There was no fucking way I was going to come, and I was glad for it. I wanted to punish myself for what I was about to do.

For what she was about to see.

Sadly, the only coming I was doing was coming down from my high, which was the last fucking thing I wanted. It was a shitty-ass time to sober up.

I changed my mind.

I couldn't do this.

I couldn't hurt her. I would find another way. I grabbed what's her name's forearm to make her stop her pointless hand job, but it wasn't her my eyes darted to.

It was Ti.

MY Ti.

Standing at the foot of the bed.

She appeared straight faced. Impassive. Almost expressionless. I knew better than to take her at face value. Thia ran deep, but covered up even deeper. What I saw behind her flat expression scared the shit out of me, because it was more than her usual spitfire self.

She was mad.

Pure unadulterated RAGE mad.

The naked bleach blonde kneeling next to me barely paid Thia any attention, and continued to stroke me as she looked back at her despite my hand on her arm trying to stop her. "You want in?" she asked Thia.

Maybe she wasn't there. Maybe I was just dreaming. Because Thia Andrews had been occupying my dreams since that first night in the shower.

It wasn't until she spoke that I knew for sure it wasn't a dream after all.

I thought she'd run.

I'd done this so she would run.

Not from the house. From me.

But she didn't. The girl was always surprising me.

She walked right up to the bed with a look of determination in her eyes that I'd never seen before. She reached over me and plucked one of my guns from one of my holders, which was the only thing I was wearing. She aimed at the naked blonde and cocked it. "Get. Out. Now." The fake seductive look on the blonde's face instantly disappeared and was replaced with fear. She jumped from the bed and ran out the door without a backwards glance.

I know it was the asshole thing to do but I couldn't help it.

Maybe it was because I was drunk.

Maybe because I was tired of not knowing what to do or who to trust or how to protect the girl who had wiggled and smiled her way into my broken heart.

I laughed.

Not just a little laugh either. I laughed at the absurdity that my life had become as well as the situation I was currently in.

Thia turned the gun on me and that's when I noticed the tears threatening to leak from the corners of her beautiful green eyes.

I froze.

"Shit."

Ti sniffled, although she was obviously trying to hide the fact that she was on the verge of crying. An unfamiliar feeling took over. My heart lurched into my stomach and I felt sick.

Guilt.

I'd committed every crime there was to commit. I'd done shit that sane men would never dare to even think of, yet I'd never felt a shred of guilt for any of it.

Ever.

Until now.

Until Thia.

Love. It was the only kind of torture I wasn't familiar with.

I was quickly learning it was the most painful kind of them all.

"You know," she started. Her voice was as shaky as the gun in her hand. "You really need to stop trying to make me hate you."

I muddled through my cloudy thoughts in search of a response, "And why is that?" was the best I could come up with.

Ti laid the gun down on my bare stomach and I resisted the urge to reach out and tug her down onto me. She was about to turn the handle on the door when she turned back. Tears stained her cheeks and my gut twisted in a way I was beginning to hate as much as I hated myself.

She looked me right in the eye and held my gaze.

"Because it's working."

Chapter Twenty-Seven
BEAR

No amount of coffee or cold water could have dragged me back into sobriety after I'd seen the look on Ti's face in that room.

Alcohol and anger go hand in hand like junior high sweethearts.

I'd drank enough Jack to set me into a coma, yet after she'd walked out of the room I was more sober than before I'd had a single drop.

I pulled on my jeans and ran after her.

Thia wasn't in the living room. She wasn't in the garage either. I was worried she'd left completely and started thinking of where the fuck she would go or who was out there waiting to hurt her when I spotted her on the dock. She was bent over, her hands moving furiously. I didn't realize what she was doing until she untied the rope from the dock and hopped off the dock.

By the time I got down to the dock she had already pushed off and was too far away from me to reach out and pull her back. "Ti, we gotta talk."

"I think you've said plenty."

"Ti, get your ass over here." Ignoring me she continued to row furiously. She was obviously inexperienced and didn't move too far too quickly. The muscles in her arms strained as she rowed harder and harder without much progress to show for it.

"There is a nasty rip current under the dock. It's a struggle for me or King to get the boat through it, so you might as well give up and come back now," I said, crouching down on the seawall.

She only fought harder, slowly she gained ground inching further away from the dock and from me. I hadn't been lying. The current was a bitch to get through if you didn't know exactly where it stopped and started. Took us months to figure out how to clear it in less than a few minutes.

As much as I hated the fact that she was doing her damnedest to get away from me I was impressed by my girl's strength.

There was no way to make this right.

I craved her forgiveness just as much as I craved her body. Her soul. Her spirit.

Her heart.

Words spilled from my lips in quick succession. I had to get to her before she was too far away to hear me. I spoke so fast I didn't have time to edit myself and choose the right words so I just went with my gut because going with my head only resulted in her beginning to hate me and as much as that was part of the plan I hadn't counted on the crushing blow to my soul that came with it.

I wanted to tell her everything.

I started with the truth.

Bear uncensored.

"For what it's worth I didn't want her. I never wanted her," I shouted. "I just don't know what I'm doing here. I don't know anything anymore."

"Looked like you wanted her to me," Ti said, huffing heavily, but making progress. If she kept up the pace for a few more minutes she would be free of the current and would quickly be out of hearing distance.

"What do you want me to say? You almost got killed in the park!"

"So did you."

"That's my LIFE though. I'm used to motherfuckers gunning for me. That shouldn't be yours though."

"You don't get to decide my life, Bear. Not you. Not anyone."

"When I'm with you it's like you put me up on this fucking unreachable pedestal. I don't deserve that kind of admiration and sometimes," I tried to catch my breath but the words kept spilling out of me. "It scares the fucking shit out of me. Whatever you think you know about me or who I am, you don't know shit about me. You don't know the things I've done, the people I've done them to. You don't know that I've killed people because I was ordered to, or because I thought it was good for club business, or just because they rubbed me the wrong fucking way. Is that what you want to hear? 'Cause that's the truth. I've done it all and you look at me like I'm somehow a good person and it makes me want to tear my fucking hair out because it's all a lie. The truth is that I'm not the good guy. I'm the fucking bad guy, and club or not, that hasn't changed." I ran my hand through my hair and took a deep breath.

It wasn't exactly a fucking love poem, but it was the truth.

"When did I say that?" Ti asked in a small whisper,

temporarily forgetting to row, the boat slid forward toward me. "Tell me, when exactly did I say that I wanted to change you?" Her voice grew louder. Bolder. "Do you think I'm some fucking sheltered idiot? I know who you are and who the Beach Bastards are. I grew up across the county, not across the country. What I want to know is why you somehow think that affects anything? I don't have you on a pedestal. I've got no rose-colored glasses when it comes to who you are. Actually, I might be one of the few people in the world who knows the real you. I wanted you because of who you are, not regardless of who you are. You weren't on a pedestal, you were in my heart!"

WERE

WERE in my heart.

Until I just fucking shattered it.

Ti floated back toward me and I battled with my original plan to push her away again, but the closer she got the more determined I was to fix what I had broken. Tomorrow was coming no matter what happened tonight.

I knelt down to pull her in, but when she saw my outstretched arm she shook her head. Rowing with even more vigor then before, water splashing into the boat in her furious attempt to get as far away from me as possible.

Fuck this.

She just said she wanted me because of who I am and that was a good thing because I was about to show her exactly who I was.

Already barefoot, and wearing only my jeans, I pushed them off my hips and stepped out of them. From Ti's position I knew she couldn't see me in the shadows. I tossed my jeans out onto the dock and into the light.

It was a warning. I was coming for her.

I was completely naked, and I didn't give a fuck.

The slightly salty air tasted like fucking freedom. The musty smell of decay of the nearby wetlands stung my nose but I wanted more.

More was the plan.

More was in a rowboat in the middle of the big bay and I couldn't help but think how little she looked. How innocent. How vulnerable.

My cock hardened.

"What are you doing?" Ti called out, the fear in her voice doing nothing to placate my raging hard on.

"Suddenly, I feel like a fucking swim," I said wickedly, stretching my arms over my head.

"No! Stay away, Bear. I mean it!" Ti shouted, lapping her oars so hard into the water she was finally able to break free of the current, gliding easily across the water. "You're not coming in here."

That's what you think.

"Oh, yes. I fucking am," I muttered. I sucked in a deep breath and dove head first into the dark water.

A predator seeking its prey.

Chapter Twenty-Eight
THIA

Bear had lost his damned mind.

From the second we left the park he hadn't been the same.

I knew he wanted me to walk in on him with that girl. It wasn't what she was doing to him that both pissed me off and broke my heart. It was the fact that I knew he'd done it on purpose. He wanted to get caught.

He wanted to HURT me.

Even though I was free of the current I continued to row, wanting to get far enough away from the shore that Bear would give up on swimming and turn back around. As I got closer to the shore on the opposite side I'd thought I would see other houses surrounding the bay, but the rest of the shore was covered in a mixture of tall thin trees that bent and swayed with the slightest breeze and short stumpy mangroves that sat on top of the water on little sticks that reminded me of the pillars that held up King and Ray's house.

I really hadn't thought Bear was going to jump in. An empty threat that turned out to be not so empty.

The spot where Bear had jumped into the water created a rippling effect over the surface, growing larger and larger as it spanned out. By the time it reached the boat it had turned from slight ripple to little wave, rocking the boat from side to side.

That's when I realized that there was no other disturbance in the water. No indication of movement of any kind.

Where is he? My anger and irritation temporarily replaced by worry.

I counted to ten.

Nothing.

I counted again.

Nothing.

"Bear!" I shouted.

No response.

Keeping one oar raised out of the water I turned the boat around and followed the path from where I came, scanning for signs of life. I'd only gotten a few strokes in when the stillness exploded beside the boat. My heart leapt into my stomach as Bear launched himself through the surface of the water like an orca, soaking my hair and clothes.

"Why do you care? Why are you really mad?" Bear asked, grabbing onto the side of the boat. "Tell me, Ti, and be fucking honest with me because we both know you can't lie for shit. Why do you care if I fuck and snort and drink myself into an early fucking grave?" Fire danced in his eyes, water dripped into his face and mouth. "Tell me," he challenged. "Right fucking now 'cause I need to know." He lifted a leg over the side of the boat. I held onto the sides to prevent myself from going in as it tipped more sideways than I thought a boat could, letting in a few inches of water. Bear lifted his other leg into the boat and it righted itself again as he climbed in. With limited space, he sat behind me on the little bench seat, my back to his chest. His knees splayed out on the side of my hips. I turned sideways to glare at him.

Bear was running a hand over his head, wringing out the excess water.

He was also naked.

Completely and utterly, devastatingly and beautifully...naked.

I wanted to hate him and I was pretty sure I did but that didn't mean that his mere presence didn't affect me.

Under the light of the moon his tattoos and smooth skin looked as if they were shining, glowing with the same iridescent light reflecting off the water. His chest and arms flexed from the strain of his swim. His ab muscles rose and fell as he tried to catch his breath and I found myself following them where they turned into a V, pointing down to his...

I averted my gaze to the trees. "You win, Bear, whatever you are trying to argue. It's fine. I agree. You win. Just go!"

"Bullshit," he said. "I don't win. I fucked up, Ti. If this is winning I hate to find out what losing feels like, so please, tell me what it is you think I won?"

It was exactly what I wanted to hear.

It was exactly bullshit.

"You wanted to push me away," I reminded him. "You wanted to hurt me. Mission accomplished. Now get out of my boat."

"First off, this is my boat. I built it with King and Preppy when they first bought the place, so if anyone is getting out, it's you. Second, I tried to push you away. I admit it, even convinced myself that I wanted to do it. I thought it would be better if you hated me. I thought you would be better if you hated me." His eyes met mine. "And part of me still thinks that's true. But nothing about the look on your face felt like I was doing the right thing. The reality of you hating me was nothing like I thought it would be." His voice grew quiet and his words sank further into the barrier I had a hard time keeping up around him. "It gutted me, Ti."

Don't listen. He's lying. Don't believe him.

"I know the feeling," I said, the words dripping with the bitterness I felt.

Don't listen. He's lying. Don't believe him.

"Here I thought you were being an asshole, but really, you just couldn't push her hand from your dick fast enough?" I snapped. "Makes total sense. Please, by all means, continue," I said sarcastically, resting my chin on my closed fist and leaning toward him to hear the rest of his ridiculous lies. The breeze picked up blowing my hair over my shoulders. Bear reached over my shoulder and grazed the side of my neck with the back of his knuckles. I shivered as he pulled my hair back around, dragging his fingertips across my skin as he adjusted my hair across my back. "You don't get to touch me." I seethed, trying my hardest not to give away the desire coursing through me by leaning into his touch.

"I told myself I can't have you, but I can't shake you. Why do you think that is?" Bear asked, his words a whisper against my bare neck. His fingers continuing to dance down the back of my arms despite my protest.

A part of me wanted to turn around and crush my lips to his.

A part of me wanted to drown him in the bay.

I was lost in sensation as my skin prickled to life and a muscle inside of me spasmed and clenched. It was a war. Desire vs. Anger.

Anger was losing, but I wasn't ready to give up the fight so easily.

Or so I thought. I'd opened my mouth to argue, yet somehow my brain thought the words and my mouth delivered the message, but I wasn't fully aware of what I was saying. Of the truth.

"You can't shake me because I love you, you fucking asshole," I said. Instant regret and fear slammed into me and I considered jumping into the bay to avoid seeing Bear's reaction.

His thighs tensed around me.

After what seemed like forever he finally spoke and my heart started to shatter all over again. "No, you can't love me."

"No?" I asked, feeling every bit of anger coming back with a vengeance, rage raced up toward my neck, my blood turning hot in my pulsing veins. "No? You really are an idiot then! You don't get to tell me that. And newsflash: I've loved you since I first saw you when I was just a kid and I will love you until I'm a hundred years old and even after they bury me in the ground." I turned in the seat and Bear shifted his leg to make room for my knees, which were dangerously close to his cock that I couldn't help but notice was already hard, pulsing as we argued. "You don't have the right to tell me not to, love doesn't work like that. The way I feel about you is the one thing in my life I still have that's completely mine, and believe it or not, even you can't take that from me." I grabbed the oars and tried to row back to shore but Bear locked his thighs around me so that I couldn't turn back around. He grabbed the oars from me and tossed them overboard, one at a time, launching them like little javelins across the water.

"What the fuck!"

"We aren't going anywhere," Bear said, looking down into

my eyes. Where there was irritation before was now only confusion. Pain. That's when I realized it.

He'd told me that I couldn't love him, not because he didn't want my love.

But because he didn't think he was worthy.

FUCK THIS. I grabbed his face in my hands and forced him closer to me. "You came into my life when I had nothing left." I told him, putting everything I had out there for him to take in. I thought I'd feel weak telling him the truth but I didn't. If anything, I felt stronger with each new confession, finding strength in the truth. "You've been everything to me." I leaned forward and planted a small soft kiss on the corner of his mouth, his lips parted and his gaze dropped to my lips as I pulled back. "You just have to remember how to be something to yourself."

"I can't," Bear said, so quietly I wasn't sure if he really spoke. "I can't," he repeated. His shoulders fell and his gaze dropped to the floor of the boat.

"Why? Tell me why?" I demanded, standing up off my seat. Bear was now eye level with my chest.

"I'm...lost," he admitted, and my heart sank.

"Then I will help you find your way," I said with new found determination, rubbing my thumbs over his temples. Bear leaned into my touch and closed his eyes, but it didn't last long. Suddenly he pulled away.

"It's not that easy. I'm a biker without a club. I feel like I'm nothing because I don't know who I am anymore." His brutal honesty should have had me skipping around in elation, finally cracking the hard shell that was Bear, but the happiness never came, because my heart was hurting for him.

Hurt quickly turned to anger.

"What do you want?" I asked. It came out a little harsher

than I intended. He shook his head and remained silent. "Answer me, damn it!"

His eyes locked onto mine and I saw the second he fixed that shell back in place. "I want what every man wants, Ti. A bottle of Jack and my fucking dick sucked. You up for it, baby girl? Ready to wrap those beautiful lips of yours around my cock? Or should I bring that other chick back to get the job done? Or, maybe you want to join us? It's the least you can do to make up for the earlier interruption." Bear's eyes glinted with a hint of evil, but I saw right past his lies to the pain lurking beneath the surface, beneath the facade he was so good at clinging to when he didn't want to show his true feelings.

I slapped him across the face.

Hard.

His hands dug harshly into my hips and he jerked me toward him, the boat rocked violently. "Careful," he warned.

"You can try and distract me by making me angry, but you can't, it's not going to work. Not this time. So, tell me Bear," I repeated my question. "What. Do. You. Want?" I was angry that the beautiful man in front of me couldn't see what I saw in him.

"What I want isn't important," Bear said. He moved his hands around to my lower back and tugged me in closer. "I can't have what I want."

"Why not?"

"Because what I want is not fucking possible!" he said. "Tell me, Ti. You gonna bring my dead friend back? 'Cause Preppy died right in front of my eyes and I couldn't save him! You gonna give me my club? I want things to be the way they were supposed to be before it all went to shit. You gonna take the nightmares away? The ones where I relive Eli and his men torturing me, shoving some broken bat up my ass and shoving their cocks in my mouth? Because I want all that and more than anything I want..." He looked away, but I wasn't about to let him stop there. I brought his gaze back to mine and held it there.

"What? What else do you want?" I asked, softly this time. When he didn't answer right away I was afraid I'd already lost him.

After an eternity, he finally spoke and when he did his words knocked the wind from my chest. "You," he finally admitted, his voice stronger, more assertive than just seconds before. "I've been a ruined man for a long time. I can't ruin you too."

"You didn't ruin me," I said. "You saved me."

I didn't even realize the boat had started to tip over until it was too late. I lost my hold on Bear and crashed into the dark water.

Bear's strong arms lifted me out. "Grab onto the side," he said, tapping on the side of the boat. I couldn't reach the ground but Bear could because he held onto the boat and walked us toward the nearby shore. I was so wrapped up in Bear that I hadn't noticed how close we'd floated. King and Ray's house looked so small from across the bay. Lights flickered in the windows. It seemed a million miles away, not just a few hundred feet.

Suddenly I was airborne and in seconds I was flat on my back on a tiny muddy beach and Bear was on top of me. His lips crushing mine until I couldn't breathe, his hand palming my breast, his cock hard and ready between my legs.

"Baby, I'm sorry," he said dropping his forehead to mine in a rare moment of vulnerability. His voice was rough and shaky. "Help me. Please. I don't know what I'm doing here."

"What are you trying to do?" I asked. He raised up, just enough to look me in the eye.

"I'm trying to love you."

We were two tortured souls. Both in more ways than one person should ever have to experience.

But we found each other.

We needed each other.

So, help him I did.

I sat up enough to pull him back down to me, the broken shells in the mud dug into my back. The water of the bay lapped over my bare feet. Bear was a million different things, and he may have been pushing thirty, but we were alike in so many ways. He was just a boy who had no clue what he was doing and I was just a girl who had no idea what to do with all the feelings I had swarming around inside of me.

I just knew that I wanted him.

That I loved him.

"Promise me that no matter what, that you won't give up on me. Promise me, Ti," Bear said, his eyes welling up with water. I wiped the corner of his eye with my thumb and he leaned into my touch.

"I won't give up on you," I promised and I meant it.

I would never give up on him.

Neither of us knew what the future held for us, if anything at all. All we knew is that we had today. Right then, right there. We were just a normal boy and a normal girl trying to figure out how to love one another.

Today.

Tomorrow we would figure out the rest.

Today, Bear pulled my shorts and panties to the side, sank his hard cock deep inside of me and frantically fucked me until I couldn't think of anything but him, the orgasm that tore through my body, the tears that ran down my face, and the elation my heart felt over knowing that the stupid boy who made mistakes loved me.

And that was good enough.

For today.

Because tomorrow never came.

Chapter Twenty-Nine
THIA

Bear pushed the boat back in the water and used a thick branch to row us back to the other side of the bay. "I really am sorry," Bear said again when we were halfway across.

"I really do love you," I said, and I meant it.

"You know that you are the only person in my life who has ever told me that?" Bear asked.

"What is going on?" I asked, noticing a commotion going on by the seawall, which Bear had his back to as we rowed.

"Fuck if I know. This is all new to me too," Bear said, oblivious to what I was referring to.

"No, turn around," I said and Bear looked behind me to where a woman wearing an all-white pantsuit stood on the seawall. Her dark hair was pulled into a severe bun and her lipstick was so bright red that I could see it even in the dim lights of the dock. Next to her were three police officers with their guns raised and aimed at our boat.

Bear turned around and as soon as he saw what we were heading toward he tried to subtly turn the boat around but it was too late, we hit the current and it pushed us rapidly toward the seawall. "I'm sorry," the woman said, "I know this wasn't supposed to be until tomorrow but I couldn't hold them off. I tried to call your cell."

"Bear, what is she talking about?" I asked. "What's going on?"

"Fuck!" Bear cursed, dropping the useless branch into the water.

"Cynthia Anne Andrews?" one of the officers asked.

"Why are they calling my name?" I asked Bear who looked at the floor of the boat and then back up at me.

"Don't forget your promise, Ti. Don't give up on me," he said as the boat hit the seawall. One of the officers reached down to grab me and I shrieked.

"Don't fucking touch her!" he warned, standing up in the boat. The officer pulled back but held up his gun again. "Ti, you gotta go with them."

"What?" I asked. My heart pounding rapidly against my chest. Ray and King had come out of the house and were standing several feet behind the woman and the cops watching the scene unfold.

"Thia, I'm Bethany, your attorney, and he's right, you have to come with me."

"I thought it was just a meeting? I thought it was tomorrow?" I asked as the understanding of what was happening sunk in.

"I'm sorry," she said and I believed her. Bear bent down to lift me onto the seawall and I shrugged him off.

I was going to prison.

And Bear knew.

That's why he'd tried to push me away. He knew they were coming for me and wanted to sever whatever it is that we had before they did.

Before I was gone.

"No, don't touch me," I argued, but Bear didn't listen.

He grabbed me by the back of my legs. "Remember your promise," he whispered again, hoisting me up toward the awaiting officers. Bethany threw Bear his jeans and he stepped into them before climbing onto the seawall, the little boat kicked out from under him and without being tied down was quickly launched into the mangroves by the current.

I hung my head and held out my hands behind my back, waiting to be cuffed. Bethany came to stand by my side and gave my shoulder a small reassuring squeeze. It didn't work.

"You are under arrest for the murders of Wayne and Trinity Andrews anything you say..." One of the officers started and that's when I looked up and noticed that their attentions weren't on me. And neither were their guns.

They were on Bear.

"No!" I shouted, lunging forward but Bethany caught me by the shirt and tugged me back. They cuffed Bear and holstered their guns. They pushed him forward through the grass to one of the awaiting squad cars that were parked by the house, the rotating lights painting everything in splashes of blue and red.

"King!" I shouted, but he looked at me in a warning that said to keep my mouth shut. I broke free from Bethany's grip and ran forward. Bear hopped to the right, dodging the officers long enough to spin back around to me. I launched myself up at him wrapping my arms around his neck and my legs around his waist and I kissed him furiously until one of the officers pried me away, our lips the last of our connection to be severed.

"You don't have to do this. Please. Please don't do this," I begged him, still not fully understanding what exactly was going on. Tears streaming down my face as the officers placed me in front of King who wrapped his arms around my shoulders and whose stone like grip didn't allow for even an inch of movement toward Bear. Ray came to stand next to me, and Bethany next to her.

The officers forcefully pushed Bear forward, smashing the side of his face against the police cruiser where they patted him down. Before throwing him into the back of the car he looked back at me.

"I love you," he mouthed and with the echo of the slam of the door shutting Bear off from me, from my life, I swear I also heard the sound of my heart shattering.

Chapter Thirty
BEAR

I rained down punches on Corp's face until it was a mangled mess of skin and blood and my orange jumpsuit was splattered with red. Serves the motherfucker right for coming at me with a fucking shank.

As soon as I knew Corps was in county I knew he'd be coming for me. Too bad they sent a pussy to do a man's job.

Two weeks I'd been waiting and watching until he finally made his move, but I was ready.

Judging from the wreckage that used to be his face I can honestly say that he wasn't.

"McAdams, you have a visitor," snapped the guard. Corps moaned and I delivered one last punch to the side of his jaw, knocking him out cold. I stood up as the guard slid open my cell.

"I see your visit went well," said the disinterested guard who tapped away on his phone as he led me to the visitor waiting area. He was the prick who put him in there to begin with, fully understanding what it was that Corps planned on doing.

"It did. He's shit for company though. Doesn't say much. Moans and groans a lot. I think he might be ill. Splitting headache," I joked as the guard looked up from his phone long enough to roll his eyes and open the door separating the cell block from the hallway that led to the visitation area. "My lawyer came earlier. Who's here?" I asked.

"Some chick," the guard said, pushing open another door. I stopped.

"Take me back," I said. I told King not to let Ti come. As much as I wanted to see her I didn't want her to see me in here and her coming for a visit wouldn't work with the confession I'd signed.

"Can't, you got a visitor. She showed ID. She signed in. You go in. You've got five minutes," the officer said, opening the little room that looked like a cafeteria. I scanned the tables, which were mostly empty. It only took me seconds to realize that Ti wasn't among the visitors. There was only one table where a lone woman sat waiting, looking down at her hands.

"Her?" I asked the guard.

"Yep," he said, shutting the door behind me.

I made my way over to her and was about to tell her that she signed in to see the wrong prisoner, but when she looked up at me all the air in my lungs left in a swoosh.

"Abel?" she asked, looking up from behind silver streaked dark brown bangs.

My head spun and I blinked to make sure what I was seeing wasn't a hallucination.

"Mom?"

Excerpt From Soulless
THIA

Handcuffs bit into my wrists. My arms strained above my head as I hung from a pipe that ran across the ceiling. When I could no longer hold myself up and my muscles gave out with a POP as my joints painfully dislocated. My chin fell to my chest. Wide tape covered my mouth, wrapped around the back of my head, pulling on my hair every time I turned my head. With one nostril stuffed up I felt dizzy, barely able to get enough oxygen through the other.

My vision blurred as I tried to focus on my surroundings. Grey. Concrete. An open ceiling with pipes and wires. Nothing on the bare walls. A metal cage in the far corner. In the center of the small room was a blue tarp. Next to the tarp was a red toolbox with a yellow electric drill set on top. It was all so clean.

Sterile.

That's when the panic set in and my eyes opened wide as the realization of Gus's plan for me. I pulled on the cuffs above my head with a newfound strength I didn't have seconds

Excerpt From Soulless

earlier. My legs flailed around uselessly in mid air as I struggled against my restraints.

The door opened and Gus entered the room. When I first met him in the park he'd protected Bear and myself. I'd even thought he was cute in a best friend chubby cheeked kind of way.

That Gus wasn't who walked into the room. This Gus looked up at me, dangling from the ceiling, like I was a steak and he was a hungry lion who hadn't eaten in months.

"I really wish it could be me who could have all the fun with you today, but you see little one, I have a phone call to make to Bear. I have to let him know that his girl has been kidnapped by the MC. I have to continue playing the role of loyal soldier, so unfortunately for me, I had to call in a substitute." He stepped up to me and I braced for whatever it was he was about to do. My heart hammering in my chest.

The tape being pulled off was painful, but it passed quickly and I was finally able to take deep breaths. Gulping for air as if I'd been drowning. "Why do this at all?" I asked, after finally being able to catch my breath. "Me, Bear, the MC? Why?"

"I don't ask why. I do what I'm told. Asking why is not my job."

"Then what is your job? Who hired you?"

Gus covered my mouth with his hand and pressed his forehead to mine. My stomach rolled. "That doesn't matter. What only matters now is what is about to happen to you. My advice? Give into the pain. Enjoy it. The human body is a fascinating machine and although I don't get to do it myself, I'll be watching the video later and I'm sure watching that machine come apart is going to be nothing short of spectacular." He let go of my mouth and set the tape back in place. "Although I'm

Excerpt From Soulless

sure Bear is not going to love it as much as I will. He doesn't appreciate the beauty in it like I do."

He stuck out his fat tongue and licked my face from my jaw to my eye and my stomach rolled again.

Gus stepped back and took one last lustful look at me. "Such a shame, little one." Before he left the room he adjusted a camera next to the door I hadn't noticed. A red light came on. "Maybe, I'll stay. Just for the first part," Gus said, opening the door. "We're ready," he called out and a blond man appeared in the room, shutting the door behind him. He was shirtless, cut and muscular, tattoos covered his arms and chest.

A wrench in his hands that he tapped into his palm over and over again as he looked me up and down.

Gus was evil.

This guy, with his classic good looks, was the fucking devil.

His eyes were black and glowing like a demon in a movie and I realized there was no getting out of this. My fate had been sealed. With every step the devil took toward me the fear I felt increased higher and higher until I'd hoped I'd die of a heart attack before this lunatic could carry out whatever sick plans he had for me.

The devil set the wrench down by the toolbox and pulled his shoulder length hair on top of his head with an elastic band. He bent his head from side to side, making a sickening cracking sound. He did the same with his knuckles.

Then he came for me.

While Gus looked at me like he was lusting after my blood the blond devil looked natural. In his element.

Possessed.

He reached up and unhooked one of the cuffs, catching me before I fell to the concrete floor. My arms still raised above my head as they'd become completely useless and disjointed.

"Nooooooo!" I tried to scream behind the tape, tears ran out the side of my eyes. He carried me to the tarp and laid me on top of it, binding my ankles together with the tape.

"You can take the tape off. She wants to make sure her screams make the video," Gus said. "Start with the teeth, they are the most painful."

"Why are you still here?" the devil asked. I was shaking so hard I could hear my jaw rattling behind the tape.

"Just wanted to watch the fun start."

"I don't do audiences," he said adamantly.

"Come on man, just one tooth, then I'll leave."

"Do it yourself then," the devil said, standing up as he tossed him the wrench. Gus's face lit up and he practically ran over to me, crouching down by the toolbox he lifted out a metal contraption.

"Just one. And then I gotta go," Gus said, ripping the tape off my mouth. He pried it apart using pressure points on the roof of my mouth to force me to comply.

It wasn't the first time he'd done this.

The blond devil stepped back and looked down at us with an annoyed look on his face. He was pissed that Gus was taking his work away from him. "I got shit to do so hurry the fuck up."

"I'd love to take my time, little one. But this is going to have to do." He pushed the wrench into my mouth and clasped onto one of my molars. He didn't just start to yank on it, he started pulling slowly, building the pain, setting each nerve on fire, prolonging the pain as he pulled harder and harder until I felt as if my entire jaw was being ripped from my skull. I screamed so loud my chest hurt. Warm copper flooded my mouth.

Gus sat back, his chest heaving up and down. My bloodied

Excerpt From Soulless

molar between the tongs of his wrench. "That was fucking fantastic."

"Great. Now get the fuck out or I'm leaving."

"Fine," Gus said, standing up and setting the wrench down on the tarp. "Just make sure she screams, she was adamant about that." The devil nodded and knelt down next to me again, picking through the toolbox. I started to choke as the blood dripped down my throat. He pushed my head to the side so the blood could run out of my mouth, the spreader bar painfully tearing into the flesh inside of my mouth.

How could someone so beautiful be so evil? I thought to myself. And then I remembered something Bear had said.

He looks like sunshine. Blonde hair and blue eyes. The kind of looks you'd see on one of them TV shows all the teenagers like these days. But that kid's got the devil in him. Only human lives he values are his wife Abby and now his kid. Jake's the only person in the world who scares the shit out of me. You know, besides you.

It was my only chance. "Jake," I said. But I was tired, so very tired, and with the spreader in my mouth it sounded like "gggggggech."

He ignored me and shuffled through his toolbox and that's when I realized it was over.

I was going to die.

I love you Bear.

THE END (FOR NOW)

Bear and Thia's story is
continued in <u>SOULLESS</u>
AVAILABLE NOW

ALSO BY T.M. FRAZIER

THE PERVERSION TRILOGY

PERVERSION (Book 1)

POSSESSION (Book 2)

PERMISSION (Book 3)

THE OUTSKIRTS DUET

THE OUTSKIRTS (Book 1)

THE OUTLIERS (Book 2)

THE KING SERIES

LISTED IN RECOMMENDED READING ORDER

Jake & Abby's Story (Standalone)

The Dark Light of Day (Prequel)

King & Doe's Story (Duet)

KING (Book 1)

TYRANT (Book 2)

Bear & Thia's Story (Duet)

LAWLESS (Book 3)

SOULLESS (Book 4)

Rage & Nolan's Story (Standalone)

ALL THE RAGE (Spinoff)

Preppy & Dre's Story (Triplet)

PREPPY PART ONE (Book 5)

PREPPY PART TWO (Book 6)

PREPPY PART THREE (Book 7)

Smoke & Frankie's Story (Standalone)

UP IN SMOKE (Spinoff)

Nine & Lenny's Story

NINE, THE TALE OF KEVIN CLEARWATER

King & Doe's Novella

King of the Causeway

Pike's Story (Duet)

Pike (Book 1)

Pawn (Book 2)

ABOUT THE AUTHOR

T.M. Frazier never imagined that a single person would ever read a word she wrote when she published her first book, The Dark Light of Day.

Now, she's a USA Today bestselling author several times over. Her books have been translated into numerous languages and published all around the world.

T.M. enjoys writing what she calls 'wrong side of the tracks' romance with sexy, morally corrupt anti-heroes and ballsy heroines.

Her books have been described as raw, dark and gritty. Basically, while some authors are great at describing a flower as it blooms, T.M. is better at describing it in the final stages of decay.

She loves meeting her readers, but if you see her at an event please don't pinch her because she's not ready to wake up from this amazing dream.

For more information please visit her website www.tmfrazierbooks.com

FACEBOOK: facebook.com/tmfrazierbooks
TWITTER: twitter.com/tm_frazier
INSTAGRAM: instagram.com/t.m.frazier
JOIN MY FACEBOOK GROUP, FRAZIERLAND: www.facebook.com/groups/tmfrazierland

Printed in Great Britain
by Amazon